A GAME OF MALICE

GLEDÉ BROWNE KABONGO

BrowneStar

Media

www.brownestarmedia.com

A GAME OF MALICE

Copyright 2024 @ Glede Browne Kabongo

ISBN: 979-8-9913219-7-6

WHY READERS FIND GLEDE BROWNE KABONGO'S BOOKS "UNBELIEVABLY ADDICTIVE."

- Next Generation Indie Book Award Winner, Best Fiction Series
- National Indie Excellence Award Winner, Suspense
- IPPY Silver Medal Winner, Suspense/Thriller
- Eric Hoffer Award, First Runner-Up, Mystery/Crime
- Readers' Favorite International Book Award, Honorable Mention, Psychological Thriller Category

"Gledé Browne Kabongo probably turned into my favorite thriller author!"
— *Amazon Reviewer*

"Freakin genius!" — *Romance Bytes*

"I can promise a swiping frenzy…just as intense and engrossing as *Gone Girl*."
— *Reedsy Discovery Reviewer*

"A masterpiece of a psychological thriller."
— *LaDonna's Book Nook*

"A thrilling page-turner. A recommended read for fans of Liane Moriarty and Shari Lapena."
— *NetGalley Reviewer*

"A spellbinding thriller."
— *Long and Short Reviews*

"Spellbinding and engrossing."
— Ana E Ross, *New York Times* and *USA Today* bestselling author

"A riveting crime thriller packed with mind-blowing twists and turns."
— *NetGalley Reviewer*

"I could see this book being made into a film. Brilliant!!!
— *NetGalley Reviewer*

"A sassy, edgy page-turner." — *Wall to wall Books*

ALSO BY GLEDÉ BROWNE KABONGO

Our Wicked Lies
Fool Me Twice
Conspiracy of Silence

FEARLESS SERIES

Game of Fear
Autumn of Fear
Winds of Fear
Reign of Fear

AVAILABLE IN AUDIO

Conspiracy of Silence

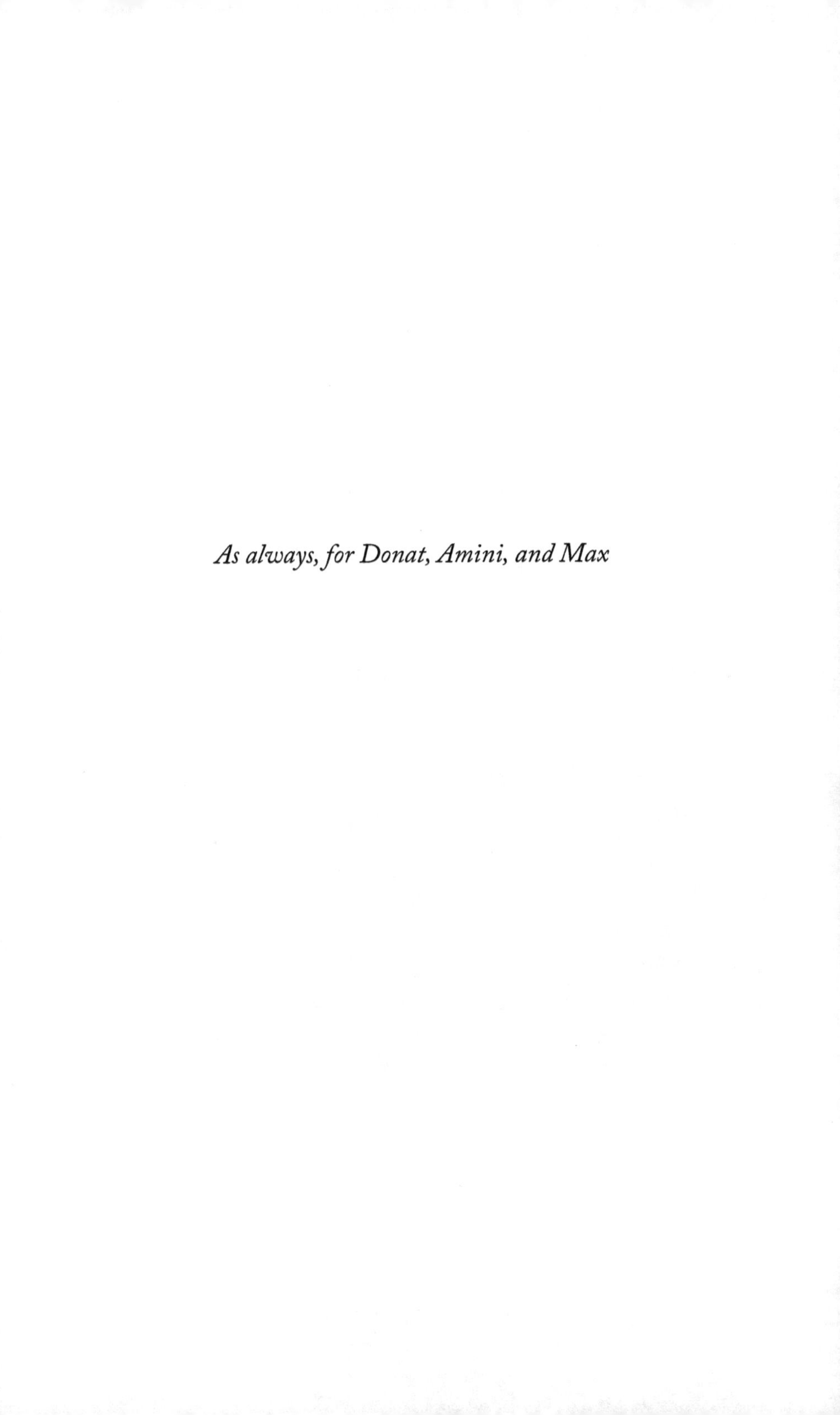

As always, for Donat, Amini, and Max

CHAPTER 1

It's not even first period yet, but Branson Academy is already a battlefield.

Alliances shatter like glass in the hallways, and behind every smile lurks the promise of betrayal. Welcome to Monday morning, where ruthless ambition wears a school uniform and Shakespeare would feel right at home. The first act? Pure, unadulterated drama.

Down the hall my best friend and STEM queen, Mackenzie Fleming, is involved in a heated conversation with Kellen Fontaine. Mackenzie's hands fidget with the straps of her backpack. A tense, palpable energy radiates off her.

I weave through the bustling crowd of navy-blue blazers, ties, and plaid skirts to grab what I need from my locker before heading out to AP chemistry. Something is off about Mackenzie lately: a nervous, paranoid vibe that sets my teeth on edge.

At first, I assumed it was the intense pressure seniors face to get into their top-choice colleges. The race began well before the fall semester kicked off a month ago. At Branson, everything is an Olympic sport, even college admission—a potent mix of desperation and depression.

If I don't get in, my parents will throw a fit and heads will roll. They rejected me? How dare they? Don't they know who I am?

Mackenzie would happily give up a kidney to get into MIT. But I don't think killer essays, flawless transcripts, or a mile-long list of awards and accomplishments are the problem.

She keeps her phone screen hidden whenever we hang out. Or shows up to class looking like she's gone several rounds with a grizzly bear the night before and barely survived.

"Whoa. Now that's a new one."

The voice belongs to Liam McSweeney, who stands off to the side with a group of acquaintances, their faces glued to their phone screens. Liam can't get enough of the school's official gossip app—BransonBuzz.

Once at my locker, I grab my books and toss them into my bag, occasionally glancing in Kellen and Mackenzie's direction. Kellen is my soccer teammate, but I mostly think of him as a giant wart I can't get rid of.

Tall and athletic, with dark hair he styles in a top knot, Kellen looms over Mackenzie like a monstrous cloud blocking her path. Her eyes dart nervously up and down the hall, searching for an escape hatch. My Spidey senses tingle, warning me trouble is in the air.

I join the steady stream of students heading to various buildings across campus for the first classes of the day. With one hand holding the straps of my backpack, I open the gossip app with the other and pretend to be engrossed in the details so Mackenzie and Kellen don't notice my approach.

According to the latest rumors, a love triangle between the captain of the boys' Lacrosse team, a bubbly cheerleader, and a shy bookworm is getting ugly. It's quite juicy and scandalous. Otherwise, it wouldn't have made BransonBuzz.

"Mackenzie, how was your weekend?" I ask casually.

A startled Kellen jerks his head up. He says, "We're busy, Lucas. Take a hike." Kellen looks at me like a gross piece of lint he discovered on his otherwise pristine uniform.

"Oh. Stupid me," I say, slapping my forehead. "I forgot I needed your permission to talk to Mackenzie. Next time I'll put in a request with the Department of Kellen Affairs. How's that?"

Kellen glowers at me. Mackenzie's honey-brown eyes plead with me to walk away, be the bigger person for her sake. Why do that when I can get on Kellen's last nerve instead?

"Shouldn't you pick on someone your own size?" I ask Kellen.

"What part of 'take a hike' don't you get? This is a private conversation and none of your business."

I don't budge.

"Weekend was great," Mackenzie says, running her fingers through her newly styled hair. "I went into Boston and got a makeover." Lavender streaks now weave through her shiny, ash-brown curls. The bold change suits her, adding an edge to her usual polished look.

She shoots me a too-bright smile meant to reassure me she's fine. I don't want to stress her out further, so I back off to give her some breathing room and time to get away from her abrasive boyfriend.

"I'll see you later," I say. "Taking off for AP Chemistry, but text me if you need anything, okay?"

She nods slowly. "Sure, Lucas. I'll catch you later."

As I walk away and rejoin the flow of students, a tight knot forms in my stomach. Why was Kellen so intense and Mackenzie desperate to get away from him?

I can't help but glance back over my shoulder, half expecting to see Kellen's menacing glare following me like an evil eye. But they're already gone, swallowed up by the throng of students.

Once outside, I sprint across the quad toward the STEM building, breathing in the crisp October morning air. The Branson campus is massive and ridiculously picturesque, spread out over several hundred acres in Concord, Massachusetts.

The manicured grass fans out like an emerald carpet, and the pathways are lined with neatly pruned hedges and colorful flower beds. Towering oak trees complete the portrait.

Ah, yes, the stunning campus provides plenty of eye candy for the glossy brochures and in-person visits from families desperate to send their kids here. Families impressed with the size of the endowment, the school's reputation for academic excellence, and record number of acceptances to top-tier colleges.

But I've also been at Branson long enough to know there are plenty of hidden skeletons. Skeletons that don't make it into the brochures or campus tours. It's the other side of Branson, where trouble always lurks, like some evil henchman in a dark alley at night. Pardon the reference. Obviously I've watched one too many gangster movies with my brother Blake.

Last year, an AP English teacher was fired for running a pay-to-play scheme. For the low, low price of only five thousand dollars, those who could afford the fee but didn't bother to do the work were guaranteed an A in the course. Why? Because AP English is almost PhD level here, as in Ms. Whitman has a PhD in English from Columbia.

And that's the reason I can't shake the chill sliding down my spine. I've learned a thing or two in my three years at Branson. I don't believe Mackenzie is fine.

CHAPTER 2

I catch up with Mackenzie at an after-school club meeting.

"What did Kellen want?" I ask.

"Nothing."

Her tone comes off whiny and irritated. Mackenzie fidgets with something in the pocket of her uniform blazer, her usual radiance dimmed by the anxiety clouding her eyes.

As if to drive home her point, she adds, "I'm fine, Lucas. You make a big deal about everything. Stop being so intense already."

Now may not be the best time to tell my friend to quit lying to my face. First off, she won't be my friend much longer if I do, and second of all, my mother says you catch more flies with honey than with vinegar. Why would anyone want to catch flies? I have no idea, but whatever.

"I worry about you. Are you stressed about applying to college?"

Mackenzie shakes her head, her curls bouncing with the movement. She then shifts her focus to the dark-pink polish on her fingernails. My cue to buzz off.

It's our weekly meeting of the Alexander Alerie Club, a student-led group where we freely discuss the complexities of our mixed-race identity. Alexander Alerie, a biracial student from France, attended Branson over forty years ago. The event known simply as "the incident" was the reason for the club's formation.

The cozy room boasts a combination of colorful bean bags, a large couch, and plush armchairs. A flat-screen TV mounted on the wall and a few thriving indoor plants add a nice touch.

At first, our club was simply a place to gather and discuss our shared experiences of living with dual-racial identities. We joked about it being our weekly biracial-identity-crisis therapy session.

But as time passed, the Alerie Club evolved into something much more. It became a haven where we can embrace and revel in our diverse backgrounds through activities like movie nights, cultural outings, and indulging in delicious foods.

And when the mood strikes us, we delve into intense discussions and debates, fearlessly tackling topics like religion, politics, and sex without holding back.

Besides, the club is the only safe space on campus we can let loose about race and ethnicity with humor and laughter and not worry that the PC police will come for us. I mean, if *we* can't joke about it, who can?

We wait for the meeting to be called to order. Some members are lost in their phones, scrolling through social media or texting friends, while others have earbuds or headphones on, blocking out the world and immersing themselves in music.

Candace Baxter, who's Black and Indian, buzzes around the room like a hummingbird, tending to her beloved plants.

As the official plant mom of the club, she's overprotective of her "babies" and threatens to harm anyone who messes with them. We all know better than to touch the plants without her permission, let alone water them, if Candace misses a club meeting.

"Come on. Tell me what's really going on." I'm hounding Mackenzie again. "I've got your back, whatever it is."

"Lucas, please," she whispers. "I know you want to help, but you can't, okay? So drop it."

Note to self. Add short-tempered to the list of Mackenzie's odd behaviors. When we first became friends, she was all sunshine, an optimist who was good at many things. Like photography. She took amazing photos of nature and even won the Shutter Star Award, a prestigious contest for middle school and high school students across the country. That hobby fell away, and I hadn't noticed until now.

I wonder if her anxiety has anything to do with her parents? Mackenzie is an only child and says her parents have been unhappy and fighting a lot lately. I only met them once when they came to Branson for an event.

Mackenzie's mother is Dean of the Heller School for Social Policy and Management at Brandeis University, and her dad is a research scientist at a life sciences company in Cambridge. Are the Flemings splitting up? Is that why Mackenzie seems to be unraveling?

"Kellen looked like he wanted to smack you," I whisper, grasping at anything that will get her to open up.

She scoffs. "Come on, Lucas. I would never allow Kellen or anyone else to put their hands on me. I'm not that weak."

"I know you're not." My tone comes off as defensive. Mackenzie is petite and looks twelve, although she's seventeen going on eighteen. She's like a sister to me, and I would have no problem punching out Kellen if he threatened her. I'd worry about getting expelled from school later.

Kellen hates my guts, and the feeling is mutual. He wanted to be captain of the boys' soccer team, but Coach felt differently and selected me instead. Plus, the team voted. It never seems to occur to Kellen that I've already led the team to two championships and plan to make it three in a row this season.

Ivy Ishihara, the club's vice president calls the meeting to order. Ivy is bossy in both subtle and not-so-subtle ways. It depends on what mood she's in when you interact with her.

She freaks me out though. I swear Ivy has feline in her. You never hear her coming, and then poof, just like that, she appears in front of you. Ivy's long dark hair cascades down her back in a way that suggests she gave her hair specific instructions on how it should hang.

"Hey, my fabulous mixed-race crew. It's good to see each and every one of your beautiful faces this week. Welcome to another therapy session—er, I mean Alerie Club meeting. Let's gather round and roast the stereotypes, dissect the struggles, and maybe even shed a tear or two. Mostly from laughing too hard."

Hooting and hollering follow Ivy's remarks as she takes a seat in the semicircle.

"Last weekend I had an oldie but goodie," Matteo Bonetti says with a grin. He's coanchor of *The Branson Insider*, our popular student-run TV news broadcast.

Ivy nods and motions for him to continue.

"It was the classic 'What are you?'" he says, prompting eyerolls and murmurs from the group.

Ivy asks, "How did you respond?"

With mischief in his eyes, Matteo says, "I told her I was a rare Pokémon."

The club erupts in laughter. Even Mackenzie can't help but crack a smile.

"That was truly epic," says George Yancey, fist bumping Matteo. George is a soccer teammate. He constantly complains about being caught between the disciplinary tactics of his strict Liberian father and his more laid-back Swedish mother who lets him get away with anything.

Ivy says, "Lucas had a similar experience. Isn't that right, Lucas?" Her eyes bore into mine, forcing me to engage in the conversation.

I try to avoid Ivy; my sister Alexis loathes her. If I so much as flash my teeth at Ivy and Alexis finds out, it won't be pretty. I can practically hear her voice in my head right now. *You're dead to me, Lucas!*

"Um, not sure what you're talking about Ivy." I need a minute to reorient my thoughts. I wasn't expecting to be called on.

Ivy folds her arms over her chest, her face the picture of exasperation. With a dramatic sigh, she says, "It's about people constantly challenging your Blackness. Or thinking it's acceptable to make racist comments around you because they assume you're white based on your appearance."

With another long-suffering sigh and shake of her head, Ivy acts as though she can't believe she has to remind me again. But I know she lives for these moments, to pull me into her ever-swirling vortex of drama.

Before I dive into a recap for the group's benefit so Ivy will leave me alone, I have a complaint about the genetic prank played on me sixteen years ago. No matter how much tanning lotion I slather on, I can only manage a whiff of color. Just a whiff, not an actual tan.

The ice-blue eyes don't help either; they're large and round and scare even the most hostile cats. Don't ask how I know. All I can say is, the gene pool conspired against me to make certain I stuck out like a tourist in my own family. Such a hater. I didn't inherit a single drop of melanin or any distinguishing features from my mother's side of the family. Not one. Zilch. Nada.

As I got older, I tried not to feel weird about it. I turned to research, desperate to find others with similar experiences. That's when I discovered other biracial children who also heavily favored one parent in appearance.

Genetics is complex and unpredictable, I suppose. It doesn't give advanced warning about how it's going to manifest, that's for sure.

The memory Ivy wants me to relive happened two years ago. I'd rather eat nails for breakfast than dredge up the episode. But here we go. Someone I considered a close friend came over to my house for a visit. The conversation shifted to our family history.

With great pride and excitement, I shared my family background—my mother; Grandma Shelby and her Louisiana roots; Grandma Jenny, my paternal grandmother, originally from the Bahamas; and my dad.

My *real* dad. The father I've had since the day I was born, not the one whose face stares back at me from the mirror. It's important to make the distinction. He's also biracial, because Grandpa Bobby is Guyanese Indian and married to Grandma Jenny.

Well, my brag fest about my heritage turned into a big old pile of betrayal and hurt.

"Lucas, you don't count as Black," the person stated with confidence.

I can handle the curious stares or shocked expressions when we're out in public and I call my mother "Mom" or the incredulous reactions when people find out Blake, Alexis, and I are related. But this particular hateful comment from my so-called friend pierced me deeply. The wound still aches, if I'm being honest.

It just made everything worse. My identity struggles, wondering about the other half of me, always feeling that I have to defend the way I look, not that I can do anything about it, or having to prove my mother is really Black.

I shy away from family-history projects, haunted by my unknown biological father.

But on that day, the venomous comment "You don't count as Black" shattered my sense of belonging by trying to displace me from the loving, supportive family I've had all my life. The comment ripped my security blanket from me, and I'm still struggling to get it back.

Ivy beams at me. As if my rehashing an avalanche of pain is something I should be proud of. The things I do for this club.

"That was harsh," Candace says, her lips pursed with disapproval. "I hope you kicked the jerk to the curb. The nerve of some people." She sinks deeper into her seat, shaking her head as though this is the most baffling situation she's ever heard.

"Dude, I'm not gonna lie. When I first met you, I thought you were white," Alex Delgado says from the far side of the semicircle.

We call Alex Mr. Chill because nothing fazes him. And he speaks slowly and deliberately as if he doesn't want you to miss a single word he says. Except when he's speaking Spanish; then his words flow like a rushing river, filled with emotion and passion.

A chorus of nods and murmurs follow Alex's words. Every one of us in the club shares a common struggle: "Not Enough" Syndrome. Feeling not enough for one race or the other.

Constantly feeling pressure to conform to a specific cultural mold in our speech, behaviors, beliefs, attitudes, and preferences.

But sometimes, when we gather, discussing race and its complexities gets burdensome. In those moments, we just want to be carefree teenagers, acting silly, laughing, sharing our hopes and dreams—to simply be human.

To my surprise, Mackenzie takes my hand in hers and squeezes. I smile inwardly. Even when she's annoyed with me, Mack still lets me know she cares.

The conversation shifts to our next event. George's eyes light up as he starts discussing the planning for our Ethnic Eats Bonanza: Holiday Edition.

Twice a year, our club hosts a food bonanza unlike anything at Branson Academy. It's our version of a food festival—a vast potpourri of dishes representing the cultures and backgrounds of our members. The whole school turns out in full force, and we donate the money to various causes.

Although the bonanza is one of my favorite things about being a member of the Alerie Club—you guessed it, I love food—I turn my attention back to Mackenzie and her stonewalling.

When something weighs on me, I can't let it go. I push and push until the object of my inquiry gets hostile and threatens to do me bodily harm if I don't back off. What can I say? It's part of my charm. Mackenzie will continue evading if I bring up Kellen again, so I change tactics.

"Are you going to put in a good word for me with Misha or what? Tell her I can make her wildest dreams come true?" I give Mackenzie my most charming smile.

My charming smile must be losing its power because Mackenzie scratches her cheek. In her eyes, I observe a hint of skepticism.

CHAPTER 3

Misha Johnson-Arya. Just the mention of her name sends my heart into a spiral. No joke. I know I should make a move, but I'm too chicken. Plus, I've been risk averse since birth. Weighing the pros and cons and coming up with a plan first is more my style.

"Misha and I aren't friends," Mackenzie says.

"She nodded at you in the hallway last week. After assembly last Tuesday."

"I don't know what you think you saw, but like I said, I don't know her. Yeah, I know of her. I've seen her around campus a few times, but we don't interact or live in the same dorm or have the same friends. Maybe she was nodding at someone close to me and you thought it was directed at me."

"Are you sure?"

For as long as I can remember, I've been crushing on Misha. She probably doesn't know I exist, but if she does, she could shut me down so fast the BransonBuzz would go into a frenzy for weeks. I couldn't take the humiliation. So for now, I'll play it cool.

Mackenzie was my ticket to test the waters, Misha adjacent. But now Mackenzie denies knowing Misha and implied I'm seeing things.

Mackenzie continues, "Besides, don't waste your time with her."

"What do you mean?"

"Hanging out with Misha could be risky."

"You said you don't know Misha. Why would you say she's risky?"

Mackenzie shrugs. "I heard rumors about her and Jayden Williams, that's all. I don't want you to get hurt. If Misha is seeing someone else, leave it alone. You're a great guy, and Ivy isn't the only girl at Branson who knows you're special."

"You sound like my sister."

"Because it's true."

"So you're saying I should forget about Misha?"

"Up to you. If Jayden is in play, I think you should back off. Not worth the drama."

Jayden Williams. I hate that guy, the quarterback of our football team. Good-looking, arrogant, and a first-rate jerk. Yes, he's a walking cliché. If a douchebag could morph into a human being, it would take the form of Jayden. Seriously, the guy's ego is so big it needs its own zip code.

Oh, and don't get me started on his stupid catchphrases. If I hear, "Live large or go home" one more time, I might pop a blood vessel.

As our meeting wraps, everyone eagerly commits to supplying their signature dishes for the food bonanza. I'll rely on my grandma Shelby to make her famous Louisiana Seafood Gumbo, bread pudding, or Sausage Jambalaya. Or I might hit up my brother Blake to bake something mouth-watering.

I hastily grab my belongings and head for the door with Mackenzie at my heels. She's given me a lot to ponder, her words igniting a whirlwind of curious thoughts.

As she's about to take off, I ask, "When should we meet to discuss the plan?"

"I'll text you."

"I'd suggest coming over to my house, but I don't want anyone to accidentally overhear us," I say, a sense of urgency and secrecy creeping in.

Mackenzie is helping me with my investigation—the investigation into who my biological father was and whether he really died in a car accident before I was born, the way my parents keep insisting. Something about their story doesn't add up, and I want answers.

Mack takes off in the opposite direction. As I turn to head to soccer practice, my heart nearly pops out of my chest when Ivy Ishihara appears suddenly and plants herself in my path. I didn't hear or see her. I hate the stealth thing she does.

"You should wear a bell or something; warn people, Ivy."

"Come on, is that any way to talk to a friend?" Ivy curls her fingers around my bicep, the unexpected touch sending a jolt of surprise coursing through my body.

"Wow," she remarks. "Impressive. Very impressive." Her voice is full of admiration.

I'm not sure what to make of her brazen move, so it's best I head to soccer practice.

"Ivy, gotta run." I move my arm from her grip before it becomes the next item on the BransonBuzz.

Ignoring me, she says, "What's up with little Mack? She looked like she just lost a high-stakes poker game to the Grim Reaper."

The statement stumps me for a minute. Ivy is quite perceptive today.

"I didn't know you cared."

"Of course I care. I care deeply for all my fellow students. At Branson, we're one big happy family, and we should look out for one another."

She must be drunk or high. Or dying and trying to score points with God.

"What are you talking about? You hate almost everyone at this school."

"I don't hate you, Lucas. You and Mackenzie are friends, and if she's not okay, then you're not okay."

Time out. Where is this weird conversation headed? My confusion must be plain on my face because she continues, "Life's a bit like a game of chess." Her eyes glint with some deeper meaning I can't yet figure out. "We each have our pieces on the board, maneuvering and strategizing, trying to outsmart each other."

"Okay. I get the metaphor, but what does that have to do with Mackenzie?"

Ivy leans in closer and whispers, "But sometimes, it's not just about making the right moves. It's about keeping an eye on the other player's pieces. Because you never know when someone might have a hidden queen up their sleeve."

Then Ivy walks away, her words lingering heavy in the air with meaning and warning. A heightened sense of unease washes over me.

CHAPTER 4

When Mom inquires about the Alerie Club meeting, I keep my response brief.

"It went fine."

I quickly shove a forkful of linguine into my mouth, using it as an excuse to avoid elaborating. Mackenzie's behavior today was unsettling. Ivy's cryptic warning, comparing it to a chess move, only added to my lingering unease.

It's dinner time, a sacred ritual in the Rambally household. Both my parents have busy careers, but Mom takes the time to cook our meals and freeze them for weekday dinners. As a neuropsychologist at Massachusetts General Hospital, her schedule is crazy with patients and research; yet she still finds time to be a part-time instructor at Harvard.

Dad, a cardiothoracic surgeon who teaches at Harvard Medical School, and is cofounder of a biotech start-up, is usually home in time for dinner.

Mom uses dinner as a time to discuss our day and anything that might be troubling us. Alexis takes my one-word response to Mom's question as an invitation to start with the drama.

"I heard Ivy Ishihara was all over Lucas," she says. "I shudder to think what she could have done if my brother hadn't escaped her evil clutches." Then she sighs dramatically, as only my sister can.

Blake almost chokes on his food, and Mom and Dad give me an ecstatic look as though I'd just told them I found a diamond mine in our backyard.

"Is Ivy a friend?" Mom asks, all casual. She's showing real restraint, her way of making sure I don't clam up and cause her to miss out on a juicy piece of gossip.

"No. She's just a member of the Alerie Club."

"Then why was she all over you as your sister says?" Mom has a mischievous glint in her eyes. She most likely thinks I'm crushing on Ivy or she's my secret girlfriend.

"Ivy likes annoying me to get to Alexis." Except our conversation today had nothing to do with Alexis.

"She's in love with you, Lucas. Admit it. I won't shame you. I promise." Alexis gives me her doe-eyed, innocent look, the same one she gives Dad when she wants to have her way about something he already said no to.

Blake says, "You could do worse. If you have a crush on Ivy, you've got my vote."

Alexis gives Blake the stink eye. I can always count on my little brother. If I told Blake I was going to rob a bank, he would ask what kind of getaway car we should get, not that either one of us has a driver's license.

I have a permit and need to wait another three months, when I'm sixteen and a half, to get my junior operator license. Blake and Alexis, the twins as they're called in our family, are only fifteen, so they don't qualify for a permit in Massachusetts.

"What?" Blake asks innocently. "I'm just supporting Lucas. Ivy seems nice."

"Well she isn't," Alexis says, with attitude.

"Oh?" Mom says. "What's wrong with Ivy?" She puts her fork down and leans in with her hands under her chin.

"She's a vapid, vindictive, vain train wreck of a human being." Alexis folds her arm and silently dares us to contradict her.

Anyone listening would think Ivy and Alexis are in the same grade and have some kind of nineties style East Coast-West Coast hip-hop feud going. Alexis is a sophomore, and Ivy and I are juniors.

Alexis neither forgives nor forgets. I don't remember the details, but Ivy and her mean-girls posse, The Phantastic Four, either did or said something mean to Alexis's friend Cadence Maxwell who transferred out of Branson.

That's when the hate war started. Although I don't know how Ivy feels about my sister, I prefer to stay out of their beef.

"Whoa, pumpkin," Dad says. "Those are some harsh words. I don't know Ivy, but do you think you're being unkind?"

"Not at all, Daddy. Those are the kindest words I can think of to describe Ivy."

"She's that bad, huh?" Dad asks, with a grin and twinkle in his eyes. Dad spoils Alexis and humors her.

"The worst. Ever."

"What's your beef with Ivy?" I ask.

Alexis turns to me with a fire in her eyes that threatens to burn me to a crisp if I don't do as she says.

"Stay away from her, Lucas. She's trouble with a capital T. You don't know what she's capable of." Then she turns to her twin. "Blake, quit being supportive."

A change of topic is called for after my sister's rant, one I'm happy to supply. "Well, there was one interesting thing that happened at the Alerie Club meeting today." I direct my gaze at Mom.

"What's that?" she asks.

"Matteo shared with our group about a recent experience he had. People questioning his heritage." I share the story with the family.

Silence wraps around the dinner table. Dad puts on his poker face. Everyone knows where this is conversation is headed.

The story circulating in the family is Mom got pregnant with me when she was in college. The man she was dating, my biological father, was *mean to her* and died in a car crash before she could tell him they were expecting.

Dad, my real dad sitting at the dinner table, helped her through her grief because they'd been best friends since high school. He proposed, and they got married while they were still students at Yale. Seven months later, I arrived.

Sounds straightforward, right? Except I'm positive that's not the truth. Not all of it anyway. Each time I bring up my biological father, Mom suddenly has something in the oven, laundry to finish, an important call to make, or some instant catastrophe about to befall one of her patients if she doesn't intervene.

I want to know why everyone in the family is tight-lipped about the man whose DNA I carry, the man who gave me this face. What if I contract some rare genetic disease that requires knowledge of both biological parents' medical history? Then what? No, I'm not some pessimist, but these are important questions I need answered.

"Sweetie, you know what happened to your biological father. We explained everything," Mom says. "That man was never your father. Your dad is right here," she says, gesturing at Dad, Dr. Tyler Jeffrey Rambally.

That man. She never mentions his name. Dad strokes her arm to keep her calm. There it is again. That look on her face, like her world is about to collapse.

Alexis and Blake absently move food around on their plates. I don't want to cause Mom stress. She's been through a lot in her life. Things she keeps hidden from us. But thanks to Alexis's gift for digging up dirt on family members, all three of us end up speculating, pondering, and panicking about the secrets Alexis shares with us.

Mom's eyes glisten with tears. I immediately regret saying anything. Without hesitation, I jump up from my seat and make my way toward her.

Wrapping my arms around her neck, I whisper an apology. "I'm sorry, Mom. I'm just curious. Please don't cry." I turn to Dad and offer a similar apology. I add, "I won't ask anymore."

My mother's gentle touch offers some comfort, but it can't erase the weight of my unanswered questions.

"It's okay, Lucas," Dad reassures me. "It's natural to have questions about your origins."

Despite their words, neither of them will tell me the truth. That's why working with Mackenzie is so important. If anyone can help me get answers, it's her.

There is so much about me that could be connected to *that man.* My bursts of rage, for example. When someone pushes me too far or hurts someone I care about, a wave of fury engulfs me, and all I want to do is make them suffer.

My mother's gaze sometimes lingers on me with a mix of bewilderment and… I don't know… confusion? As if she can't fathom how I ended up her son. Other times, she showers me with attention and affection as if trying to make up for something. But what is that something?

And why do her eyes prickle with tears every time I mention *him?* So far, the only explanation that makes sense to me is this: my biological father was a terrible person.

Mom snaps me out of my thoughts when she adds, "You shouldn't worry about who your biological father was. It doesn't matter and has no bearing on who you are. Besides, you have a great relationship with your uncle Christian, so there's that connection to Za—"

She catches herself. Mom was about to give up the name, but I know better than to push. At least I have the first two letters, something I can share with Mackenzie.

Uncle Christian is another angle I can pursue, although he avoids and deflects my questions. He's the half-brother of my birth father, if that's a thing. Even Aunt Callie, Mom's best friend who's married to Uncle Christian, won't divulge any details. Neither will my grandparents. Not even Uncle Miles, Mom's younger brother. The whole family had built a wall of secrecy around this man, and I'm determined to uncover the reason for the guarded silence.

CHAPTER 5

Mackenzie's response to my question is, "Nothing."

"What do you mean? You could have told me that in a text."

We sit in a corner of the common room on campus, the place where both boarding and day students gather to unwind and connect after a long day of classes. A sleek espresso machine hums softly, its rich aroma drawing a steady stream of students eager for a caffeine fix before pulling all-night study sessions.

Nearby, a group of students gather around a foosball table, their laughter and cheers mingling with the thud of the ball against the table. On the opposite side of the room, others lounge on a plush area rug, their backpacks discarded haphazardly beside them, their faces absorbed in their phones.

I knew trying to dig up dirt on a dead man, pun intended, would be hard, but I wasn't expecting *nothing*. Mackenzie's shoulders tense. She scans the room as though looking for someone.

"Who are you looking for?"

"Nobody," she says quickly.

"Are you afraid Kellen will show up and cause a scene?"

"No, don't be silly. I'm not afraid of Kellen."

"Then who?"

"What?" she asks, distracted.

"Who are you afraid of?"

She gives me a weak smile to put me at ease. "I'm not afraid of anyone. Anyway, I was about to say I couldn't find anything. I did a deep web search using several combinations that included your mom's name, Yale, and the Wheeler family, and I couldn't get a single hit."

"Mack, please sit down," I say. "Your nervousness is contagious."

She fidgets with the sleeves of her sweatshirt and jumps when someone laughs too loudly from across the room. No caffeine for her.

Mack ignores my request and continues as if I hadn't spoken at all. "There's nothing about your mom's time at Yale, and nothing about a Yale student being in a car crash during that timeframe. Unless you can convince your mother to give up his name, the plan will crumble before it gets off the ground."

"I have two letters. Mom started to say his name and stopped herself."

"She did? How come?"

"I told the family at dinner I was wondering about him. Mom wasn't happy about it, but she almost blurted out his name. All I got were Z and A."

"That's good news, Lucas. More than we had before. But what if we're looking at this all wrong?"

"Wrong how?" I ask.

Mackenzie doesn't answer right away. Instead, she pulls up the hood of her Branson sweatshirt over her head and partially covers her face.

"Are you going to keep acting weird all evening?" I'm sick of her saying everything is fine when it's obvious something is wrong. She pulls off the hood.

"Okay, I may as well tell you. I'm trying to break things off with Kellen, but he just gets more clingy. It's stressing me out. He's applying to BU and Northeastern so we can attend college in the same city. Kellen doesn't even like New England that much."

"Do you want me to talk to him?"

She touches her left temple, her eyes closed as though contemplating my offer.

Why did I say that? It's a stupid idea. Kellen won't listen to anything I say.

Knowing Mackenzie, she feels terrible about breaking up with Kellen because of his tragic backstory. His mother died of leukemia the summer before his freshman year at Branson. His father, Lee Fontaine, who made millions in real estate construction, dumped Kellen at Branson and remarried a year after his first wife passed.

Kellen, like Mackenzie, is an only child. They bonded over that commonality, I assume.

If Mackenzie wants to put distance between them, Kellen must be heart-broken. He doesn't have a lot of friends and probably suffers from loneliness like a lot of the boarding students. Wait. Why am I sympathizing with a guy who wishes my face would end up under the wheel of a bus?

"I can handle Kellen," she says. "It's not just that. College applications are taking a toll. My parents are constantly on me about it, especially my mother. Having a mom who is also a dean is a curse, let me tell you. She has friends at a few of the colleges I'm applying to, but none at MIT."

Before I can think of an appropriate response, she says, "I'll figure things out. It's intense. You know how it is at Branson. The rich and connected will use their influence to get their kids every advantage, legal or otherwise. The rest of us claw our way into whatever is left."

It's an open secret that Branson parents will do just about anything to get their kids into top universities, and that puts a lot of pressure on students. Branson has been a feeder school for the Ivy League for decades. There are only three slots maximum per Ivy League school. Same for other top colleges in the country, so competition is fierce.

"My dad went to Yale and Harvard and has a strong network. Mom graduated from BU. Do you want me to speak to them, see if they can reach out to their people on your behalf?"

"Thanks, Lucas. You're the best." She plants an affectionate peck on my cheek. "Now let's get back to the investigation. Let's consider the possibility we're tackling the problem all wrong."

CHAPTER 6

How do we evaluate whether there's a right angle or a wrong one?" I ask. "There's not enough to go on."

Mackenzie adjusts her body and looks at me intently. "You said everyone in your family is tight-lipped and your mother clams up. What if it's because the story they told you is bogus?"

"Are you saying they lied?"

"It wouldn't be the first time parents lied to their kids. I'm not saying your parents are bad people. Just that the story they told you might be wildly different from the truth, and there's a serious reason behind all the secrecy and evading."

I let out an impatient huff, thinking Mackenzie has completely lost it. All the stress she's experiencing must have warped her mind. I believe what my parents told me is the truth, just not all of it. Now Mackenzie is suggesting what I've learned isn't even in the neighborhood of the truth.

"Okay, explain," I say calmly, despite my muscles tensing and my skin prickling.

"The kidnapping. Brynn Harper said she kidnapped you because she's connected to your biological father. That could mean Brynn is related to you."

"Brynn is doing life in prison. I don't see how this plays into what my parents told me."

It might be worth mentioning that I was kidnapped when I was ten. Yeah, there's been enough drama in my family to produce a highly rated show on Netflix.

"If Brynn is related to your late father, that means she had knowledge of your existence. Stay with me for a minute."

"Okay, I'm listening." But I'm also pulling my ear, a nervous habit.

"Your parents never said anything about Brynn, prior to her kidnapping you. What if there's another reason she snatched you?"

"Like what?"

"Like your mom isn't your mom?"

"Are you insane?" My yell catches the attention of a few students who look curiously in our direction. I relax back into the couch and blow out a calming breath. The gawkers return to what they were doing.

"What if it's not your dad who died in a car crash but your biological mother? And the woman you know as your mom raised you, but she did so because your real mom was her friend and she's the one who died in the crash?"

I stiffen in the seat, not quite comprehending Mackenzie's logic.

"Look, I know it sounds far out. Let's assume for a minute what your mother said is true; he didn't know she was pregnant. It could explain why Brynn kidnapped you years later; your biological dad, her relative, found out the Ramballys were raising you."

"How do we find out?"

"Not sure yet."

"Brynn could be the key," I suggest. "My parents would never allow me to visit her in prison though. Plus, I'm a minor."

"Leave it to me. I'll come up with a plan."

"Are you sure? You have a lot going on."

"Yes. I want to help you with this. That's what friends are for."

For the first time since this journey began, I feel optimistic. But what if Brynn Harper reveals something truly horrible?

I'm about to share my morbid thoughts with Mackenzie, but her attention is elsewhere. She appears mesmerized by a cluster of students conversing and laughing. I crane my neck to see if I recognize anyone in the group. Misha! She's dressed in jeans and a hot-pink V-neck T-shirt with a sweater tied around her waist.

As if Misha senses my gaze on her, she turns around and looks straight at us. At me. Then a breathtaking, can't-breathe, mind-frying smile spreads across her face. I almost fall out of my seat because my heart is battering so hard in my rib cage.

Don't blow it, I tell myself. She flips back one of her long, curly braids.

Is she coming over, or should I go over and speak to her? But I don't want to ditch Mackenzie, who just elbowed me in the rib.

"What?"

"Stop drooling."

"I'm not drooling. All I did was smile." I smiled back at Misha, right? "Is there a law against smiling?" I ask Mackenzie.

"No there isn't, but I've never seen you fawn over any girl like that before. Normally you're all Mr. Cool and in control. One look from Misha and you turn into goo."

"Exaggerate much, Mackenzie?" Why is she giving me a hard time? I might be Mr. Cool to my friends, but when it comes to Misha, I'm a tangled ball of nerves and self-doubt. Besides, I've never asked a girl out on a date before.

"I'm going to say hello," I announce.

"Aren't we supposed to be hatching a plan to see Brynn Harper?"

"We will. But Misha smiled at me. That's huge. It's a sign. You should be excited for me."

I meant it as a guilt trip, but when I look at Mackenzie, her hands are trembling.

"What's wrong?"

"Nothing. I haven't eaten yet."

"Mack! You know better. For goodness' sake, I thought you already had dinner when you texted me. The dining hall is closed now."

Mackenzie has Type I diabetes and has to eat healthy, balanced meals; take insulin daily; and check her blood sugar regularly. She doesn't skip meals or miss taking her medicine. What caused her lapse today?

"Don't freak out. I have food in my room."

"What kind of food?"

"Fruit. Some vegetables in the mini fridge."

"Good. You didn't forget to take your insulin, did you?"

"I'm fine, Lucas. I didn't forget."

"I should let you go so you can eat." I want to walk her back to her dorm to make sure she does eat, but boys aren't allowed in the girls' dormitories at night. That rule gets broken several times a week if the BransonBuzz is to be believed.

"Hi, Lucas. Hi, Mackenzie."

The sound of Misha's voice is both magnetic and melodic. She stands just inches from us. Mackenzie looks like she wants to be anywhere but here and doesn't return the greeting. She needs to get food in her belly asap.

"Hi, Misha," I say, hoping my voice sounds normal. A few beats of awkward silence follow. I'm not sure what to say, so I go with, "Would you like to sit with us?"

Before Misha answers, Mackenzie stands, hurriedly gathers her things, and then says, "See you later, Lucas."

She storms out of the common room. What's that about? Mackenzie is seriously off, and my unease is growing. I make a mental note to check in on her later.

"Do you and Mackenzie have some kind of…issue?" I ask Misha.

"No," she answers quickly. "Maybe she really did have to go. I'm not taking it personally."

Misha surprises me when she continues, "Good game against Auburndale the other day. You mistimed a couple of passes and tried to dribble your way out of trouble. But you turned it around in the second half."

She watched me play. The thought both thrills and terrifies me. Misha has an air of mystery about her that's intimidating yet irresistible.

I often see her walking down the hallway effortlessly, looking stylish, even in uniform. When that happened, my heart would race like I was about to take a penalty kick in the biggest game of my life. Or my palms would get sweaty and my mind would go blank.

CHAPTER 7

Thanks for watching the game," I say. "We'll take all the support we can get. I let Auburndale's captain get inside my head. He's a trash talker. It didn't work, obviously. We still crushed them in the end."

"Of course you crushed it. You're Lucas Rambally. Kylian Mbappé better watch out."

"You follow professional soccer?"

"Not really." She looks down at her feet. "I might have overhead you and Liam talk about it." She lifts her head. "And I might have seen a poster of him in your locker when you left it open by accident."

I chuckle. "Yeah, you got me. He's my favorite player. My brother's too. I didn't think you noticed things about me."

"I notice a lot about you, Lucas."

"Like what?"

"How kind you are when you don't have to be. Helping freshmen with their homework. And laughing at Caleb's bad jokes."

"Caleb is the master of terrible jokes," I say, grinning.

My heart is beating fast again, loudly in fact. I hope she can't hear it. I never noticed how long and thick her lashes are, although this is the first we've been this close. And she smells amazing, a peach and grapefruit combination that produces a sweet, calming scent. Is it her shampoo or lotion?

I shake the creepy thoughts from my head and pinch my nose in a nervous gesture.

"You don't have to be nervous, Lucas."

"I'm not," I say too quickly. "I didn't think…I mean, I always thought you were out my league, so I'm surprised you came over to talk to me." *Stupid idiot.*

Her eyes go big with disbelief. "You thought I was out of your league? The guy the girls at Branson can't stop talking about?"

"Huh?"

"Lucas is so blindingly gorgeous, I need sunglasses just to look at him. I heard Lucas volunteers at a center for underprivileged teens. Can you say heart of gold? Saw him open the door for Mrs. Hendricks the other day. Chivalry isn't dead, people. I could listen to Lucas count sheep, and I'd still swoon." Then she asks, "Do you want me to go on?"

"Did you get that from the BransonBuzz?" I ask, embarrassed. "You shouldn't listen to them."

"Nope. Heard it all with my own ears. And maybe that explains why Mackenzie flew out of here."

"What do you mean?"

"I'm just saying perhaps she has a little crush on you."

"What? Nah. Mack and I are close friends. The idea that she likes me that way is ridiculous."

"Is it though? Maybe Mackenzie is hiding things from you."

Misha's statement confuses me. It came out of nowhere, and now, I don't know what to say or how I should interpret her assertion. Misha and Mackenzie say they don't know each other well, so what is Misha talking about?

"What things would Mackenzie be hiding from me?" I ask.

Misha shrugs. "That she likes you. The way she stormed out of here when I came over to say hi. Is it so hard to believe she has feelings for you?"

"Yes, it is. Mack has a boyfriend. Kellen. And she definitely doesn't think of me that way. Trust me."

A thousand thoughts attack my brain at once, like a swarm of bees that escaped the hive. None of them make sense though. How did we go from a conversation about our mutual crush to Mackenzie liking me? So much drama in one evening.

My phone chimes with an incoming text. I remove it from my pocket. The words on the screen glare back at me, dark and ominous.

Mackenzie: Trust no one.

CHAPTER 8

The late afternoon sun casts long shadows across the soccer field, a meticulously maintained expanse of lush green. As I lead the team through a series of intense drills, my thoughts are all over the place.

Mackenzie's strange text is playing on a constant loop in my mind, like a bad scene from a horror movie. Why did she escape the common room like Misha was radioactive?

I force my thoughts to remain in the present. The air buzzes with the rhythmic thud of soccer balls meeting our feet and the occasional shouts of encouragement from Coach.

As team captain, it's my responsibility for not only leading my teammates on the field, but to also embody the spirit of Branson's storied soccer legacy. No pressure whatsoever. Except, I can't afford to mess up. A senior has always led the team. Coach broke with that tradition, amidst objections and skepticism, and took a chance on me.

Can't say that I blamed the haters—I mean, detractors. Branson is a member of the Pinnacle League, a group of eighteen Northeast prep schools that compete athletically and academically. Branson has won four soccer championships. I scored the winning goal that delivered our fourth championship last year as a sophomore. I'm determined to win our fifth this year, my first as captain.

I dribble the ball skillfully, weaving through cones with precision. Our training regimen is grueling. Early morning drills, and Coach's sharp commands are part of the routine.

Coach Gordon Prescott was captain of the U.S. Men's soccer team at the 1994 World Cup. Rumor is Branson ran an aggressive campaign to wrestle him away from his position as assistant head coach of the men's team at the University of North Carolina-Chapel Hill. By aggressive, I mean they wouldn't take no for an answer and paid him an obscene amount of money. But he gets results.

My teammates, including my younger brother Blake, hustle to keep pace with me. Although Blake is only a sophomore, he earned his spot on the team based on his skills alone and not because we're related. Coach wouldn't go for that anyway.

As the intensity of the drills heighten, I dart toward the goal, attempting a swift maneuver that leaves Kellen, who's right behind me, frustrated. He's been trying to take the ball from me, unsuccessfully. As I'm about to kick the ball into the net, Kellen executes a violent tackle that sends us both flying. We crash into the ground.

I land flat on my back. For a moment, everyone freezes. Kellen attempts to crawl away, but something in me snaps. The move was deliberate, and he should be punished. I grab him around the neck, startling him.

We grapple on the grass, limbs intertwined as Kellen tries to shake me. Murmurs float in the air, but I can't make out what's being said. I'm too angry. I pin Kellen down on the grass. Coach's whistle shrills, cutting through the mist of my anger.

"Enough!" he bellows.

As team captain, I should set an example. My action fills me with anger and embarrassment. I get up from the ground, removing the grass from my hair and jersey.

"What's your problem?" I ask Kellen.

The team has now gathered, watching the exchange with mild amusement. Coach says nothing. He has taught us to resolve our conflicts.

Kellen's eyes flare with resentment. "No problem here, Lucas. Just trying to enhance my already awesome skills so we can beat Thayer."

Kellen wipes dirt from his face and gives me a devious smirk that makes me want to drop him like a stone. He tackled me on purpose. A move designed to push me to lose my temper and look bad in front of Coach and the team. Coach holds me to a higher standard as the captain. Kellen is determined to undermine me so he can steal my position. That ain't happening.

"Grow up, Kellen. If you don't possess the mental toughness to handle a simple practice, perhaps you don't have what it takes to play for Branson."

Tension hangs thick in the air. George Yancey, a defender on the team and fellow Alerie Club member says, "This is not cool, Kellen. What are you trying to prove?"

Kellen's hands ball into fists, his jaw set tight. His eyes are wild, as though he's contemplating punching me.

Coach Prescott, a towering six-five man with graying dark hair and piercing gray eyes, tells the team to rerun the drills. Everyone except Kellen and me. His expression falls somewhere between *what were you thinking* and *get your act together. Now!*

"What I just witnessed on the field is unacceptable, shameful. You embarrassed yourselves and your teammates. I don't care who started it or why."

Coach's observation that Kellen initiated the scuffle makes me feel slightly better. That is until Coach looks me dead in the face, his countenance full of disappointment.

"Lucas, you're captain of this team, and I expect you to control yourself, provoked or not. This whole incident is beneath you both, and it will *never* happen again. How do you think it will look if word gets out that Branson's captain and his striker got physical with each other?"

Neither one of us says a word for a few beats.

"It won't happen again, sir," I say.

"You have my word." Kellen parrots my response.

Coach adds, "You both owe your teammates an apology. If you can't practice restraint, you're no good to this team, am I clear?"

Coach issued the warning I was afraid of. One more misstep and I'm out. This incident is a clear reminder I should work harder the next time someone provokes me to keep from exploding. I wanted to pound Kellen's face into the ground for tackling me on purpose. Those kinds of thoughts scare me.

"Perfectly clear, Coach," Kellen says.

"Good. When you come to practice, your job is to focus and train. Train and focus. Everything else, leave it off the field."

CHAPTER 9

You okay?" Blake asks, as he towels off the beads of sweat glistening on his forehead. The locker room buzzes with activity, the air thick with a mingling scent of sweat and chlorine. The metallic clatter of lockers opening and closing echoes through the room, punctuated by the occasional burst of laughter and the sound of running water from the showers.

Blake and I stand in a corner of the locker room, speaking in hushed tones. Blake has what our mother calls quiet charm. He's not the loudest or most confident guy even though he has every reason to be. Blake is kind, loyal, and humble. Also, he's the most amazing baker.

Yes, my brother bakes; he can whip up any new creation or put his own twist on old classics, from cakes to pies, bread, and everything in between. He started watching our mom cook and bake when we were kids and took to baking like a duck to water.

Blake was first runner-up on The Cooking Network's Kids Baking Cup Championship a couple of years ago. On the soccer field, he's one of the most versatile players we have. My younger brother is a teenage Renaissance man. Except when Alexis and I tease him about his crush on Sabrina Sala. She likes to cook and bake too, so they're a perfect match.

"I'm fine. I let Kellen's antics affect me. I'm embarrassed. What's his problem anyway? Besides being miffed that I'm the captain and he isn't."

I lean against one of the lockers with my arms folded. "I don't like what happened during practice nor the way he treats Makenzie. I'm worried about her."

"Did she say anything to you?" Blake asks.

"Mack and Kellen had an argument yesterday after the assembly. He was all over her, stressing her out. She wants to break up with him but says he's clingy."

"So let her handle things with him. It's no reason to get benched. Coach was not happy."

"True. But if Kellen hurts Mackenzie, I'll make sure he pays."

"Is that so?" Kellen swaggers into the area, peeling off a sweat-soaked jersey, his signature smirk plastered across his face.

"I'm talking to my brother, Kellen. It's a private conversation."

"I heard you making threats." He shakes his head as if I'm some bratty kid who disappointed him. I ask Blake to leave us alone, and my brother hits the showers.

"You're in over your head, Lucas. Mackenzie is not the sweet, innocent girl you think she is." Kellen steps closer, invading my personal space, his eyes narrowing.

I don't flinch or move a muscle.

"There's more going on than she's telling you," he says. "Mackenzie is hiding dark secrets. And she doesn't need you to rescue her, to be the hero."

"Admit you're a lousy boyfriend instead of coming up with this ludicrous story. Have some self-respect, man."

"Are you calling me a liar, Rambally?" Kellen switches to my last name when he wants to sound adult and in control.

"Stop stressing her out, Kellen. She has enough on her plate without you adding to it. And I didn't much appreciate you trying to intimidate her yesterday."

I suspect Kellen was trying to convince Mack not to dump him and got intense about it.

Doubt creeps into my thoughts, though, as I consider Kellen's words. *Dark secrets.* I flash back once again to the cryptic warning to trust no one. And now, Kellen says the same. Do these secrets have anything to do with why Mackenzie comes to school some days exhausted?

The image of Mackenzie, the girl I thought I knew, begins to fracture. Mackenzie, who a couple of weeks back hid her phone from me when I was too close to the screen. I shake off the thoughts. I won't be disloyal to my friend. Although she hasn't responded to my text asking for an explanation of *Trust no one.*

"You know what your problem is, Rambally? You have blinders on," Kellen taunts. "Step out of your little bubble, your perfect little fantasy world where everyone is good and follows the rules and bad behavior should be punished. Open your eyes, man. Take off the blinders before you get blindsided."

After Kellen leaves the locker room, my thoughts wander to the past. I've known Mackenzie since I was a freshman. We often met up in the abandoned garden at the far end of campus. The one Mack discovered by accident.

The garden was our spot when we wanted to escape the pressures of school and life in general because it's peaceful and quaint. We even named the giant gnome with the red hat Mr. Gnomington. I think back to that warm, sunny day last spring.

"I wonder how many secrets Mr. Gnomington has heard over the years," Mack said. "Before the garden was abandoned, I'm sure a lot of kids came here. Secret meetups. Secret plans. Secret confessions."

The future spymaster in me agreed with her. "Tons of people could have visited the garden and nobody but Mr. Gnomington would see."

Mackenzie's mood changed abruptly. She said, "I hate it here. It's hard to make friends. Everyone is so cliquish. I hate the gossip and backstabbing, the intense competition about everything. How fake so many people are."

I gazed at her, surprised she felt that way. She added, "Yeah I know. It's a great opportunity that will open a lot of doors for me, but geez, does it have to be so…I don't know… Machiavellian?"

Mackenzie painted an accurate picture of Branson. I didn't let those things bother me, but for her, it was a different story.

"Don't worry so much," I said. Easy for me to say. I lived at home, attending Branson as a day student. I went home every day after school and ate dinner with my family most nights. Liam and Caleb, childhood friends since third grade and day students also, lived only a few streets away from me. Mack didn't have the same privilege.

"Soon, you'll be out of here," I said, attempting to encourage her. "Graduation is coming faster than you think."

However, recent events paint a sinister picture. One that suggests my friend could be living a double life.

CHAPTER 10

We agreed to meet at Bonnie's Tea House on a quiet side street a few minutes from downtown Lexington. Mackenzie and her family lived in England for two years when she was younger because of her dad's job. She developed an appetite for tea, scones, toffee pudding, and all sorts of British baked goods.

When she texted this morning to say she had information on my biological father, I couldn't contain my excitement; I barely concentrated during classes.

The meeting will also give me a chance to ask Mackenzie again about the warning text she sent last night after she scampered from the common room and why everyone thinks she's hiding dark secrets.

I thought treating her to Bonnie's would be a great way to thank her for helping me and provide the best atmosphere for asking difficult questions.

It's 2:45 p.m. when I arrive at Bonnie's, fifteen minutes before the agreed time. The interior is quaint and charming, with vintage teapots and artwork adorning the walls. I grab a seat at a large window with a view of shops and stores across the street and traffic whizzing by.

The gentle murmur of conversation weaves through the space, with the occasional clink of teacups adding to the ambience. Glancing at the menu, I can't decide between the fruit tart and raspberry French macaron. But I'm definitely having the cranberry autumn tea.

Bonnie, the owner, saunters over to my table. "Hey, Lucas. Haven't seen you around in a while. How are you? How's school?"

"I'm fine. School's great." I glance at the door. Mackenzie should arrive any minute.

"Expecting someone?" she asks.

"Mack. I hope she gets here before you close up for the day."

"I'm sure she'll arrive soon. In the meantime, what can I get you? It's on the house."

"Really? You don't have to do that. Mack loves this place, and I'm treating her."

"Aww. That's sweet of you, Lucas. Mackenzie is lucky to have you as a friend. Don't you worry about it. Anything you and Mackenzie want is on me. I won't take no for an answer."

To argue with Bonnie would be rude. She's offering to do something nice. Besides, I could scarf down several tarts in one go, which isn't gentlemanly in a place like this.

"Okay, I'll have the cranberry autumn tea to start. I'll wait for Mack before ordering pastries."

"Coming right up."

It's ten minutes after three, and Mackenzie isn't here. At first, I thought she was just running late. I didn't want to text her and appear desperate and anxious. But now, I'm beginning to get nervous. I tap out a text.

> Lucas: Are you on your way? Bonnie says our orders are on the house. You can have all the scones you want.

No response. A minute goes by and then two and three, and still no answer. No speech bubble bobbing up and down. Anxiety swirls in my belly. Where is she? Did she forget? Or got held up after school? Perhaps something unavoidable popped up?

What if Kellen found out she was meeting me and made a big stink about it, convinced Mack to leave me hanging?

But she wouldn't leave me hanging. She could be meeting with her guidance counselor, I reason. Given her stress about college applications, it's possible she forgot about our meetup and her guidance counselor meeting is running over.

I order another tea. It's now twenty after three, and still no response to my text. Bonnie comes by the table.

"Mackenzie still isn't here?"

"No. And she didn't respond to my text."

"Don't worry, she'll show up." Bonnie gives my shoulder a gentle squeeze, but I'm panicking inside. I try texting again.

> **Lucas:** Are you coming? No problem if you got held up at school. We can talk tomorrow. Just let me know you're okay.

Then, a few minutes later, I try again.

> **Lucas:** Seriously. You're freaking me out. Why won't you answer my texts? Are you okay?

By three forty-five, fifteen minutes before Bonnie closes, Mack still hasn't arrived and never responded to a single text. I stand and head toward the door to have a look outside. I see nothing but gray skies, the beautiful afternoon sun gone. I text Liam and Caleb.

> **Lucas:** Have you seen Mack? She was supposed to meet me at Bonnie's forty–five minutes ago, but she never showed. She's not responding to my texts or calls.

> **Liam:** Haven't seen her. Maybe she spaced.

> **Caleb:** It's not like Mack to flake.

> **Lucas:** I agree. That's why I'm worried. Let me know if you guys hear anything.

I call Mackenzie after I text my friends. It goes straight to voicemail. The café is emptying of customers, with just me and an older couple left. Bonnie gives me a sympathetic glance, as if to say, *sorry your girl stood you up.*

Only Mack isn't my girl, not the way Bonnie thinks. There have been whispered rumors at school though, that Mackenzie and I are secretly a couple and that's why Kellen hates my guts. The Branson rumor mill goes overboard, churning out all sorts of mostly nonsense gossip. The more outlandish, the better.

As my fingers tap on the table, the café's cheerful atmosphere fades away, overtaken by a distant rumble. Raindrops patter against the window, quickly escalating into a relentless downpour. The crowd has thinned, leaving only Bonnie and me in the now-empty café.

"I'm sorry, honey," Bonnie says, sympathy softening her face. "Can I give you a ride home? I'm sure your parents are worried about you in this weather."

"Thanks, Bonnie. I'll text Blake to let him know you're dropping me off."

Why did Mackenzie stand me up on the day she was going to reveal what she discovered about my biological father? Is she okay?

The answer hits me like a punch to the head. *She's not.*

CHAPTER 11

I lie on the bed, mindlessly scrolling through my phone. It's Saturday afternoon, twenty-four hours since Mackenzie stood me up at Bonnie's. All my texts and calls went unanswered. No one has any news about her whereabouts.

Liam, Caleb, and the twins asked around to friends and acquaintances at school also and still no sighting. Misha has neither seen nor heard anything either. It's unlike Mackenzie to ignore me. But the truth is, she's taken off before without warning. Ignoring me, though, is new.

Perhaps playing music will distract me for a little while, free me from the velocity of terrifying thoughts that won't simmer down. Thoughts that insist something is horribly wrong.

My favorite playlist of eighties pop tunes and nineties rap and hip-hop fail to do the trick. As I'm about to pause "Mama Said Knock You Out" by LL Cool J, my phone buzzes with an incoming call from an unknown number. Spam, probably. Not in the mood.

I silence the call, go back to scrolling, and then decide to pull out the manuscript for one of the graphic novels I'm working on. It's a hobby I developed in eighth grade. The creativity serves as an outlet to help me channel stress and anxiety. Minutes later, I quit.

Nothing helps to soothe the growing dread and unease. My cell buzzes again. Same number. Persistent, whoever this is. I ignore the call once more. When it buzzes a third time, curiosity gets the better of me and I answer.

Sighing, I say, "Hello?"

A shaky voice comes through the line, filled with worry and exhaustion. "Lucas, this is Mrs. Fleming, Mackenzie's mom."

I shoot up into a sitting position, alarm bells pummeling my brain.

"Hi, Mrs. Fleming. Is everything okay?"

"No, Lucas. Have you seen or heard from Mackenzie today?"

"Uh, no. She was supposed to meet me for coffee yesterday afternoon, but she never showed."

She pauses and then takes a deep breath, as if trying to steady herself. "Lucas, Mackenzie didn't come home last night. We're calling her friends, relatives … everyone we can think of. I was hoping you've heard from her."

Mackenzie didn't come home? I'm trying to remain calm, but panic creeps into my voice.

"No, I haven't. I… I don't know where she could be. This isn't like her."

"I know. We're so worried. If you hear anything, anything at all, please let us know immediately."

"Of course, Mrs. Fleming. I'll keep my phone on me. If she contacts me, I'll call you right away."

"Thank you, Lucas. And please, if you think of anywhere she might be, don't hesitate to check. We're going to call the police if we don't hear from her soon."

"I will. I promise."

I stare at the phone in my hand after Mrs. Fleming hangs up, willing it to buzz with a message from Mackenzie. But the screen remains dark and ominous.

CHAPTER 12

Things go from bad to worse.

Dr. Crawford, our headmistress, stands nervously at the podium, fiddling with her scarf.

She clears her throat. "Good morning, students," she begins, her trembling voice echoing in the hushed silence. "I regret having to share this news with you. One of our students has gone missing. Senior Mackenzie Fleming was last seen during school hours last Friday."

The stillness hovers over the assembly. Then murmurs erupt like wildfire, spreading uncertainty and fear in their wake.

A wave of numbness washes over me, freezing all thought and emotion. *Mackenzie is officially missing. Mrs. Fleming called the police and the school.* Although I had the feeling something was seriously off with Mackenzie, especially with my unanswered calls and texts and her mother reaching out, I still held on to the hope she would resurface. Like she always had in the past. What I wasn't expecting was confirmation of my worst fears.

Like the rest of the assembly, I wait for the remainder of the story to come tumbling out of Dr. Crawford.

"Mackenzie's parents reported her missing Saturday evening. They became concerned after she failed to come home on Friday as planned for a family gathering on Saturday. Her last communication was a text assuring her parents she was on the way home. But she never arrived."

My heart sinks further as I try to imagine what could have happened to Mackenzie.

Dr. Crawford continues, her voice firmer this time, "Law enforcement is working tirelessly to find her, and we are fully cooperating with their efforts."

My gaze sweeps over the auditorium, taking in the tense atmosphere. Whispers and expressions of disbelief ripple throughout the room. My hands lie limply in my lap. Slowly, my thoughts thaw from their frozen state.

My brain latches on to something Dr. Crawford said. Mack texted her parents that she was on her way but never showed.

If I'm following this scenario logically, Mack received my texts on Friday afternoon, ignored them, and then responded to her parents later on Friday, perhaps early evening, to say she was on the way home.

Then where was Mackenzie between the time school ended on Friday, when we agreed to meet at Bonnie's and later Friday when she texted her parents?

Something about this scenario doesn't add up. Mackenzie wouldn't unnecessarily worry her parents. She's one of the most responsible people on the planet.

Liam, breaking his silence says, "You were right to worry, Lucas. Mackenzie didn't ghost you."

I remain quiet, my mind swirling with questions. Dr. Crawford is replaced at the podium with the school lawyer. He issues a stern warning to avoid the press and direct all inquiries to his office or Dr. Crawford's.

"What do you think happened?" an anxious Liam asks. We're heading down the crowded hallway toward our lockers.

The usual vibrance and chatter of Monday morning has been replaced by a dull, unsettling hum of fear and unease.

Mackenzie is hiding dark secrets. Kellen's words crash into my thoughts like a tidal wave. It's one thing to have suspicions about a friend's absence, but to have official confirmation that she disappeared is hard to process.

Trust no one. What did Mackenzie mean by that? The timing of the message was odd, appearing after she ignored Misha's greeting and rushed out of the common room. Or maybe it had nothing to do with Misha and everything to do with why Mackenzie vanished.

I lean up against my locker for support, and Liam does the same. We stand together, united in our shock and fear and the million questions buzzing around our collective minds.

The news still doesn't seem real, so I pull out my phone and look through texts, emails, and my call log. Anything to see whether Mackenzie tried reaching out to me. Nothing. Disappointed, I do something I rarely do: open the BransonBuzz.

BRANSONBUZZ

Posted by: @BransonFabulous

Where has our little Mack gone? Oh where, oh where could she be? Is this one of her "breaks," or is something more sinister at play? #PrayforMackenzie #Shook #SolvetheMystery

Reply from: @TrueGlamorQueen

I'm not one to spread rumors, but perhaps Mackenzie needed a break from her rivalry with a certain STEM-queen wannabe who's thirsty for that award. One less competitor to worry about, right? #ShadyasHeck #CompetitionThins

Reply from: @StraightUpBaller

Weren't Mackenzie and her boyfriend about to break up before she disappeared? Relationship drama gone wrong? I hope she returns safe and sound. #BransonSupport #Shook #TrusttheProcess

Reply from: @GuardianofTruth

The police are already here. The first twenty hours are the most important in finding a missing person. Any information could be helpful. #StayStrongBranson

#BringMackHome

Reply from: @ChessGirlMagic

Mackenzie could be just a girl who
wants to escape the drama, so she took
off. We've all been there. Our favorite
Branson heartbreaker with the six-pack
and killer soccer moves has little Mack out
of sorts. That's my story, and I'm sticking
to it. The alternative…it's too awful.
#ComeBackMack #SolveTheMystery

Reply from: @BransonFabulous

Or maybe she wanted to escape from a
certain cringe teacher. Y'all know who I'm
talking about. #ComeBackMack #Shook

CHAPTER 14

BREAKING NEWS:
STUDENT GOES MISSING FROM
ELITE PREP SCHOOL

We're live at Branson Academy, where the atmosphere is tense as news of a shocking disappearance rocks this elite campus. Seventeen-year-old senior Mackenzie Fleming has vanished without a trace. Mackenzie was reported missing by her parents Saturday night after she failed to arrive from school the previous evening.

Makenzie is described as a hard-working and conscientious student who had her sights set on attending MIT next fall.

Mackenzie was last seen heading to her dormitory late Friday afternoon, and no one has seen or heard from her since. Concord police are investigating the teen's disappearance.

This prestigious institution, known for its academic excellence and esteemed faculty, is now thrust into the spotlight for all the wrong reasons. Branson Academy, nestled on several hundred acres on the outskirts of the affluent town of Concord, has long been revered as a beacon of privilege and opportunity.

However, beneath the facade of academic prowess lies a darker underbelly of scandal and intrigue. Just last year, Branson was embroiled in controversy when allegations of a pay-to-play scheme surfaced, implicating several faculty members in a nefarious plot to boost grades in exchange for exorbitant sums of money. Wealthy students, desperate to maintain their status and secure their positions at prestigious universities, allegedly paid thousands of dollars to teachers to guarantee passing grades in courses they were failing.

Now, with Mackenzie's disappearance sending shockwaves through the campus, questions abound about what truly goes on behind closed doors at Branson Academy. The police are asking for the public's help in locating Mackenzie. Anyone with information is asked to call the Concord Police tip line at the number at the bottom of your screen.

Stay tuned for more updates as they become available.

CHAPTER 15

Tension hangs heavy in the dining hall. Murmurs and speculation float around as students ignore their lunch plates and clutch their phones, scrolling through social media for updates.

Thank goodness the media circus outside died down. Just before lunch, the scene was surreal with a chaotic cluster of news vans, their satellite dishes extending skyward like alien antennae.

Reporters and cameramen weaved through campus, ambushing students and faculty on the way to and from classes, their microphones outstretched like spears as they sought out anyone who could give them a soundbite to play on the various newscasts.

They sensationalized Mackenzie's disappearance like she was just another story to help them get more eyeballs than their competition.

I stare into nothingness, ignoring everyone at the table, hoping I will wake up from the nightmare. Mackenzie had been acting out of character, but she had kept insisting she was fine. *Stop being so intense already*, she'd told me.

Backing off was a mistake. I see that now. I can't even think straight, let alone figure out what to do; I haven't had time to think about where she could have gone or why. And whether it had anything to do with why she was acting so strange.

Liam grips my arm. "Have you seen the latest on the BransonBuzz?"

"It's just stupid rumors. People running their mouths about things they know nothing about."

"We have to be optimistic," he says. "The story made the news. Somebody out there knows something. The police will find her, Lucas."

Fear and confusion rain down on me in a long, painful stream. Mackenzie suffers from Type I diabetes. Her blood sugar levels can get dangerously high, and if she can't access her medication, I don't want to think about what could happen to her.

"And what if the police don't find her?" I ask Liam.

CHAPTER 16

There's another rumor floating around," Liam says, glancing around the crowded dining hall before leaning in closer to me.

"What's that?" I reach for a fry on my plate, but my stomach churns at the thought of food.

"That Mackenzie isn't doing well in history, and she's cracking under the pressure. Her whole focus has been her STEM classes and her senior Capstone project. Mr. Glendale won't give her a retake on the history test, and she's afraid it will affect her GPA."

The noise of the dining hall fades away as I contemplate this latest tidbit. Many rumors have already circulated in the short time since we learned Mackenzie vanished.

"No way. Mackenzie wouldn't take off because of a bad grade."

It's true. Mackenzie is a hard worker, hates complaining, and would work twice as hard if she got a bad grade on a test. Not run away. Not worry her parents to death.

It makes sense she would focus on the STEM classes. Mack believes MIT will give her a leg up on the path to becoming a digital forensics analyst. She wants to investigate cybercrimes and gather evidence on how criminals commit those offenses.

Mackenzie dreamed of majoring in Computer Science and minoring in Economics. She has off-the-charts computer skills. I'm not bragging because she's my friend. Mack has created award-winning software. Plus, the kids in the computer science club are in awe of her. And these are people with serious cred when it comes to hacking and building tech.

My mind recalls a post on the BransonBuzz. A reference to competition and rivalry, STEM-queen wannabe, and the hashtag #CompetitionThins. What's that about? Is it a clue to Mackenzie's disappearance?

Liam says, "It's their job to find her, isn't it, the police?" I detect a catch in his voice. One that casts doubt as to whether we'll find her.

"I hope Mackenzie is okay, that she's plotting her escape," Caleb says, speaking for the first time since we sat down to lunch. "Remember that Escape Room adventure we did last year? She was the first one to solve the puzzles and figure out the clues."

I'd all but forgotten about the day-long outing to Boston. We all wanted to be on Mackenzie's team precisely because we knew she could effortlessly solve the puzzles and decipher clues that would lead our team to victory.

Turns out she was a mastermind at solving mysteries. I only hope she can put those skills to good use and return unharmed.

"What if the police want to speak with you?" Liam asks.

"Why would they?"

He shrugs. "You and Mack were … *are* friends, I mean. They would want to talk to anyone in her circle."

"I guess so. My parents will have to get involved. They won't allow me to talk to the police without them present."

"Yeah. So what are you going to tell the cops?" Liam presses.

Shrugging, I say, "I know nothing about Mackenzie's disappearance."

Transcript of Police Interview

Interview Location: Concord Police Department
Interviewer: Detective Corey Kang
Interviewee: Lucas J. Rambally
Present: Lucas's mother, Dr. Abigail Cooper Rambally

Detective Kang: Please state your name for the record.

Lucas: Lucas Jason Rambally.

Detective Kang: Thanks for cooperating, Lucas. This won't take long. I just have a few questions about Mackenzie Fleming.

Lucas: Okay.

Detective Kang: How long have you and Mackenzie been friends?

Lucas: Three years. We met when I was a freshman. We're also members of the same club at school.

Detective Kang: That would be the Alerie Club?

Lucas: Yes.

Detective Kang: When was the last time you saw Mackenzie?

Lucas: Last Thursday. We were together in the common room at school. We were supposed to meet at Bonnie's on Friday, but she never showed.

Detective Kang: Last Thursday about what time?

Lucas: Around seven in the evening.

Detective Kang: Are you certain of the time?

Lucas: Yes, approximately.

Detective Kang: What did you and Mackenzie talk about last Thursday in the common room?

Lucas: Um, Mackenzie seemed tense.

Detective Kang: Tense how?

Lucas: Jumpy, nervous.

Detective Kang: Did you ask her why?

Lucas: Yes. She said the stress of college applications.

Detective Kang: Hmm. And that was it?

Lucas: Yes.

Detective Kang: Are you sure? Mackenzie didn't provide any further details about why she was jumpy or nervous?

Lucas: No.

Detective Kang: What happened last Friday at Bonnie's Tea House?

Lucas: Not much to tell. Mackenzie and I were supposed to meet there. She never showed and didn't answer any of my texts or calls.

Detective Kang: Was that unusual for her?

Lucas: Yes, she's never ghosted me before.

Detective Kang: Did you notice any odd behaviors prior to the meeting in the common room? Did Mackenzie seem scared or worried?

Lucas: She was anxious. I asked her about it, and she said she was fine.

Detective Kang: Are you aware of any issues she was having at school with anyone?

Lucas: No.

Detective Kang: Let's go back to last Friday. Any particular reason you and Mackenzie agreed to meet at Bonnie's after the two of you spent time in the common room the day before?

Lucas: Um, no. I just wanted to treat her since she was so stressed out. I was trying to cheer her up.

Lucas: And, um, she mentioned that her parents aren't getting along and she was worried they would get divorced.

Detective Kang: I see. Did Mackenzie confide about any other problems with her family? It could lead us in the right direction to finding her.

Lucas: No. I don't think Mack would run off because her parents had problems.

Detective Kang: What makes you say that?

Lucas: Mack, well, she's not an impulsive person. She's a planner.

Detective Kang: Can you expand further? Are you saying Mackenzie planned her disappearance?

Lucas: No! Absolutely not. I'm not saying that at all.

Detective Kang: What was your recent fight with Kellen Fontaine about?

Lucas: Excuse me?

Detective Kang: Your soccer teammates we spoke to said you and Kellen Fontaine got into a physical altercation during practice last week.

Lucas: Kellen was a jerk. He tripped me on purpose during practice. I didn't like that, and we got into it. No big deal.

Detective Kang: Are you sure that's all it was?

Lucas: Yes, I'm sure.

Detective Kang: Thank you for cooperating, Lucas. We may have follow-up questions.

CHAPTER 18

No matter how many times I say Mackenzie is missing, it's still surreal. I'm waiting for someone to wake me from the nightmare so everything can go back to normal. But my interview with Detective Kang yesterday was all too real.

By the time Mackenzie was officially reported missing by her parents, twenty-four hours had already passed, including all of Friday night.

Detective Kang confirmed the first twenty to twenty-four hours after a person goes missing are the most crucial for investigators. After that, the case gets more difficult. What he really meant was the chances of finding Mackenzie safe and unharmed are dwindling.

As if to emphasize the point, there have been no leads so far. Not from the campus search, including the back woods. No trace of blood or footprints. No sighting on security cameras or in town for that matter. No response from her phone. I've called at least a dozen times, and it goes straight to voicemail.

It's as if Mackenzie was abducted by invisible aliens and taken to some far-off galaxy. And holding back from Detective Kang during my interview was not the smartest thing to do. I omitted Kellen's comment about Mack hiding dark secrets and her paranoia that had nothing to do with the stress of applying to college, and I certainly didn't tell him Mack hid her phone from me.

But my biggest omissions were the fact that Mackenzie and I were looking into the identity of my biological father and the BransonBuzz post about Mack taking a break. I assume they wouldn't put too much time and energy into finding her if they knew she had gone missing before.

I can recall at least two incidents. Both occurred when she was experiencing stress and overwhelm. Like me, Mackenzie takes mostly AP classes. Add a rigorous STEM program on top of that, and it's enough to make even the most brilliant student crack.

Mack went to her cousin's place, some small town in New Hampshire way in the boondocks, to get away from everything and everyone. She was gone for four days. I only found out because I kept hounding her.

Then there was the bullying episode that stressed her out to the max. She had a snooty, stuck-up rich girl for a roommate. I can't remember the name of that insipid creature. Anyway, she demanded to be moved to another room. Apparently, Mackenzie *smelled poor* and her roommate didn't want the stench to rub off on her.

While waiting to be assigned a new room, she would leave snarky, passive-aggressive notes for Mackenzie and talk loudly on the phone late at night so Mack couldn't get to sleep.

Mack's response to that insufferable witch was to take a bus to New York City and meet up with a childhood friend for a few days.

If I'm going to find out what happened to Mackenzie, I must face reality: she *is* missing. The vigil tonight may be a good place to start my covert investigation. I can observe people, see if anyone is acting suspicious. Eavesdrop on conversations that could provide clues.

I arrive at my locker to swap out the books for my afternoon classes. A few students are doing the same, their faces a mixture of fear and concern. No one will be able to focus on afternoon classes anyway.

When my phone pings in my pocket, I place my backpack on the ground and take out the phone to see the message. It could be from Mackenzie.

> **Unknown:** The past holds the key to the present. What you buried deep may soon come to light.

I glare at the screen. Is this a joke? Was this message intended for me? I type back a response.

> **Lucas:** Who is this? What do you want?

> **Unknown:** In the game of vengeance, every move has a consequence. Yours may have set events in motion.

> **Lucas:** What are you talking about? This isn't funny. Who are you?

After a minute, there's still no response to my questions. I lean up against my locker and close my eyes. *Vengeance. Consequence. The past holds the key to the present.*

What if someone knows what Mackenzie and I did and she's paying the price?

CHAPTER 19

Mackenzie

Two weeks before the disappearance

C an I get you anything?"

"No, thanks."

"There's nothing to be nervous about. I just want to have a little chat." He gives me what is supposed to be a disarming smile, but it comes off more like a menace.

I admit the suspense is killing me. What does he really want?

When you get an urgent text telling you to meet Damian in the back of the library in a dusty, forgotten room where old technology goes to die, it's either the setup for a horror movie or something seriously messed up is about to happen.

Spoiler alert: it's the latter.

There's something about being summoned by *him* that makes you question all your life choices. Damian only cares about one thing: make it rain cash.

Many unsuspecting people don't know the many calculated and devious ways they were targeted, manipulated, or betrayed.

Branson is built on cut-throat competition, and ruthless tactics are highly encouraged. But we pretend those are just nasty rumors. It's no coincidence that at least seventy-five percent of faculty have advanced degrees because Branson has been a feeder school for the Ivy League for decades.

Damian leans back in the worn leather chair and twirls a pen. "You've been restless lately. Unfocused. Skipping meetings. Sometimes it takes you five or six hours to get back to me. That kind of behavior makes me nervous, and I question your loyalty."

My heart skips a beat. He didn't drag me here to air his grievances. It's a warning. A serious one. I have a lot on my plate, and he doesn't care: a full course load plus my senior Capstone project, college applications, working for him, and trying to keep Charlie Covington from stealing my scholarship.

Things have gotten so bad that I shuffle into class every day like a zombie running on empty and desperately searching for the nearest caffeine fix.

"You never have to question my loyalty. I'm juggling a lot and struggling to balance it all. It has nothing to do with you or the society."

"Oh, don't get me wrong, Mackenzie, I understand."

No he doesn't. Otherwise, I wouldn't be here looking at his judgmental, irritated face.

He continues, "But we have certain obligations and deadlines to meet. We need you to pull your weight. And you've been slacking. You even admitted it yourself."

"I…What?" I'm too shocked to speak. That was a low blow, twisting my confession about juggling a lot. Psycho.

A ripple of worry takes root in my mind. Is he about to kick me out of this society or worse? I'm so exhausted from it all. Scared we'll get caught and I'll be expelled and go to jail. At this point, I wouldn't mind if a bus ran me over. That might not be so bad. *I should stop with the morbid thoughts.*

But everyone in this group knows not to mess with Damian. Oh, he can be as charming as those husbands in the psychological thrillers my mother loves... you know, the ones who turn out to be complete psychos who abuse their wives and convince her it's all in her head or just outright kills her.

One thing's certain. Damian doesn't play around when it comes to his money. I've scaled firewalls that protect confidential information, accessed archived files hidden in digital vaults, and uncovered the deepest, darkest secrets of powerful people. All so he can act like he's king of the universe.

At one time I thought I was invaluable. But once I understood what this group was all about, it was too late to back out.

"I pull my weight," I protest.

How dare he accuse me of lapsing? I carry this whole operation on my back, like Atlas with a side hustle of financial genius. Without me, this society would be as profitable as an ice-cream truck in a snowstorm. Now, if I'm reading him correctly, he's threatening to ruin my life.

"Did something happen? Why are you questioning my loyalty? I've done everything you've asked and more. I understand the stakes."

"That's right," he says pointing a finger at me. "You have a lot to lose. See that you never forget that fact."

A chill runs down my spine. Damian is going scorched earth on me. Lately, I've been ignoring some of his messages because the stress is too much. With all that I have going on, I don't have the energy to jump every time he snaps his greedy little fingers.

So here I am, trapped in a twisted game with no easy way out. But don't count me out yet. Because if there's one thing I've learned, is that sometimes the only way out is to play the game better than they do.

CHAPTER 20

Stepping into the central quad, I breathe in the crisp October evening air. The usual daytime bustle of activity is replaced by a somber silence. The old oak trees, with their sprawling branches, provide a canopy for the vigil. The LED candles flicker in the soft breeze, the flames dancing like restless spirits.

My pulse kicks up a notch as I observe the crowd gathered around. Students, faculty, staff, and even parents have come together, their faces illuminated by the soft glow of the candles they hold. The murmurs of the crowd blend with the distant chirping of crickets, creating a haunting soundtrack to the evening.

I spot a few familiar faces. Emily, Mackenzie's roommate, stands near the front. Beside her is Mr. Glendale, Mack's history teacher, his usually stern face softened by grief. As I move closer, I hear snippets of whispered conversations, fragmented pieces of concern and speculation concerning Mackenzie.

I scan the crowd, looking for anyone who might be acting out of the ordinary. I don't know what I'm looking for exactly, just something, anything. Someone whose actions seems suspicious. My eyes land on Charlie Covington, who is standing slightly apart from the main crowd, her expression unreadable. Mackenzie never liked her. I make a mental note to talk to her later.

Mr. Moore, my math teacher and head of the math and computer science department, steps up to the makeshift podium and addresses the crowd.

"Thank you all for coming out. We're gathered here this evening to pray for Mackenzie's safe return. She is a cherished member of our school community, and I've had the privilege of being her STEM advisor."

As Mr. Moore continues speaking, I let my eyes wander again. Alexis and Blake stand next to each other, Caleb and Liam to their left. Misha listens attentively to Mr. Moore, her gaze laser focused on him.

The vigil continues, with a few more people stepping up to share their thoughts on Mackenzie and calling for anyone with information, no matter how insignificant it may seem, to come forward.

Mr. Moore's speech fades into the background. From the corner of my eye, I see a shadow flit past the edge of the crowd. My pulse quickens. I turn, straining to see who— or what—it is, but the figure slips into the darkness beyond the quad. I glance around, hoping no one notices my sudden movement, and then quietly make my way toward the edge of the assembled crowd.

The farther I go from the glow of the candles, the darker it becomes. The only light comes from lampposts casting shadows on the cobblestone paths. I move swiftly, my footsteps echoing in the silence, ears straining to catch any sound that might betray the shadow's location.

I catch another glimpse of movement near the main building that houses administrative offices and the main auditorium. I speed up, my breath coming in shallow bursts as

I round the corner. There, 1 notice the shadow again, this time slipping around the corner of the building. I'm close now, so close I can almost hear the figure's footsteps mingling with my own.

As I approach the corner, I slow down, trying to move silently. I peek around, expecting to see the figure just ahead. But the pathway is empty, the darkness swallowing any trace of the person I'd been following. I scan the area, my eyes adjusting to the dim light, but there's nothing—no movement, no sound.

Frustrated, I stand there, my mind racing. Who was it? Why were they lurking around the vigil? Could it be someone connected to Mackenzie's disappearance? I turn back toward the quad, my eyes still scanning the area, hoping for another glimpse. But the figure is gone, leaving only the chilling possibility that this person is watching me.

Returning to the vigil, I force myself to blend back in with the crowd, though my mind is elsewhere. The flickering candles seem dimmer now. When my text tone goes off, I frown and remove my cell from my pocket.

> Unknown: Mackenzie is not the only one who can disappear. Better watch your back, Lucas.

CHAPTER 21

Leaning against my locker with eyes closed, I replay last night's vigil. But it's not the speeches or hundreds of lit candles that dominate my thoughts. It's the figure at the edge of the crowd, taking chase, and the anonymous text threatening me. The feeling of being watched.

"Are you okay, Lucas?"

I open my eyes. Misha stands in front of me, her face etched with worry.

For a moment, the anonymous texts and the potential connection to Mackenzie escapes my brain. I'm touched by her concern. She nervously bites her bottom lip and hops from one leg to the other.

"Oh, I'm okay. Just…worried about Mackenzie," I stammer.

"It doesn't seem real, does it?" Misha says. " I mean, you hear about people disappearing on those true-crime shows, but you never think it could happen to someone you know."

I wince. No one ever comes back safe and sound on those true-crime shows.

Mackenzie isn't the only one who can disappear. Better watch your back, Lucas.

In the game of vengeance, every move has a consequence. Yours may have set events in motion.

I swallow hard and shake off the memory of the anonymous texts.

"Are you sure you're okay?" Misha asks again, this time with a frown. "Sorry if what I said upset you."

"No, no it didn't. It's just hard when your friend disappears without any warning. You can't help but think worst-case scenarios. Although I really don't want to go there, my mind does anyway."

Misha reaches out and strokes my arm in a gesture of comfort, which takes me by surprise. A pleasant surprise that makes me feel warm and tingly. And just as quickly, she pulls back as though my blazer contains static electricity that zapped her.

"Sorry," she says.

"No, please don't apologize. I—"

"Hey, Lucas, I want to ask you something. Can we talk for a minute?"

Ivy. She approaches with her usual confidence, books in hand, and a pink Chanel backpack slung over one shoulder.

The tender look of concern slides off Misha's face, and just like that, she scuttles away like an animal on the Savannah who senses a predator is on the prowl. I'm too stunned to speak. I look down the hall at Misha's disappearing form and then back at Ivy who stands inches from me.

"What is it, Ivy?" I sound hostile even if I don't mean to. I can't believe Misha ran off like that. Why would she run from Ivy?

"Calm down, Lucas. I just wanted to see how you were doing. You and Mackenzie are close, and her being gone must be terrible for you." She touches my arm the way Misha had just moments before. "How are you coping?"

I feel bad for my hostile tone earlier. Ivy looks really worried.

"It's my fault she's gone."

"Why would you say that?" Ivy asks.

Last night's events must have turned my brain to mush. Mackenzie needs me to find her, wherever she is. I can't be rattled by anonymous messages that make no sense. But the timing is suspect. First, Mackenzie vanishes and then the texts show up. I can only assume they're connected.

"Come on, Lucas. It's not your fault," Ivy says. "Nobody knew Mackenzie would vanish. All we can do is let the police do their job. The media being here may not be a bad thing. They could help find her quicker."

I don't have that much faith in the media, but I don't say it. This whole encounter is weird: Ivy's concern, Misha rushing off when Ivy arrived.

Ivy loops her arm around mine as if it's the most natural thing in the world, a habit she's adopted lately. "The whole school knows you're protective of Mackenzie. She's lucky to have you as a friend. But if you ever just want to talk or vent, I'm here."

"That's decent of you, Ivy," I say, untangling my arm from hers.

Ivy's gaze is steady as her eyes lock with mine. She says, "Just like in a game of chess, it's important to keep an eye on the other players, Lucas. Sometimes, the queen isn't the only piece with hidden power. There are pawns and knights lurking in the shadows, waiting to make their move."

The anonymous texts float into my head once more. *In the game of vengeance, every move has a consequence.* Something about Ivy's latest chess reference has my brain straining to make a connection in the text. But I can't.

"Plain English, Ivy. I'm not up for your latest riddle."

It's true. My thoughts are as scattered as confetti after a parade. I've had little time to play out possible scenarios that might be worth pursuing. The clock is ticking. I'm reminded every minute what Detective Kang said about the first twenty to twenty-four hours being the most important in finding a missing person.

Does Ivy have secret information? Why does she keep hinting that some kind of game is being played? She'd started hinting even before Mackenzie went missing.

"Who are these players I should watch out for? The pawns and the knights? Do you have information about why Mack is missing and who's involved?"

Ivy Ishihara—popular, beautiful, bossy, and loathed by my sister—plants a kiss on my cheek and says, "Text me if you want to talk, okay?"

She takes off down the hall with purpose, her long black ponytail swinging from side to side.

CHAPTER 22

Texting Kellen and asking to meet in the library after school was a long shot, but he agreed. I'm the last person he wants to talk to, but the situation calls for us to put our petty differences aside for Mackenzie's sake.

The library is quiet and private, exactly what's needed. My conversation with Kellen could be my official first move at playing amateur detective. I have to do something to bring Mackenzie home.

Kellen plops down in a navy-blue common area chair across from me. A small, round table separates us. Only a couple of students are around this section of the library, so we're mostly alone.

"Thanks for coming," I say, not sure how else to start the conversation.

"What's up?" Kellen asks, trying to sound causal, but the small tremor in his voice gives away his discomfort.

I force myself into a state of calm, choosing my words carefully so we don't end up in an argument, as is customary whenever Kellen and I interact.

"Last week after soccer practice, you said Mackenzie was hiding dark secrets. Do you think it has anything to do with her...you know, her absence?"

Kellen shrugs. "Hard to say. I've never known anybody who vanished before. It's creeping me out big time. And I'm worried sick about Mackenzie."

A brief silence follows. Then I say, "It's creeping me out too. Can you think of any place she could have gone, maybe a secret place, or did she mention any plans that didn't seem a big deal at the time?"

"Why are you asking me all these questions? The police are investigating Mack's disappearance. What can you do that the police can't?"

My turn to shrug. "I have to do something, Kellen. Did you forget Mackenzie is diabetic? What if she doesn't have access to her medicine? She could die."

Kellen looks down at his feet, his hands steepled together.

I add, "I'm not trying to be depressing about the situation, but she's been gone for days now. No word, no clues, nothing."

"I know," he whispers.

When Kellen's gaze locks with mine, his eyes glisten. "We had a fight before she went missing. We said awful things to one another. I accused her of cheating on me with you."

"Why?" Mackenzie never mentioned this accusation. It could explain the heated conversation last Monday in the hallway after general assembly let out.

Another shrug. "You and Mackenzie are tight. She was always going on and on about you and your family..." He trails off and stares off to his right, his gaze landing on a rotating bookcase.

"It's not true, Kellen. I don't think of Mackenzie that way and vice versa. To suggest there was something going on between us is beyond stupid." When Kellen remains silent, I add, "Is that why she wanted to break up with you? Because you were acting jealous and accused her of having feelings for me? Did you make her disappear because she wanted to dump you?"

I regret the words almost immediately.

Kellen whips his head back in my direction, his face like thunder. I think he even bares his teeth at me. "Don't be a scumbag. You know, Lucas, maybe you're the one who caused her to vanish. You and Mackenzie have your own secrets, don't you? Did she threaten to rat you out and you got rid of her? And now you're sitting here acting like the concerned friend?"

"Are you that stupid?" I ask, even though I probably deserve his wrath. The guy is in pain, and I accused him of causing his girlfriend to vanish.

But Kellen doesn't seem fazed by my insult. He assumes a knowing expression, stroking his chin and shaking his head as though he just solved the mystery. Did Mackenzie say anything to Kellen about what we did to Cole Parker?

Cole Parker. He could be the sender of the anonymous texts. He's been gone from Branson for over year now. An image of Cole's bruised-and-battered face flashes before my eyes, but I force the image to dissolve. What's done is done. It's not as if he didn't deserve it.

I pick through my next words carefully. "No, Kellen. I had nothing to do with Mack's disappearance. I was waiting for her at Bonnie's. She never appeared. That's when I knew something was up. Bonnie can vouch for me. When I arrived and when I left."

"Big deal. You could have hired somebody to snatch Mackenzie while you sat at Bonnie's, acting all innocent. You're not fooling me, Lucas. Word is, you have a dark side."

"What's that supposed to mean? You're talking nonsense." *Is he? You did lose control with Cole.*

My anger spikes, and I want to kick Kellen, but it would only give him ammunition, convince him I do have a dark side. First, he accuses Mack of cheating on him with me, and now I'm the one responsible for her disappearance. I remind myself not to be so quick to take the bait.

Ignoring Kellen's comment, I ask, "Did Mackenzie complain about anyone at Branson giving her a hard time?"

Kellen scowls at me, as though I've deprived him of a fight by ignoring his taunt.

"Well?" I ask impatiently.

Reluctantly, he says, "Charlie Covington."

"What about her?"

"Things were getting intense. About the Emerson-Langston STEM Award."

"How intense?"

Charlie Covington and Mackenzie have a rivalry about the STEM Award. Charlie must be the STEM-queen wannabe mentioned in one of the posts on the gossip app right after Mack went missing. Mack had mentioned it to me, how Charlie put her down for sport and made Mackenzie feel as if Mackenzie was underserving of the award.

Personally, I think Charlie is a trifling B-word I'm not allowed to say, one with a superiority complex that masks major insecurities. An entitled brat who also feels threatened by Mackenzie's talent.

Did I mention my mother is a therapist? Her training must be rubbing off on me.

Mackenzie said that Charlie doesn't need the award, a full ride to a top college to study in one of the STEM fields. Her parents are filthy rich. She just wants to prevent Mack from winning the award. At least, that's what Mack told me, but Charlie was too smart to voice this out loud.

"Charlie implied Mack cheated on a couple of tests," Kellen says. "No one took her seriously, but the rumor is out there."

Would Charlie hurt Mackenzie to get the competition out of the way? It's one thing to cut someone with words, but orchestrating a disappearance is next level psycho. Yet, with her family's money and connections, who can say with certainty?

"So you're saying Charlie had a strong motive to get Mackenzie out of the picture?"

Kellen raises a brow. He says, "The Charlie Covingtons of the world would run over anyone who got in their way with a steamroller. It doesn't matter if a barista at Starbucks gets their order wrong or someone is competing against them for a prestigious award.

"Girls like Charlie don't mess around. And they know they can get away with anything."

CHAPTER 23

Later that evening, after dinner and homework, the twins and I decide to create a crime board. With our materials gathered ahead of time—a foam board, multicolored Post-it notes, yarn, pushpins, and index cards—we get to work in what we refer to as our Bat Cave.

The Bat Cave is a large room on the second floor of the house tailored just for us. The room exudes a cool, laid-back vibe with the walls adorned with posters. In the corner is a cozy sectional with colorful throw pillows.

Our parents sprung for a state-of-the-art entertainment system, complete with a large flat-screen TV, gaming consoles, and a massive collection of video games. We often have movie marathons here and intense gaming sessions. The surround sound provides an immersive experience. The shelves lining one wall are filled with books, board games, and collectibles.

Alexis writes the case title, *Mackenzie's Disappearance*, on the cork board. She caps the Sharpie and asks, "Where do we want to start?"

"Suspects," Blake says without hesitation.

"We should establish a timeline of events," I offer.

Soon, all three of us are on the crime board, writing notes, pinning photos, and drawing connections. When we're finished, we take a step back.

"Let's assume Mackenzie went missing last Friday when we were scheduled to meet up at Bonnie's," I begin. "So she's been missing five whole days."

Silence covers the room, solemn expressions all around. Five days with no news, no clues, and no idea where to look.

"If Mackenzie left on her own, and it's a big if, she would know how to avoid security cameras and leave undetected," Blake says.

A look passes between Alexis and me.

Blake continues, "Or if someone took her, they too knew how to avoid the cameras."

"Or, perhaps the cameras were disabled," I say.

Mackenzie definitely has the skills to do something like that. The more I think about it, the more the possibility comes into focus that she could have left of her own free will.

Alexis breaks into my thoughts. "You said Mackenzie was acting strange, nervous, and paranoid. You also saw her in a heated argument with Kellen, the same week she went missing."

"Right," I say. Alexis sticks a pin in Kellen's photo. "Mack said she was trying to break up with him, but he got clingy. And this afternoon, Kellen admitted he thought Mack and I were…well, you know."

Alexis rolls her eyes. "Is Kellen our number-one suspect?"

"Not so fast," I say. "Charlie Covington had a strong motive also. With Mackenzie out of the way, she would be in the clear to win that STEM scholarship."

"We should find out who else is in the running, see if Charlie threatened anybody else," Blake says.

"Even if she did, none of them went missing, only Mackenzie did," Alexis adds.

"Don't forget Kellen said Mack was hiding dark secrets." I never quite believed that Mack's paranoia, during our meetup in the common room to discuss my biological father, was all about Kellen stressing her out over an impending breakup. Mack was craning her neck, as if looking for someone she wanted to avoid, and I don't think it was Kellen.

Then I remember what Liam said, the rumor that Mackenzie was failing history and she was afraid it would affect her GPA and jeopardize her chances of getting into MIT.

"What?" Blake asks. "You were a million miles away just now."

"It may be nothing. Trying to understand how Mr. Glendale fits into all this."

Mr. Glendale had attended the vigil and appeared genuinely upset. But could I have misread the situation? Once I saw the figure move at the edge of the crowd and took chase, I pretty much forgot about who did what at the vigil.

"The history teacher?" Alexis asks.

"Yeah. If Mack failed a test and was worried about her GPA, how does that play into her disappearance?"

"A secretive Mackenzie is the best clue we have so far," Blake says. "Whatever she was hiding could be the reason she disappeared."

It's time to tell the twins about the phantom I spied at the edge of the vigil and how I followed.

"That sounds creepy and suspicious," Alexis says.

"And dangerous," Blake adds. "Whoever it was could have led you somewhere isolated…" Blake lets the rest of the sentence trail off.

He doesn't need to spell it out.

"It was risky, but it could have paid off. Did you guys notice anyone acting suspicious at the vigil?" I purposely stood separate from the twins because I wanted the freedom to move about freely and observe.

Blake and Alexis exchange a guilty glance.

"What is it?" I ask.

"You have to promise not to make a big deal about it," Alexis says.

"Okaaay," I say, drawing out the phrase.

"Promise, Lucas."

"Okay, I promise. Don't be so melodramatic."

Satisfied, Alexis says, "Liam and Ivy were kind of cozy at the vigil."

"What does that mean?"

"They were talking really close together, almost touching. Then they left together."

CHAPTER 24

This *newsflash can be interpreted one of two ways*, I think. Either it was all innocent and I have nothing to be concerned about or something is going on behind my back.

Besides Mackenzie, Liam McSweeney and Caleb Andersson have been my closest friends since we worked on a project together in elementary school.

Why would Liam and Ivy take off from Mackenzie's vigil, especially since, like me, Liam lives locally and is also a day student? I'm curious about where they could have gone and what they needed to discuss that was so secretive.

"Don't make a big deal about it," Alexis says. "Liam is your friend, just ask him."

"Yes, that makes sense. I'm sure it was nothing."

My mind races with various thoughts and scenarios, but I soon sideline those thoughts and return to the question of Kellen.

"I'm not certain we can trust Kellen," I admit. "He could be deflecting suspicion from himself."

I think back to Kellen accusing me of having a dark side and being involved in Mackenzie's disappearance. The dark side came out that night with Cole Parker. But no one knows what Mack and I did, how far we went to make Cole pay.

Had Cole waited an entire year for revenge? After all, they say revenge is a dish best served cold.

CHAPTER 25

Mackenzie

Ten days before the disappearance

I consider the library my second home. When I'm not working in the computer lab, I'm here doing research or studying. It's getting late, but I need to finish up my essay on *The Ethical Implications of Artificial Intelligence in Modern Society*. Strangely enough, this essay is not for my Intro to AI class; it's for English.

With my career aspirations centered around technology, I need a solid understanding of ethics. We've all seen the movies, what can happen when tech gets out of control. I'm only interested in tech for good, though.

Tapping my favorite pen against my temple, I reflect on the chilling premise of the 2014 film, *Ex-Machina*, which presents a scenario where an AI, designed to pass as human, uses its intelligence and charm to deceive its creator.

I type quickly as ideas flow from my brain, into my fingers, and onto the laptop screen. Ex-Machina *raises profound questions about the boundaries of AI consciousness and the ethical implications of creating machines that can outsmart their creators. It challenges the notion of control, illustrating how easily humans can be outmaneuvered by their own creations when ethical considerations are neglected.*

I begin a new paragraph. I'm in the zone, unstoppable, as though a muse showed up specifically for this essay. Now that I think about it, I should find a way to include snippets of it in some of my college essays. But I must secure an A first.

The film Ghost in the Shell *explores the blurred lines between human consciousness and artificial intelligence. The Puppet Master, an AI that has gained self-awareness, challenges the concept of what it means to be alive. This narrative forces us to confront the ethical ramifications of merging human and machine, questioning the sanctity of the human soul and the potential loss of individuality.*

The movie serves as a profound commentary on the ethical boundaries we must consider as we advance in AI technology, urging us to ponder the true essence of humanity in an age of machines.

Pleased with how this essay is turning out, I scroll to the section on algorithm bias and discrimination. I feel a sharp tap on the shoulder. I swing around and come face-to-face with Charlie Covington. I swear this girl put a tracker in my bag. Everywhere I go, everywhere I turn, she's there.

"Working hard, Mackenzie?" Charlie's voice drips with mock sweetness as she leans in close, her eyes sparkling with malice.

I force a tight smile, pushing back the urge to tell Charlie what I really think of her. Since I don't have a death wish, I'm forced to engage.

"Always, Charlie. Unlike some people, I actually have to work to secure my future."

Her lips curl into her signature smug smirk, and then she takes a seat opposite me. She taps her expensively manicured nails against the wooden table.

"Oh, I care about my future, Mackenzie. But unlike you, I don't have to resort to begging for handouts to get what I want."

Charlie wants to rattle me, undermine my confidence, and chip away at my resolve to win that scholarship no matter what so I can rub it in her stupid, smug face. I have this fantasy where I'm awarded the prize and Charlie weeps uncontrollably at my feet and begs for my forgiveness. But I kick her instead. I would never do that in real life, obviously. I wasn't raised by wild animals.

Instead, I say, "Is that so, Charlie? Because last time I checked, academic scholarships were awarded based on merit, not entitlement."

Charlie's laughter rings out like a sharp crack in the stillness of the library, drawing the attention of nearby students who glance curiously in our direction.

"Oh, Mackenzie, you're so naïve. But I suppose that's what happens when you spend your whole life living in someone else's shadow."

"Oh, Charlie, bless your heart for your concern. But trust me, I'm quite comfortable basking in the shade of my own achievements. It's a shame not everyone can experience that level of brilliance firsthand. But hey, I'm always here if you need sunglasses to shield yourself from the glare of my shadow."

I can't help it. Charlie has been relentlessly targeting me because she sees me as her only competition for that scholarship. She's petty and vindictive, and she might go nuclear on me for that retort, but I had to put her in her place. I'll pay for it later, but whatever. I refuse to let her diminish my accomplishments.

With a fake smile, I return to my essay and ignore Charlie. But she won't give up so easily.

"Ah, Mackenzie, always so humble. It must be exhausting carrying around that oversized ego of yours. But don't worry, I'm sure there's plenty of room in your shadow for both of us. After all, someone needs to provide the contrast to your mediocrity. I mean, it's so cute that you think you belong here," Charlie drawls, her voice dripping with contempt. "But let's be real for a moment. Branson is for the elite, the cream of the crop. And last time I checked, you don't exactly fit the bill. Frankly, everyone would be better off if you left for good."

My fingers wobble slightly as I continue typing, my eyes glued to my laptop screen. I won't give that witch the satisfaction of seeing me squirm. It's as if she took an extra dose of her mean-girl potion before she showed up at the library.

The thing about Charlie is, she doesn't care if there's a single grain of truth to anything she says. She just lets her tongue loose, her words landing like vicious stab wounds.

And, she keeps on talking. "Oh, don't get me wrong, Mackenzie. You do try hard. But let's face it, darling, you're in over your head."

I give Charlie a scornful look, but inside I'm silently counting to ten to compose myself. Every once in a while, the old insecurities I've had since starting at Branson show up uninvited. Very few people know that I got accepted as part of a special program for students interested in STEM.

Don't get me wrong, my grades were strong enough, but so are most of the students who apply. It takes much more than high marks to get into Branson. I think the interview and my projects were what clinched my acceptance.

Besides, Branson wanted to appear progressive and inclusive for the glossy recruitment brochures and school website. I'm not naïve. But even now, I'm one of only two Black girls in the senior class.

It's very cliquish at Branson. Girls like Charlie and their minions run the school. The girls on my floor are cordial enough but never invited me into their private world. I can honestly say Lucas is my one true friend here. He's a year behind me, but when we met, it was the breath of fresh air that I desperately needed.

We met at an Alerie Club meeting. He pulled up a chair next to me, extended his hand, and introduced himself. I remember thinking he was way too confident for a freshman. He must have caught the weird look I gave him because the next sentence out of his mouth was, "I know, I know, but I swear my mother is Black."

I said, "Mine too," and then we burst out laughing.

I looked him up and down and told him he didn't look biracial.

He said, "Maybe I should have a T-shirt made. It would say, *Flipping the script, Inverted Oreo.* Or, *Inside Out Oreo: The Sweetness Lies Within.*"

There was something magnetic about Lucas, even as a freshman. That's what I thought then and still do. We've become the best of friends, a friendship for which I'm so lucky to have.

Knowing Lucas cares for me is the perfect anecdote to the likes of Charlie. He makes me feel like it's not so bad here after all.

"You know what, Charlie? I've decided I belong here. Unlike you, I can't afford to be mediocre. After all, Branson is my big opportunity, and I must take full advantage. I don't have rich parents who reward my mediocrity and give me every advantage possible, deserved or not. So can't you show some compassion? Why are you so threatened by little old me?"

Not waiting for a response, I grab my things and walk out of the library, leaving Charlie with her eyes wide and mouth agape.

CHAPTER 26

The dining hall is a cacophony of clinking cutlery, overlapping conversations, and the occasional burst of laughter. Liam and Caleb are already seated at our usual spot, a corner table by the window overlooking the expansive green quad.

I weave through the maze of tables, dodging a group of rowdy guys from the crew team who are as loud and obnoxious as usual.

"Think they'll ever talk about anything other than rowing?" Caleb mutters as I sit down.

"Doubt it," I reply. "They probably dream about it too."

The rich aroma of roasted chicken and freshly baked bread wafts through the air as Caleb digs into his meal. I place my tray down on the table and take a seat, my mind already drifting to the conversation ahead.

I glance at Liam, who is preoccupied with his phone, his fingers flying across the screen.

"So, Liam," I begin casually. "I saw you and Ivy slip out of the vigil the other night. Everything okay?"

Liam looks up from his phone, a hint of surprise in his eyes, which he quickly masks. With a nonchalant shrug, he says, "Yeah, Ivy wasn't feeling well. Needed some space and fresh air. The vigil was overwhelming for her."

"Overwhelming how? Was she emotional, or was there something else?"

Liam sighs, running a hand through his unruly red hair. "She's been under a lot of stress lately, with school and everything else. We just needed to talk somewhere quiet."

"Talk about what?" I press.

Liam hesitates and then says, "Actually, we went off to play chess. Ivy's been teaching me strategies. She says playing relaxes her."

Interesting. Neither Liam nor Ivy had ever mentioned they meet up to play chess. Ivy has been dropping hints using chess metaphors, and I have yet to untangle what she's talking about. I sense there's deeper meaning behind those metaphors, but I can't quite grasp it, especially since they started before Mackenzie disappeared.

"Strategies?" I echo. "Like what?"

Liam thinks for a moment. Caleb doesn't say a word, but he is clearly enthralled by this conversation. It appears that he didn't know Ivy and Liam played chess either.

Liam says, "She said, 'Sometimes, to win the game, you have to sacrifice your queen.'"

"Sacrifice the queen?"

"Yeah," Liam nods. "She said sometimes you have to give up something important to protect the king or to win the overall game."

"Did she say why she brought up that specific play?" I ask, trying to keep my tone casual and steady.

Another shrug from Liam. "Not really. Why do you ask?"

"No reason."

I try to focus on lunch, but my appetite has disappeared. Is this latest metaphor more than just a chess strategy? It feels like a hint at something deeper. Last time I asked Ivy to explain herself she just sauntered off with no explanation. Now she's teaching Liam and doing the same thing.

The only explanation that makes sense to me is Mackenzie's disappearance is a game we're all caught up in. Is she the queen that must be sacrificed to protect the king? If so, who's in control of the board, and how do I identify the king that needs protecting?

CHAPTER 27

Another text message appears on my way to the common room. Whoever is texting me definitely knows what went down with Cole Parker. I'm at a loss. Can't go to the police. I'll end up expelled from Branson and possibly sent to jail if Cole is behind the messages.

I'm searching for Charlie Covington. I learned from a trusted source, Liam, that Charlie sometimes hangs out in the common room during her after-lunch study period.

I find her seated in a wing-back chair scrolling through her phone near a window, her long blonde locks partially covering her face. I take the seat across from her without saying anything. She looks up from her phone.

"What do you want, Lucas?" She tucks her hair behind her ears and narrows her eyes at me. Eyes that glint with suspicion.

I turn on the charm full throttle. For Mackenzie's sake.

"Can't a guy say hello to a beautiful girl? What's the world coming to? And what's with the hostility, Charlie?" I give her my most winning smile.

She relaxes. Still suspicious, but her shoulders relax. "You avoid me like spoiled milk, so why are you here talking to me?"

"Negativity is not a good look for you, Charlie. How do you know I haven't been secretly pining for you?"

She giggles and then shakes her head. "Good line. But it's a crock. The only reason you're here is because of Mackenzie. You heard we don't get along, and you want to know if I had anything to do with her disappearance."

Charlie just took the air out of my balloon. I press on anyhow. "Wow, Charlie. You've been watching too many crime shows on TV."

"Oh, yeah? So you don't want to talk about Mackenzie?"

"I didn't say that."

"Look, Lucas. Let's cut the crap. I don't like Mackenzie. I make no bones about it. I had nothing to do with her disappearance, and to tell the truth, I couldn't care less whether or not she's found. Now get lost and leave me alone."

What a heartless…I quickly reel in my thoughts, imagining my mother standing next to me, daring me to finish the bad word I'm thinking but am not allowed to say.

Feeling deflated, I get up from the chair without saying a word. Charlie had already gone back to scrolling through her phone anyway.

As I exit the room, I retrieve my phone from my pocket and compose a text. I'm not sure what I'm expecting, but I must try.

> **Lucas:** Hey, Mackenzie. Where are you? Are you okay? Everyone is worried. The police interviewed me. Are you hurt? Please text me back.

Nothing. No ellipses floating up and down, indicating she's composing a response.

My eyes remain glued to my phone as though, through telepathy, I can cause words to flow in response to my questions. *She's really gone.*

An exhausted misery floods my entire body. I hate to say it, but…I'm this close to…my eyes are welling up. I loosen my tie, shed my uniform blazer, and stuff it into my backpack.

Fresh air. That's what I need, so I start hurrying toward the exit. I almost crash into Misha in my haste.

CHAPTER 28

Decision time. Do I say hello and keep moving or address the question I haven't had time to explore, such as Misha taking off when Ivy hijacked our conversation?

"Hi," I say awkwardly. A few students brush past us.

"Hey, Lucas. It's nice to see you again," Misha says.

"You too."

Silence. And more awkwardness. Then, I ask, "Do you have a minute to talk? No pressure if you're busy."

"Sure. Let's find a seat."

I sit across from Misha in a semisecluded section of the common room. She won't look me in the eye. Instead, she focuses her gaze on a group of girls talking animatedly near the espresso bar. I follow her gaze and understand why. Ivy is holding court with her friends, The Phantastic Four minus Aurora Sanchez.

"What happened yesterday? Why did you run off when Ivy appeared?"

"Does it matter?"

"It does to me. Ivy scares you. Why?" I ask gently. "Believe me, nothing you say is going to shock me."

Misha returns her gaze to me and shrugs. "You wouldn't understand, Lucas."

"Try me."

I wait patiently for Misha to share her story. "Ivy and her friends are popular, untouchable. I don't want to cause any ripples, you know."

"Ripples? Why would you cause ripples?"

"It's better that I stay clear of her and her friends, most of the kids at Branson for that matter."

"Why?" I ask, puzzled.

"I'm an outsider. I don't have rich parents or connections. We all pretend Branson welcomes everyone. It's a farce."

She continues, "There are two kinds of students at Branson. Those whose parents are rich and connected, and those whose aren't. I will never be part of the club. They ignore me, and I ignore them. Simple."

I need a minute. My head swims, trying to make sense of it all. "So you ran because Ivy's parents are rich?" Ivy's dad Paul founded Ishihara Labs, a natural-products skincare company. Her mother is an appellant court judge in the seventh district of Chicago.

My question sounds silly on the surface. Of course it's more complicated than Ivy and her friends coming from wealthy families. But Misha needs to spell it all out for me. There's a hardness in Misha's eyes, as though she's cultivated that expression to protect herself. What was the cause?

The Phantastic Four are a popular clique at Branson. Kingsley Carmichael, Aurora Sanchez, Maeve Williams, and Ivy Ishihara. They're beautiful, affluent, and get the best of everything. From grades—there have been rumors that they'll do anything to stay on top—to exclusive parties and summers spent in exotic locations on their families' yachts, these girls inhabit a world few people will ever experience. They're not quick to invite new people into their world either.

But they also take the mean-girls cliché to new levels. What did they do to Misha? I haven't gotten a date with Misha yet, and Ivy is already causing drama.

"Do you want me to talk to Ivy? I can get her to back off."

"No!" Misha grabs my arm as if she's afraid I will stump off this minute and drag Ivy through the room or something.

"Sorry. I mean, no, you don't have to do that."

"Why not?"

"Look, the whole school knows Ivy is into you or whatever. I don't want to get in the middle."

I allow the comment to sink in for a moment. Then I say, "Misha, whatever rumors are floating around have nothing to do with you or me. Ivy and I are nothing. Besides, Alexis would disown me as her brother if I went anywhere near Ivy."

A radiant smile spreads across Misha's gorgeous face. My nose picks up on the intoxicating, sweet grapefruit-and-peach fragrance she wore when we met in the common room before.

I resist the urge to move closer to her so I can fully inhale the scent. It would be creepy and weird, and she'd never speak to me again.

"I like your sister. Sounds like she speaks her mind." Misha's eyes drift to Ivy and company once more. They're now seated and drinking espresso.

"Alexis has always been that way—fearless. My brother and I are scared to get on our mother's bad side, but not Alexis. She likes to push Mom's buttons."

"She's so tiny and seems quiet and innocent."

"Don't let her size fool you. She's a pint-sized tornado."

Misha laughs, the sound music to my ears. Talking about Alexis put her at ease. Is it too soon to ask Misha out?

"So," I begin. "Um…do you mind if I text you sometime? No big deal if you don't want me to," I add quickly. "I thought it would be fun to hang out. The autumn dance is coming up. It's totally cool if you say no, no pressure or anything."

My speech is rushed, and she studies me for a moment. Is it too late to adopt a nonchalant expression, like it won't bother me if she says no? I will seriously consider becoming a monk if she does. If what I'm experiencing is how it feels when a guy likes a girl and she rejects him, my heart can't take it.

"Sure, why not?" Misha nods her head slightly, pulls her phone from the side pocket of her bag, and then says, "What's your number? I'll call you, and you can get mine."

Relief floods over me, releasing all my pent-up tension. "Thank you," I say, assigning her name to the logged number.

"You should learn to relax. You look super intense. Why?"

"Why what?"

"Why were you so intense, like it's the first time you've asked anyone out?"

Because it is.

"Well, you could have turned me down."

"I could have. But I didn't. I'm glad you asked. Finally," she says.

"Finally?"

"You didn't pick up on any of my hints. I was beginning to take it personally, like I grossed you out or something."

Wait, there were hints? How come I missed them?

"Where did you get that idea?" I almost blurt that I've been too chicken to approach her.

"It's like I explained the other day. You're Lucas Rambally, the soccer hottie with the six-pack who's also kind, smart, and always in control. Enigmatic, a mystery. That's what the gossip says anyway."

I can't tell if she's serious or not. My brain is swirling with the idea that she'd wanted me to ask her out all this time and would have said yes. I wasted time being a colossal wimp.

"Don't listen to all that. It's just noise."

"Is it? Look how long it took you to ask me to hang out. I bet you were weighing the pros and cons, coming up with a plan, and accounting for every variable."

She continues when I remain silent. "And the only reason you asked me now is because you had questions about why I ran off when Ivy showed up in the hallway. Am I right?"

She nailed it. But I won't admit the truth. We don't know each other well enough for me to be spilling my guts. Besides, I still have questions, like what's the deal between her and Mackenzie?

"I think things through," I say. "I've been risk averse since birth. Just ask my family. I find it hard to go with the flow."

"I understand," she says. "It's better that way than to trust the wrong person."

There's something in Misha's tone that I can't quite interpret. Is it a warning to me, or is she commiserating that she trusted the wrong person in the past and things didn't go well? Was it Jayden Williams? I hate that guy.

It all started last year when we won our fourth soccer championship, beating Auburndale one to zero. Jayden and his friends were hanging out at his locker when I passed them. They started laughing, and Jayden stated loudly that football was the only real sport at Branson.

Since then, he makes it his personal mission to rant against and belittle soccer every opportunity he gets. That really annoys me, especially since that was a hard-won victory against Auburndale, and I scored the goal that clinched our victory.

As if on cue, Jayden appears, sucking all the air out of the room. I hope he's not stalking Misha. He's six foot three, all broad shoulders and a perpetual cocky grin.

Jayden approaches with his usual I'm-the-man-and-no-one-better-forget-it swagger. He smiles at Misha. I wish he would trip over his own ego and land on a pile of cactus needles. Or a porcupine.

Ignoring me, he says, "Hey, Meesh. Missed you at the party last night. What's up? You promised you'd come."

Meesh? Is it really so hard to say Misha?

Misha shifts uncomfortably. Her gaze bounces between me and Jayden. "I planned to come, but something came up."

Clenching my jaw, because I'm hanging on to my cool by a thread, I say, "Misha and I were discussing the autumn dance. Can you bother her some other time?"

Jayden finally acknowledges my presence with a dismissive glance, but the challenge is clear in his eyes. Turning to Misha, and ignoring me once more, he says, "Come to the next pep rally. You'll have more fun than the autumn dance. I guarantee it."

If Jayden is in play, I think you should back off. Mackenzie's warning during the Alerie Club meeting last week rings in my head. Is Jayden interested in Misha, or is this just a flex? Mackenzie was right, though. I hate drama.

"Catch you later, Meesh," he says. Jayden gives me a triumphant smirk before swaggering away.

"I'm so sorry, Lucas," Misha says.

"You don't have to apologize. Jayden was obviously being a rude jerk on purpose. Did he make you uncomfortable?"

The question might help me figure out if *Jayden is in play* as Mack suggested.

"I had the same question for you. I wasn't expecting him to barge in on our conversation like that."

"He didn't make me uncomfortable. Irritated, yes. The guy has a major ego."

"Yes. He's used to getting whatever he wants."

"Really? How do you feel about that?"

"Jayden is a big flirt. I don't take him seriously."

"Glad to hear it." A puff of air whooshes from my body.

"So, how about the autumn dance?" I ask.

"I need some time to think about it." With a playful grin on her lips, Misha exits the common room.

CHAPTER 29

After Misha takes off for her next class, Liam and Caleb magically appear like genies who'd been waiting in the wings. Liam plops down in the chair Misha occupied, and Caleb stands.

"Hey, man. Saw the whole Jayden thing," Liam says. "What a jerk."

"Yeah. Everything is a competition to him."

"But you got Misha's cell number," Liam says and offers a closed fist for a fist bump.

Caleb chimes in, "Only took three years."

"How long have the two of you been spying on us?" I ask.

"The whole time," Liam says, not a hint of embarrassment anywhere. "We were ready to swoop in if you needed help with Jayden." He turns to Caleb to back him up.

"No joke," Caleb says. "So, what do you want us to do?"

"About what?"

"Put fire ants in Jayden's football gear, spread vicious rumors about him, or what?"

"Whatever it is, we've got your back," Liam agrees. Another fist bump with Caleb follows.

"Or we're also willing to offer dating advice," Liam says.

I look at my friends since elementary school, incredulous. Liam, Caleb, and I became fast friends when we were assigned as a team for a group project in third grade where we had to create a diorama of a historical event. Even then, Liam's wild reddish-brown hair couldn't be tamed, and it still hangs in his face. He's constantly brushing it aside.

As we got older, Liam gave new meaning to the idea that guys like gossip as much as girls do. We both love soccer, but Liam never made the Branson team, so he supports me instead.

Caleb is Chinese and was adopted as an infant by the Anderssons who live in Lexington, same as my family and Liam's. Caleb is the adventurous, up-for-anything prankster in our group. That's why he's suggesting putting fire ants in Jayden's gear.

"We're sixteen," I say. "What dating advice could you possibly give me?"

"Hey, we may not have dating experience, but we know people who do," Liam protests. "Plus, we're plugged into the Branson rumor mill," he adds.

"Right," Caleb says. "Did you know that Mackenzie's social media accounts were shut down? People are saying she's on the run and doesn't want to be found, like she left town or something."

The news hits me like a thunderbolt. I didn't think to check. As far as I know, Mack doesn't spend a ton of time on social media. I scoop up my phone and pull up Instagram and Snapchat. Caleb and Liam are right. The accounts were deleted.

"Also," Liam says, "the other big rumor is Mackenzie ran away because she couldn't handle the pressure, you know, the STEM Award. She and Charlie had a big blow-up last week. Charlie has been spreading rumors that Mackenzie was cheating."

"That's ridiculous! Mackenzie would never cheat." My anger spirals for a minute. The nerve of Charlie. That girl is a robot. No feelings.

"Charlie actually said she doesn't care whether or not Mackenzie is found. What kind of person says that?" I ask.

"Maybe she knows something we don't," Caleb says.

"Like what?"

"Like why Mackenzie really disappeared."

"I confronted her about it. She said she had nothing to do with it, and then she told me to get out of her face."

"She could be lying," Liam says. "A lot of drama goes on here after school. Charlie's not a nice person. Nobody messes with her."

CHAPTER 30

Mackenzie

Seven months earlier – March of junior year

Have a seat, please."

My guidance counselor, Mr. Lennox, gestured for me to take the seat across from him. In his early forties, ancient according to most of the student body, Mr. Lennox was known around Branson for taking a lot of abuse from parents because he's one of the counselors for juniors and seniors.

The poor man was harassed on a daily basis from parents during college application season and well before that. He had a round, kind face and deep-brown eyes, and already started to gray. Surprise, surprise. I hope Branson paid him well.

I was curious as to why I was in his office. My mother already called him to get a report about his strategy for my college applications, although the actual applying to college won't happen for another six months.

The air crackled with an unspoken tension. "What's going on? What's this meeting about?" I asked.

"Your performance this school year has been exceptional, impressive even," he said. "AP Calculus and AP Computer Science are not easy classes, but you've risen to the challenge."

A weird feeling gathered speed in the pit of my stomach. Not sure what to call it, but I didn't like it. Okay, so I crushed my opening quizzes and assignments, but the other five students in those classes were just as impressive and exceptional.

Priya Batra built an AI-driven tutoring system that adapted to a student's pace and learning style to identify their strengths and weaknesses and help them get better.

Kai Wilson created a Cryptocurrency Trading algorithm to analyze markets and execute trades automatically, with the idea of generating a massive return on investment. I think Kai came out of the womb clutching a sign that read, *Future Billionaire, suckers.*

So why did Mr. Lennox single me out for praise?

He leaned in and said, "Mackenzie, I want to help you. Getting into MIT is next to impossible, but I think you have what it takes."

Oookaaay. Not sure how I should respond. "I thought you were already helping me, Mr. Lennox. Besides, why me? You know how competitive it is. Everybody is clamoring to get into the top colleges, and each school will only take one or two from Branson. I knew a couple of people who would literally kill a close relative for a shot at getting into their top-choice school."

He chuckled and then said, "You're skeptical. That's a smart play. And you just proved my point as to why you're smart, ambitious, and a hard worker. There's still a huge gap between men and women in STEM fields, especially for young Black women. I want to see you succeed."

"And how would you help me succeed?"

Honestly, I could use the leg up. With Charlie Covington and her mean-girl tactics, some of which I'm sure were illegal, breathing down my neck, I could use an ally.

For me, winning the Emerson-Langston STEM Award was about more than the substantial financial support, which would almost be a full ride for four years. It would also mean access to mentorship programs, research opportunities, and professional-development resources. Mom and dad made a good living, but MIT wasn't cheap. Heck, most of the top colleges in the country were within striking distance of costing six figures annually. Who could afford that for four years?

Mr. Lennox continued, his voice lowering to a conspiratorial whisper. "I know someone who's working on a research project outside of school, and they could use someone like you. Your teachers say you're an innovative thinker, and you bring a fresh approach and thinking to problem solving. This project could be a great addition to your college application and make you stand out even more."

Music to my ears. But how many people was he pitching this to, despite his claim that he wanted to help *me* succeed? If there were other candidates…wait. I didn't even know what the project was, and I was already thinking about the competition.

"I'm listening," I said. "What's this project, and who's running it?"

Mr. Lennox smiled, enthusiasm lighting up his face. "It's a project that will give you the opportunity to take your computer skills to the next level under real-life scenarios, almost like an internship. And the best part, you will be compensated for your time."

I could hardly believe what I was hearing. It sounded too good to be true, but Mr. Lennox wouldn't pitch this to me if it wasn't on the up and up. Besides, one of the reasons my parents wanted me to attend Branson was because the school had a massive alumnae network, globally. Branson graduates run Fortune 500 companies and dominate politics, entertainment, law, economics, and pretty much any other field you could think of.

The prospect of being involved in such a project made my mind race with possibilities, another chance to beef up my application, which was already off to a good start. But I wanted to be better than great, and this project could put me over the top, into that elite six percent of those accepted into MIT.

"But there's a catch," Mr. Lennox said, his voice taking on a serious tone. And just like that, my dreams crashed down to earth with a resounding thud.

"Of course. Isn't there always a catch?" I wanted to sound jaded, like someone who knew how the world worked, but I must have come off snarky because Mr. Lennox gave me a raised eyebrow.

He added, "This project requires total discretion. They can't afford any distractions or leaks. The work is too important and includes the handling of sensitive data. If you choose to accept, you must be prepared to keep the work a secret at all costs."

I wondered whether I was in a bad spy movie. Whenever words like *absolute secrecy, leaks,* and *sensitive data* were tossed around, it was usually a sign that you should run, and fast. But in the movies, they never did. The hapless recruit said yes, and before long, bad things started happening, and they couldn't stop it once it was set in motion.

CHAPTER 31

The air hangs heavy with tension. I slouch at the end of the sofa sectional in the Bat Cave, my mind racing with all kinds of terrible what-if scenarios.

Blake and Alexis sit across from me, their expression mirroring the anxiety I felt after I told them what Liam and Caleb said and about my meeting with Charlie.

"So we're still keeping Charlie on the crime board, right?" Alexis asks.

"Yeah. We don't know anything for sure. The police still have no clue what happened to Mackenzie, and I'm terrified now."

"Don't give up hope, Lucas," Blake encourages. "There's still the possibility Mackenzie left on her own if they're saying she was under a lot of pressure. And Charlie Covington. She probably plays with poisoned darts for fun."

"She's a witch." Alexis screws up her face in disgust.

Mack's disappearance is still getting some news coverage, but the media is losing interest. Her parents have offered a reward for any information, but so far, there haven't been any real leads for the police to follow.

Alexis picks up her phone and starts scrolling after a couple of taps. Then she says, "Which one do you want to hear first?"

"What are you talking about?"

"The BransonBuzz has fresh news."

"What are they saying?"

"Well, there's the drug rumor, basically that she went to rehab, and one about her checking into a psych ward under a fake name."

"You know what, forget I asked. This is why I don't pay much attention to that garbage app. It's just mean, vicious lies."

"But it *is* weird that her socials are gone though, right?" Blake says.

"Yeah, weird doesn't even begin to cover it," I mutter. What if something terrible happened to Mackenzie? On the other hand, if she deleted her social media accounts, it means she disappeared on purpose. Unless someone deleted her accounts.

Alexis, sensing my stress levels spike, comes over and sits next to me. "What do you think happened, Lucas? Why would Mackenzie delete everything? Why would she not respond to your messages, knowing how much you care for her?"

"I have no idea, Alexis." Her questions cause my mind to swirl further with more what-ifs and bad scenarios.

To make matters worse, I can't get thoughts of Cole Parker out of my mind or the text messages I've been receiving. Alexis must never discover what Mackenzie and I did to protect her. It was mostly me, truth be told. I came up with the plan and roped Mackenzie into helping me. If she's paying the price because…

"I tried texting Mack again today, but no response."

Alexis heads back to the crime board. She writes on a neon-green post-it note and sticks it on the board. Blake and I walk over to see what's written.

Deleted Social Media accounts.

"Didn't Kellen mention that Mackenzie had dark secrets?" Blake asks.

"Yeah. So?"

"If Mackenzie deleted her social media accounts, then it lines up with the theory that she ran away. Probably running from bad people."

Alexis writes two additional notes, *secrets* and *running from dangerous people*, and places them next to Mack's photo on the crime board.

Moving away from the board, I allow my thoughts to drift to places they shouldn't. Mackenzie used her hacking skills to help me out with the Cole problem, for example. But our actions didn't just affect Cole; they had far-reaching consequences for his powerful family as well. People who weren't used to facing repercussions for their misdeeds. I was determined to make sure Cole never hurt Alexis or anyone else again.

The texts started appearing after Mackenzie was gone. The two events must be related. But I can't share those thoughts with the twins.

My family must never discover I destroyed that guy's life on purpose and that Mackenzie may have paid the price.

CHAPTER 32

After everyone had long gone to bed, my parents and the twins, I sit at the desk in to my bedroom and boot up my laptop. The screen glows softly in the darkness. Blake's room is across the hall from mine, and I don't want to risk waking him by turning on the light.

In the distance, an owl hoots, its call echoing through the quiet night. The only other sound is the soft hum of my laptop as I pull up social media and search for Cole's name.

A string of old photos appear on the screen, and as I scroll through, I realize they're at least a year old. There's nothing recent, neither photos nor posts.

Next, I google "Cole Baxter arrest record," my fingers trembling with anticipation. Given his knack for causing trouble, it wouldn't be a shocker if his name popped up in a mugshot. But then again, his parents would do everything in their power to cover it up to protect their image as well as Cole's.

That's exactly what I didn't want, which is why the evidence was foolproof. I had to ensure Branson wouldn't bow to the Parker family connections; they had powerful senators and CEOs as close, personal friends who could make any problem go away.

I stop typing and push back from the desk. Nothing. It's like Cole Parker disappeared off the face of the Earth a year ago. Although my eyes are heavy and sleep is a good idea, I power through.

"Cole Baxter new school" is the next search term I enter, and nothing comes up. My frustration deepens. Did Cole move to another country? Who would know?

The answer comes to me in a light-bulb moment. I pick up my phone to compose a text and decide it's too late. However, there is a message waiting for me.

Unknown: Payback is a dish best served cold. Watch your back, for retribution may be closer than you think.

Hot panic stabs at me. This latest text is confirmation Mackenzie's disappearance is a revenge play. And Cole Parker is coming for me next.

CHAPTER 33

Mackenzie

One week before the disappearance

My predicament went from bad to worse.

I should have quit a long time ago. I tried, but he always dragged me back with threats of exposure. I'm a senior, and if one of the colleges I'm applying to discovers what I'm involved with, it'll be *sayonara, Mackenzie*. No bright future. My parents will be furious. All the money and resources they put into sending me to Branson would go up in smoke.

Stress builds up inside me, a cocktail of anger and frustration, as I look through my college applications. I've thought of leaving Branson and redoing senior year someplace else. The idea is both terrifying and exhilarating. But with each passing day, it becomes clear this idea should be more than just a fantasy. It's something worth pursuing.

I've worked hard to get where I am. Between my course load, working for Damian, and working on my college applications, I can't breathe.

I can no longer lead this double life. It's slowly killing me in more ways than one. My grades are slipping. I'm constantly on edge, worrying about getting caught by the authorities or betrayed by someone from within the group. The Riemann Enigma. Damian came up with that name. How clever. No one will be able to figure out what it means.

Isn't it better to go away for a while to ease the pressure? There will be other scholarships, other schools. The one upside to doing this job is the pay. I've made thousands of dollars in the past year, most of it stashed away in secret accounts.

Money isn't the problem. Escaping is.

CHAPTER 34

Mackenzie

Four days before the disappearance

I text Jacqueline, using the special app that offers end-to-end encryption and deletes the message after it's viewed. She's the only person I trust to help me get out of this mess. A few minutes later, she responds.

Mackenzie: Can we meet? It's urgent.

Jacqueline: Where?

Mackenzie: The Secret Garden. See you in fifteen.

The secret garden is tucked away on the west side of campus, accessible through a narrow, ivy-covered gate. The Branson campus is massive, and there are other places most students would rather hang out, but for me, the long walk from the center of campus to the garden is worth it.

The garden is practically hidden. I stumbled upon it by accident one day, just wandering around campus. I took a wrong turn and decided to follow the path less traveled, and voila, I ended up here.

There's only one other person I've told about this spot. Lucas. It's kind of our special place to hang out, dream, confide our joys and frustrations. Or just goof off. But I can't ask for his help. Mainly because he has no idea and I'm in so deep.

Other times, I come here alone to think. I sit on the stone bench, observing the old fountain and Mr. Gnomington, the garden gnome Lucas and I named. The autumn foliage is vibrant in red, gold, and yellows; the air is crisp; and there are fallen leaves on the ground.

Jacqueline will arrive soon, and I'm still unsure of what I'll say to her. Is it risky? Yes. There's nothing to stop her from ratting me out to Damian. My future—and perhaps even my life—hang in the balance because the society is dangerous.

She arrives and takes the seat next to me on the bench. I met Jacqueline when I initially applied to Branson. We aren't friends *per se*, but we get along because of our connection to the society. In her early forties, Jacqueline swims every day and is super fit. She lives five miles from school and loves her job.

"Thanks for coming. I... I don't know who else to turn to."

Jacqueline's expression softens with genuine concern, her brows furrowing slightly. "Of course, Mackenzie. What's going on?"

I inhale deeply and lay it on her. "I want out. I can't handle the stress anymore. With college applications, schoolwork, and everything else, it's too much."

She studies me intently, as if working out how to respond to my confession. I can't blame her. What I'm saying amounts to betrayal, at least that's the way Damian will see it.

"You realize this will unleash serious consequences, right? Damian won't just let you walk away. And it puts the rest of us in a dangerous position too. He'll start questioning our loyalty, causing chaos within the group. You know how much he values order and loyalty."

Jacqueline's voice is laced with worry and warning, her intense brown eyes searching mine for any sign of hesitation or doubt. A shiver runs through me and settles in my chest. I've been loyal and haven't said a word to a single human being outside of Riemann Enigma. But I wasn't cut out for living a double life, and I'm cracking under the pressure.

I'd rather scrub every toilet at school with a toothbrush twice than continue as a part of this group. Seriously. I'd choose to endure a marathon of AP Calculus and linear algebra classes on a loop, with a soundtrack of nails on a chalkboard, rather than do Damian's bidding any longer. A lecture on the mating habits of microscopic amoebas in Latin sounds more appealing.

But I don't say any of that to Jacqueline.

"I'm a senior, and I'll be out of here come next spring. Damian will replace me anyway. I'm just asking for an early exit so I can focus on school and college."

"Still, he's not going to be happy, and he won't make it easy for you."

"Why? I'm not staying at Branson forever. He must have a contingency plan, right? About what he's going to do once I graduate?"

"You know Damian, Mackenzie. He always has a plan. But maybe the plan doesn't include an early exit for you," she says, darkly. "Or any of us."

If her goal is to scare me, it's working. But what does it matter whether I leave the group now versus the spring? Damian doesn't need me. The group, under his leadership, has made a ton of money, so my departure shouldn't be an issue. Unless there's something going on I don't know about.

Perhaps the answer is much simpler. Damian is afraid of losing control, fearful that I might reveal the society's secrets. I rub my temples. Asking Jacqueline to meet may have been a bad idea. She doesn't seem enthusiastic about me leaving or helping me.

That shouldn't surprise me. The society is made up of people more concerned with lining their pockets than setting a good example for the next generation.

Jacqueline studies me in a way that makes me shiver.

"Forget I said anything. Maybe I didn't think things through. You're right, Damian always has a plan, and I'm sure he'll tell me what it is as graduation draws near. I guess I panicked. I have a lot going on, you know…" I trail off, waiting for a response, a reaction, something.

Her face is an unreadable mask. She says, "Sometimes Mackenzie, it's about what's best for all, not just the individual. Loyalty can open doors you never knew existed. Please consider all angles before you make a final decision."

With a faint smile and lingering gaze, Jacqueline says she needs to get back.

As I watch her walk off, my brain screams, *you've made a terrible mistake.*

CHAPTER 35

Diving into Cole Parker's digital footprint gave up no clues. It's like he ceased to exist a year ago after he left Branson. The guy is a ghost.

But is he? It's day six of Mackenzie's disappearance. The school hallways buzz with the usual morning chatter, lockers clanging open and shut, the mood subdued.

Walking to my locker, I can't help but glance over my shoulder every few steps. The texts have me on edge. Is Cole back in town, holed up somewhere carrying out his revenge plot? Or does he have someone right here at Branson doing the dirty work for him?

I open my locker, expecting to see a handwritten note with another cryptic warning written in a red Sharpie to jump out at me. Luckily, it's just my usual books.

Someone laughs, and I whip my head around to see who it is. Are they laughing at me? A locker bangs shut, and I flinch.

As I step into my first period class, Linear Algebra & Matrix Theory with Mr. Moore, I take my usual seat by the window.

The view outside mocks me with its idyllic perfection: a clear blue sky dotted with fluffy clouds, the sun shining brightly on the meticulously maintained lawn. But no amount of picturesque scenery can ease the inner turmoil associated with Mackenzie's disappearance.

Mr. Moore enters the classroom. His imposing, confident figure and contagious enthusiasm usually get me pumped up and ready to learn, but today, I can't muster the energy. Instead, I pull out the notebook and start re-creating from memory the crime board that the twins and I came up with in our Bat Cave.

Next, I write down ideas for a new graphic novel with Mackenzie's disappearance at the heart of the plot. I hope the creative process will offer me a fresh perspective on solving the mystery of her disappearance.

Opening scene – bustling high school corridor
Protagonist: Leo
Missing friend: Olivia
Last seen: ?
Olivia's secret life: ?
Unusual events before disappearance:

I'm so absorbed in my plotting that I don't notice a gradual silence take over the classroom.

"Mr. Rambally." Mr. Moore's deep baritone voice pierces through my thoughts. My head snaps up to see him at the front of the classroom, a raised brow. An expression of annoyance disturbs his usually composed face. "Are we keeping you from something important?"

A few snickers and whispers from classmates follow the question.

I quickly slam the notebook shut and stammer out an apology. "Um, no, sir. Sorry."

A ghost of a smile appears on Mr. Moore's lips as he makes his way over to my desk.

"I see you're quite immersed in your... artistic endeavors," he says, gesturing to the notebook. "But let's test your focus on some linear algebra, shall we? Can you tell the class what the eigenvalues of a matrix are and why they're important?"

Everyone stares at me, eagerly awaiting my response. I clear my throat before I begin to speak, trying to sound confident.

"Um, eigenvalues are scalars associated with a linear transformation of a vector space. They're important because they can help us understand the properties of the transformation, like whether it's invertible or not."

Mr. Moore nods, pleased I came up with a coherent answer. "That's correct. Now how about you keep the artistic endeavors for after school?"

After class is dismissed, Mr. Moore asks me to stay behind. I hope he won't make a big deal about what happened earlier.

"I'm really sorry about not paying attention," I say. "It won't happen again."

Better to get ahead of him because I'm not in the mood for a lecture. Mr. Moore leans up against the desk.

"I'm concerned about you, Lucas," he says. "Since Mackenzie went missing, you've been distracted in class. It's understandable. Is there anything I can do to help during this difficult time?"

This is an unexpected turn of conversation. I thought he would chew me out. Mr. Moore is all about discipline, respect, and hard work. He doesn't tolerate nonsense.

"I just want Mackenzie to return," I say. "The investigation isn't going well, and it's difficult to handle."

"Of course. We're all worried about Mackenzie. Why do you say the investigation isn't going well?"

I shrug. "The police haven't found her yet and have no clue where she is. They searched the entire campus and surrounding areas. Nobody saw anything or heard anything. How does someone just disappear from school? Why didn't the cameras capture something, anything? It's been six days already."

"Let's not give up hope, Lucas. We don't know why Mackenzie went missing in the first place. We can't dismiss the possibility she could return."

"I sure hope so, Mr. Moore."

"You've been asking questions, spending more time than usual in the common room. Are you trying to piece things together?"

My stomach flip-flops. I gape at Mr. Moore, but his expression remains neutral. Why would he ask me that? How does he know where I spend my time?

"No reason to be alarmed," he says, raising a hand. "I see you in the library and the common room on occasion. You chatted with Charlie Covington yesterday. You must know Charlie and Mackenzie are top candidates for the Emerson-Langston STEM Award, and I've taught them both. You made a smart move by talking to Charlie."

"I did?" I ask, hoping I don't look as shocked as I feel.

"One hundred percent. You have the mind of an investigator, Lucas. I can see that."

My mind swirls. I don't recall seeing Mr. Moore in the common room while talking to Charlie or in the library. It's also possible I was too wrapped up in my own issues to have noticed him.

Mr. Moore lives on campus like many of the teachers at Branson. Hanging around the library or the common room wouldn't be unusual. Yet he would be hard to miss. So how come I did?

"But Lucas, be careful," he says.

"What do you mean?"

"The police won't look too kindly on a student playing amateur detective. I admire your initiative, but others might not see it that way. And I meant what I said. If there's anything I can do to help, don't hesitate to ask. Even if you just want to talk. You miss Mackenzie terribly. We're all praying for her safe return."

"Thanks, Mr. Moore. That's decent of you."

"Anytime, Lucas."

CHAPTER 36

Ivy wants to meet on a bench in the courtyard. Why? I have no idea. I would have preferred to meet privately so no one can overhear us, but Ivy—being Ivy—insisted she likes to hang out in the courtyard between classes because it helps her stay zen. It's obviously not working. Ivy is the furthest from zen I've ever seen anyone.

After my strange conversation with Mr. Moore yesterday, I decided to double down on Cole Parker as my number-one suspect. I can't exactly go running to the police and share my suspicions with them. I must do this alone.

I plop down next to Ivy. The weather has been thumbing its nose at me lately. With its glorious sunshine, vibrant fall colors, and cooler but comfortable temperatures. The quad looks like a stock photo of a perfect New England fall. Mackenzie isn't here to enjoy it with me. I wish the weather would stop taunting me and match my mood: dark and fearful.

"What did you want to talk to me about?" Ivy asks, casting aside the book she was reading.

"Cole Parker."

She frowns. "Cole Parker? Why?"

"Do you know anything about his time at Branson before he got expelled? Stuff that may not be common knowledge?"

I nervously scan the area in case someone is closer than I think and overhears us.

Curiosity springs to life on Ivy's face. "What's going on, Lucas? Are you okay?"

"Please, Ivy. This is important. I can't tell you exactly why, but it is. Just trust me, okay?"

My desperate plea must have affected her because she nods slowly.

"Cole was a first-rate jerk. Sure, he was popular, but he was constantly getting into trouble, pushing the boundaries of what he could get away with. Some members of his crew were afraid of him. He could be nice and all, but there was a dark side to him."

"How do you mean?"

Ivy looks around as I had earlier, looking for potential eavesdroppers. Turning back to me, she says, "Cole would pressure girls, if you know what I mean. He sometimes got aggressive. Nasty temper. Made threats if anyone told."

Boy do I know what she means. I wish I didn't.

When Alexis was a freshman, she got on Cole's radar. He started showing up at her locker, sending her inappropriate text messages. Alexis told him to stop, that she wasn't interested in him and the messages made her uncomfortable. Cole hadn't stopped.

It all came to a head at a school dance. Alexis had a drink in hand. Someone bumped into her, and the drink spilled on Cole.

He shoved my sister in front of everyone at that party and humiliated her with a pack of lies, implying that Alexis was pursuing him and how repulsed by her he was. Alexis had broken down into sobs right then and there. She was inconsolable for days afterward.

Cole had to pay. In my humble opinion, he failed to embody the Branson value of integrity: upholding honesty, transparency, and ethical behavior in both academic and personal conduct. So, I asked Mackenzie to look into Cole and his family for information I could use as leverage.

All the other girls Cole messed with were too afraid to say anything. Without Alexis's knowledge, Mackenzie cloned my sister's phone so we could access all the nasty text messages Cole had sent her, the ones she hadn't yet deleted. There were emails too.

It was easy to create a narrative of harassment because Cole had already provided the ammunition. We created a trail of threatening emails and text messages, along with information about his father's shady business dealings and his mother's struggles with drug and alcohol abuse.

I felt guilty about roping his parents into the plan, but we couldn't risk them protecting Cole and covering up what he did, leaving him free to continue his reign of terror.

Then we sent a nice little package documenting Cole's misdeeds to the administration, anonymously of course. We made it clear that if they didn't make an example of him, and include his conduct on his school record, we would go to the press. Branson would be caught up in a scandal that painted the school as an institution that protects predators, not victims.

It worked. Soon after, more girls came forward to disclose details of their own brush with Cole. Of course the administration wanted to keep it quiet, make sure it never went beyond school walls.

We kept Alexis out of the fray, and to this day, no one suspects that Mackenzie and I orchestrated the takedown. Our scheme was devious and calculated, but we believed the end justified the means. Except, I'm receiving threatening text messages that allude to payback, and the past is coming back to haunt me.

"I heard rumors about that. So where's Cole these days anyway?" I ask, infusing my tone with a lightness I don't feel.

Ivy shrugs nonchalantly, but I catch a hint of unease in her eyes. "Who knows? Maybe you should talk to Charlie Covington."

"Charlie? Why should I talk to her?"

"She and Cole were close. They grew up together. Their families have always been tight-knit. But it's strange, she never discussed him or defended him when everything went down. That says a lot. Anyway, that's all I know."

A shiver dances its way up my spine, leaving a trail of goose bumps in its wake. I take a moment to collect my bearings, focusing on the gentle swaying branches in the breeze.

The question that immediately springs to mind is whether Charlie is acting as Cole's pawn at Branson, carrying out his dirty work. Her hostility towards me when I asked about Mackenzie raises questions. Suspicious questions. Do they have Mackenzie hidden somewhere?

Ivy adds, "Lucas, be careful."

"Mr. Moore said the same thing to me yesterday." Then I remember. Liam mentioned Ivy has been teaching him to play chess and dropped another metaphor.

"What did you mean when you told Liam that sometimes you have to sacrifice the queen? Give up something important to protect the king to win the game?"

"It was just a chess strategy, nothing more."

"And that's it?"

Ivy tilts her head to one side. She says, "Yes. But every chess move can be applicable to life, Lucas. For instance, the Knight's Move."

"What's the Knight's Move?"

"The Knight's Move is unpredictable, like some people. You never know who is a threat."

CHAPTER 37

Still reeling from Ivy's revelation about Cole and Charlie's friendship, I head to the Performing Arts Center after school to meet up with Emily, Mackenzie's roommate.

The Performing Arts Center is a grand architectural structure with soaring ceilings and elegant details. The rows of plush red velvet seats slope gracefully down towards the stage.

Emily turns as I approach and gestures for me to join her near the front.

"Thanks for meeting me."

"Of course. I want to help Mackenzie in any way I can. I picked this place because no one is around today. We won't be interrupted."

Emily's expression goes from curious to sad and back again in the span of a nano second.

"Did Mackenzie seem off to you in the days leading up to her going missing? Anything bothering her?"

"Yes, she was a bit off. More secretive than usual. Stressed out to the max. And she was always on her laptop, at all hours."

I ponder her statement, trying to connect the dots with what I'd learned so far. Mackenzie was paranoid, anxious. Kellen said Mackenzie had secrets. Now Emily just confirmed it.

"Did she mention anything or anyone specific she was worried about?"

"No. Other than the Emerson-Langston STEM Award and her battle with Charlie. Charlie is a psycho. She would ambush Mackenzie at random times just to say mean, nasty things to her."

I gulp. "Charlie was bullying Mackenzie?"

"I guess you could say that. But it went beyond verbal attacks. It was full-scale psychological warfare, like Charlie hated the fact that Mackenzie was a real threat to her."

The chill I felt earlier during my conversation with Ivy returns. If Charlie discovered Mackenzie had helped me set up Cole, it could explain the harassment. The award may be a pretense to hide the real reason she hates Mackenzie.

"Do you think someone was bothering her or threatening her? Besides Charlie, I mean."

"It's possible. She did hint that she felt like someone was watching her. But then she brushed it off as paranoia. You know, because of all the stress she was under."

I nod as my mind rewinds to the person I followed during the vigil. What were they doing there?

A strange thought sneaks into my head. It could be a good sign a random person showed up at the vigil and disappeared into the night. It points to Mackenzie being alive and held somewhere. Why else would this person show up at a gathering pleading for Mackenzie's return if they had no knowledge of her whereabouts?

"What about known enemies?" I ask. As Mackenzie's close friend, I should know if she had enemies. But I'm learning a lot of things about Mackenzie I wasn't aware of.

"No one I can think of. Of course there's Kellen. They fought constantly before Mackenzie vanished."

"What did they fight about?"

"Kellen thought Mackenzie wanted to dump him for you."

A shot of trepidation washes over me. Kellen accused me of making a play for Mackenzie. But was he deflecting?

"I guess Kellen needed an excuse to save face."

"He wanted to see her all the time, so she started ignoring his texts and calls," Emily explains. "That irritated him. Mackenzie liked her space, so she would retreat into herself when stuff was bothering her."

That's an accurate picture of Mackenzie, I think. "Thanks Emily. You've been very helpful."

"I want Mackenzie to be okay. And, Lucas?"

"Yeah."

Emily looks back at the entrance to the theater as if expecting someone. Then she turns back to me and lowers her voice.

"The day Mackenzie disappeared, she stayed in our dorm room. We just talked. She received a text message. After she read it, terror took over her face. Then she grabbed a hidden bag from the closet, as though she had prepared in advance, and asked me not to tell anyone about her leaving.

"Of course I wanted to know what was going on, asked if she was in trouble. Mackenzie said it was better for me to stay out of it."

Emily stops to catch her breath. She continues, "Mackenzie said there are bad things going on at Branson right under our noses, but she couldn't go to the police. She asked me to cover for her if things went south, to say I hadn't seen her since she left for classes last Friday morning."

I sit statue-still, too stunned to move a muscle. This is the biggest break I've had since I started digging into the case. A clue, right here at school all this time. A clue the police don't have. How could Emily sit on something this big?

On the flip side, that's fantastic news. It means Mackenzie left willingly, she wasn't abducted. Then my excitement quickly deflates. Who is she running from? Who sent her the ominous text that triggered the disappearance? It sounds like Mackenzie was prepared to run. Who has a bag ready to go at a moment's notice? Someone expecting trouble, that's who.

"And you haven't told anybody what you just told me?" I ask.

Emily shakes her head miserably.

"Did the police interview you?"

"Yes. I told them I hadn't seen Mackenzie since the morning. They asked if we got along, and I said yes, obviously. They didn't ask a ton of questions like I thought they would."

"Huh. That's interesting."

"Mackenzie likes you a lot," Emily says. "She told me if you came around asking questions, I should mention the Riemann Enigma."

I frown. "What's that?

"I don't know. Mackenzie only said I should tell you and you would figure it out."

I turn the name over in my head, but it doesn't ring any bells. I file the information away in my head to retrieve later. Right now, I'm on information overload. Or maybe it's shock. Hard to tell.

I thank Emily again for sharing what she knows.

As I leave the theater, the only thought circling my brain is the text message Mackenzie received right before she took off.

Someone warned her to run.

CHAPTER 38

Last time I met up with Misha in the common room, Jayden interrupted our conversation. Misha only said she would think about going to the autumn dance with me. Although we've been messaging each other since, the issue of the dance never came up. Hopefully, I'll have my answer in the next few minutes.

A thousand thoughts about Mackenzie kept me up all night. Replaying my conversation with Emily over and over again, dissecting each word and looking for hidden clues besides Reiman Enigma, which makes no sense to me. The strange conversation with Mr. Moore. Finding nothing on Cole Parker.

Every day I scour social media and local news websites for fresh information on the investigation. I even tried calling Detective Kang. He would only say it's still an active investigation. I can't imagine what Mackenzie's parents are going through, especially since she's their only child. The Flemings have been interviewed on TV, pleading for anyone with information to come forward.

Mom tried to get me to talk about my feelings last night. That's the thing about having a therapist for a mother. Although Mom is technically a neuropsychologist, she earned her PhD in clinical psychology before she took on postdoctoral training to become a neuropsychologist.

She wants me to open up. It got a lot worse after I hinted that I wanted to learn more about my biological father. With Mackenzie missing, Mom's concern about my emotional state and mental health is next level.

I'll never admit to my parents that it takes a lot of effort to rein in my temper when somebody makes me angry. A rage now directed at whoever is responsible for Mackenzie missing, the person or persons she's running from. She should be at school doing normal stuff. Going to classes, working on her senior Capstone project, sending off her college applications. Winning that STEM award instead of Charlie "Psycho" Covington.

Hanging out with me in the Secret Garden as we make up stories about Mr. Gnomington and all the secrets spilled in his presence. If only that gnome could talk. What would he tell me?

My hand reaches for the door handle to the common room when my phone pings with an incoming text. I reach into my pocket and pull out the phone. When I look at the screen, I can't believe what I see.

Unknown: It's me. Mackenzie. I'm okay.
Please don't freak out.

I swallow the shock climbing up from the back of my throat. The phone lies frozen in my hand as I continue to stare at the message, unblinking. Is this a trick of my imagination?

Unknown: Lucas, answer me. I don't have
a lot of time before I need to hide this
phone.

As if my brain recognizes the seriousness of the situation, I shift gears and tap out a frenzied response.

Lucas: Mackenzie? Is it really you? Where are you? Everyone's worried sick.

Unknown: I can't tell you where I am. I need you to trust me, Lucas.

Trust her? She ran off without a word and wouldn't answer any of my calls or texts.

Lucas: What's going on, Mack?

Unknown: I can't explain right now. It's not safe for me to come back. Not yet.

Lucas: What are you talking about?

Unknown: I stumbled upon something. Something awful.

My head swims with confusion and fear. Mack really is running from something, and she's been hiding all this time.

Lucas: About whom? About what? Get back here. We'll figure it out.

Unknown: It's not that simple.

Lucas: Why not?

Unknown: Promise me you won't tell anyone about this conversation. Not even the twins. No one.

Lucas: What about your parents? They must be worried.

Unknown: They can't know either. It's better if they're trying to find me. Safer.

Lucas: This is nuts. Why can't you come back?

Unknown: I saw something I wasn't supposed to. And they're looking for me.

Lucas: Who's looking for you?

Lucas: Someone's been sending me threatening messages. They know what we did.

I quickly delete the last text before sending. I can't afford to incriminate myself or Mackenzie in the whole Cole Parker setup.

Unknown: I promise I'll explain everything when the time is right. Trust me. And Lucas, be careful.

The ominous words hang in the air as I stare at my phone screen. This is the third time someone warned me to tread carefully since Mackenzie went missing. Ivy, Mr. Moore, and now Mackenzie herself. What the heck is going on?

CHAPTER 39

I try and fail to banish the sense of unease rolling through me—my racing thoughts, the adrenaline spike, the dull headache, and the fear settling in the pit of my stomach.

The most important thing, however, is that Mackenzie is fine. Fine as someone can be who's hiding and afraid to come home. It's not safe for her to be here, but she will come back when it is. Right?

Misha smiles at me when I walk through the door. For an instant, all my worries melt away. I grab the seat across from her. She smells amazing, as usual. Today, her braids hang loosely around her shoulders, making her look younger than sixteen.

"I have a present for you," she says.

"You do? Why?"

Not the best reaction when someone says they have a gift for you, but my brain is crowded with too many thoughts. Plus, I don't have a gift for Misha. Should I have brought some small token to express how much I care? Picked a flower on the way here?

This falling-for-a-girl situation is new to me, and I have no idea what I'm doing. I've never even held hands before. Sure, I had a couple of crushes in middle school, but I never said anything. Just waited until the feeling passed, like a fever. With Misha, I feel like I'm at the edge of a precipice, unsure whether I should take the leap or step back and act cautious.

"I mean, you didn't have to get me anything."

"I feel terrible about Jayden being a jerk the other day. I just want to say again how sorry I am."

The warmth in her eyes makes my stomach flip-flop. Misha reaches for the backpack on the floor next to her, opens it, and removes a package wrapped in brown paper. She hands me the package and returns the bag to the floor.

"Thank you. You didn't have to get me anything," I repeat. "Jayden likes getting in my face, claiming soccer is a wimp sport. I don't pay him any attention."

She ignores my protest and says, "Go on, open it."

I oblige, ripping the paper off, and I'm rendered speechless. I hold in my hand a fiftieth anniversary edition of the classic novel, *The Spy Who Came in from the Cold* by John le Carré.

"A little birdie told me it's your favorite book. My online research said it's one of the best spy novels of all time. I hope you like it."

I'm in awe. During one of our long, after-school conversations, we had discussed our hopes and dreams. I shared my dream of serving in counterintelligence, protecting our country from the constant threat of terrorism and foreign espionage.

She had disclosed her own dream of becoming an Oscar-winning composer and plans to apply to the prestigious Screen Scoring program at University of Southern California (USC) Thornton School of Music.

I'm touched Misha went above and beyond to discover something so personal and meaningful to me. A twinge of guilt hits me again that I haven't gotten her anything in return. But then again, it would have been presumptuous of me to buy her a gift so early in our relationship.

Without thinking, I lean in and give her a quick peck on the cheek, which I immediately regret because I invaded her personal space, people are looking at us all weird, and I'm totally embarrassed.

"Sorry, I didn't mean to do that. I just …so sorry."

"It's fine. Don't overthink it."

"I'm usually more composed."

"I know. That's why it's great to see you do something spontaneous and genuine."

"Thank you again," I say, waving the book. "It means a lot to me. Sorry if it was awkward with half the school looking on."

"I don't feel awkward. You're the one making a big deal about it."

"I promise, no more awkwardness. I'll cherish it." It doesn't matter that I already have a signed first edition copy of the novel. What matters is that Misha went out of her way to show she cares. Now is the perfect opportunity to bring up the autumn dance once more.

"So, have you given any further thought to attending the dance with me? It could be a lot of fun. You already know that I think you're great. I'd be honored if you would go with me." There. Simple, straightforward, respectful. Maybe I laid it on a little thick with the *honored* but, overall, not bad.

"I would be honored to go to the dance with you, Lucas," she says, her eyes sparkling.

Play it cool, I think, not wanting to appear ecstatic, even though I am. Girls can smell desperation.

"Thanks for accepting."

"You're welcome."

We talk a bit longer about the dance. Misha can't believe it will be my first time going and says she's flattered that I asked her to go with me. She'd never been either, so we'll both experience it for the first time together.

My phone pings with an incoming text. I'm too afraid to check. It could be Makenzie or, worse, my anonymous texter. Either way, I don't want to lie to Misha about who the text is from. I'm a terrible liar. I can't even fool a baby.

"Is that your phone? Sounds like a text message," she says.

"Yeah. No big deal. I'll check it later."

"It could be important, especially with Mackenzie missing."

I can't escape, so I tell myself to act normal no matter what the text says.

I look at the screen.

Unknown: We should meet. I'll tell you what's really going on at school.

I pretend to stare at the screen, frowning in confusion, as though whoever texted me is saying something that makes no sense.

I look up and say, "Sorry, Misha. My brother has a question. Let me answer him quickly."

She nods and shifts her attention to the foosball game in progress across the room. I quickly respond to the text.

Lucas: When? Where? Tell me the time and date and I'll be there.

Unknown: I'll text you. Make sure you come alone and you're not followed.

Make sure I'm not followed is an added layer of… weirdness in an already weird situation.

Lucas: Who would follow me? Are you in danger?

Unknown: Just come alone, Lucas. It's important. I'll tell you everything, but you have to come alone.

Is this a trap, some kind of game orchestrated by Cole and Charlie? What if someone has Mackenzie and they're pretending to be her to lure me into the same trap?

Misha says, "Is everything okay with Blake? You seem worried."

"Nah. He's fine." I must make up a story because Misha looks at me expectantly for an explanation, and I don't have one. *Think, think.*

"Blake wanted to know if we're still up for hanging out with our cousins this weekend. We'll sleep over at our grandparents' house so they can take us. Our parents are out of town this weekend."

I hope it sounds convincing and I didn't go overboard with an explanation. That's when people know you're lying— too many details.

"And you'd rather hang out with your cousins than throw a party while your parents are out of town? Lucas, what kind of teenager are you?" Misha asks, playfully. "You must be a special breed. Tell me your secrets."

The secret is simple: my parents don't tolerate what they refer to as nonsense. In our family, there's no backtalk, disrespect of any kind, swearing, and the twins and I better not pretend to be asleep when it's time to go to church on Sunday mornings.

Smiling at Misha, I say, "That's just a cliché from books and movies. Besides, my parents would never trust me again if I did something that stupid. And there would be serious consequences. Our parents are old-school young."

"What's that?" she asks.

"Mom and Dad are only in their late thirties, but they raise us old school. They're the best, but once in a while, they become the mess-around-and-find-out type of parents."

"I get it," she says. "My mom is like that too."

Then we launch into a hysterical rendition of all the Black-mom sayings we grew up hearing. When Misha does her impression of "I'm not one of your little friends, and I don't have to do anything except stay Black and die," we almost fall out of our chairs laughing, not caring that everyone is looking at us as though we've lost our minds.

Once the laughter dies down, I realize it's the first time since Makenzie went missing that I'd had an honest-to-goodness laugh. I want her to come back so we can laugh out loud together, like we always have.

Misha's sense of humor is a pleasant surprise. It's as if she knows exactly what I need. Could she read the nervousness on my face? Even though she made a joke about me not throwing a party while my parents are out of town, did she really believe the story I made up on the fly?

I can't afford for her to doubt me and then dump me. I'm falling for her. Hard.

I just hope I don't mess it up.

CHAPTER 40

Surrounded by the dense woods on the outskirts of Branson's sprawling campus, I make my way toward the designated meeting spot.

Tall trees loom overhead. The sun sinks behind the trees as I trudge deeper into the woods, my heart racing with fear. The scent of damp earth fills the air, a reminder that it rained recently and the ground is still muddy in some places.

I won't be able to find my way out in this thick maze of trees. I hope Mackenzie shows up on time. She's aware it gets dark early this time of year.

Branches twist and reach toward me like gnarled fingers, casting eerie shadows on the forest floor. Every rustle of leaves and snap of twigs makes me jump, my mind imagining all sorts of creatures hiding, waiting to jump out and get me.

Finally, I reach the spot—an old fallen tree trunk surrounded by large rocks forming a small semicircle.

"Mackenzie, I'm here," I whisper anxiously. "Where are you?"

Silence greets me, broken only by the chirping of a lone bird. Frustration builds as I text her, hoping she'll respond quickly. And she does.

> **Unknown:** I'll be right there. Stay hidden. I'll find you.

Hiding in a thick underbrush, I still feel vulnerable and exposed. The wind picks up, creating a symphony of rustling leaves around me. My heart pounds with impatience and fear.

Suddenly, distant footsteps echo. My heart leaps with relief as I catch a glimpse of Mackenzie's familiar figure in her yellow trench coat and her signature ash-brown curls with lavender streaks cascading down her shoulders.

But instead of coming toward me, she gestures for me to follow her. Confusion mixed with excitement surges through me as I trail after her figure deeper into the woods.

Just when I'm about to catch up with her, she starts running.

"Mackenzie, wait! Where are we going?" I call out between breaths, but she doesn't slow down. I trip on a fallen tree but manage to steady myself in time.

However, when I look up again, Mackenzie is gone.

Panic and a deep sense of unease overtake me as I speed up, desperately searching for any sign of her.

"Mack, where did you go? This isn't funny!" I yell, my voice trembling.

But there's no response, just the rustling of leaves and the distant chirp of a bird. Something spooked Mackenzie, something so terrifying that she wouldn't even stop to explain herself or wait for me.

The realization hits me like a punch to the gut. Who or what scared Mack so much that she ran? My mind races with worst-case scenarios as I frantically try to retrace our steps and find a way out before whatever scared Mackenzie comes for me too.

I'm about to head back to school and catch the shuttle home when I hear movement. She came back.

"Mack, is that you?" I peek in the surrounding areas, but no response. Then something heavy crashes into my skull, and everything goes black.

CHAPTER 41

When I wake up, I have no idea how much time has passed. My head throbs, and my vision is blurry. As my eyes adjust, I take in my surroundings. It's almost dark. I'm still in the woods. I have to get out of here.

I slowly rise to my feet and try not to stumble. I'm still a bit woozy. I trace my fingers around the back of my head. There's a big bump. I look at my finger. No blood. That's a good sign.

When I start moving, something on the ground directly in front of me catches my attention. A piece of paper. I bend down slowly in case I got a concussion because of the blow. I don't need to pass out again. Not when it's almost dark and I'm unfamiliar with the woods.

The past whispers its secrets, and the future holds its price. Are you prepared to pay?

Another threat. Whoever sent me those threatening text messages spooked Mackenzie. Is this the connection I've been looking for, between Cole Parker and Mackenzie? It's best to get out of here first before I can further dissect what the note means. I pull my phone from my pocket. Several text messages from Blake light up the screen.

> **Blake:** Where are you? Liam says he never saw you after school.

Drats. I fibbed to Blake. How else was I supposed to explain why I wanted to take the late shuttle home? Each text from him is a variation of inquiring about my whereabouts, and I suspect the voicemail is too. Mack said I couldn't tell anyone we'd been in contact, not even the twins. So I made up a story.

By the time I make it to the shuttle stop near the school's main entrance, I'm breathing heavily and my head throbs. Blake gives me a questioning frown, but I wave him off. We'll talk when I get home and have a chance to collect my bearings.

CHAPTER 42

You what?" Alexis's shrill voice pierces the air, echoing off the walls of the Bat Cave. She sinks dramatically into the plush leather sectional, her hand resting on her forehead as if she's about to faint. Her long dark hair falls around her face, framing her incredulous expression.

"Shhhh," I admonish. "Mom or Dad could hear you."

Blake sits across from Alexis and me. I explain the incident in the woods. "Look, something weird is going on. Mackenzie warned me not to say anything about our secret meeting and insisted I come alone, to make sure I wasn't followed. But apparently someone did follow her. The person bashed me in the head."

I instinctively reach up to touch the tender spot at the back of my head. I won't be able to hide the bump from my parents if the pain and swelling persists. I've come up with a plan, though. I'll tell Dad I was goofing around with a soccer ball, lost my balance, and fell. He will look me over and treat me if necessary.

"What about the note?" Blake asks. "That's a serious threat. Now both you and Mackenzie could be in danger, and that means we can't keep this from Mom and Dad."

"Blake is right, Lucas," Alexis says. "Things could escalate."

"Did Mack say anything to you?" Blake asks.

"Like what?"

"When you got to the spot and you saw her, did she say anything? Anything at all before she started running?"

I squeeze my eyes shut and then pick up the ice pack on the floor next to me. I place it on the bump. I think back to the non-encounter encounter in the woods. Mack didn't speak a word to me, only gestured for me to follow her. She started running; I took chase but stumbled and fell. Then she vanished. Not once did she answer me, no matter how many times I called out her name. Why not? Was she afraid of whoever knocked me out?

I open my eyes and place the ice pack back on the floor. "No. She never spoke to me."

"Are you sure you didn't see anyone?" Alexis presses. "Why would she start running after she asked you to follow her and not say a word?"

"It's obvious Mackenzie was followed," Blake offers. "She must have seen the person and didn't have a chance to warn Lucas; that's why she ran. Stumbling and falling could have been a good thing."

"How do you figure?" I ask.

"Mackenzie is running from someone dangerous. The warning note is proof. Maybe if you had caught up with her, this person, whoever they are, could have seriously hurt you. Falling slowed you down, and perhaps that saved you from even worse danger."

I ponder my brother's explanation. What would have happened had I caught up with Mackenzie? She was too scared to say anything to me, so she'd just started running and ignored my shouts for her to wait up.

I recall the very first text she sent since taking off. Bad things were happening that she couldn't discuss with me. So whoever spooked her in the woods and bashed me over the head is definitely connected to Branson. I share my suspicions with the twins.

Alexis says, "Lucas, you need to walk away from this. I feel terrible for Mackenzie, but someone attacked you today. Next time could be worse."

Blake doesn't look me in the eye. He does that when he sides with Alexis but doesn't want to say it out loud.

"What am I supposed to do? I can't just leave Mackenzie twisting in the wind at the mercy of… whoever."

"Mackenzie has parents," Alexis counters. "If she found the time to contact you and show up at a meeting place, she can reach out to her parents and let them know she needs help. Also, the police are still investigating. Even though they have no leads, it's still no reason to put yourself in danger."

My sister folds her arms and purses her lips, daring me to come up with a better argument.

I can't. That's the thing about Alexis. She's always been too smart for her own good. But there is something else I can't share with the twins. Mackenzie disappeared the same afternoon she was about to share what she uncovered about my biological father. Our project was top secret. The twins would have insisted I drop it, especially Alexis, had I informed them.

Did my biological father attend Branson? Or better yet, is he on staff? If he is, I'm unaware. The man could be hiding in plain sight. Or it may be pure coincidence Mackenzie's disappearance occurred on the same day we planned to meet at Bonnie's.

CHAPTER 43

Mackenzie

Three days before the disappearance

Charlie is angling for the STEM scholarship with a charm offensive. Only it's more offensive than charming. Gross. Too bad algorithms aren't impressed with hair twirling and eyelash fluttering. And I certainly hope that Mr. Moore isn't either.

The computer lab is a sea of activity, with students hunched over their keyboards and screens, their fingers moving in a blur. In the corner, Charlie and Mr. Moore stand close together, their heads bent in intense conversation.

My heart skips a beat as I watch them. What are they talking about? Is Charlie trying to undermine me again?

Mr. Moore, head of the math and computer science department, has this way of making you feel like any attention from him is a rare treat you should savor. That's the way he carries himself, and he has the reputation to match. Students love him, and the faculty and administration respect him.

A recommendation from him is better than gold. Not just for college applications but for the STEM Scholarship as well. I bet that's why Charlie is desperate for his attention.

She might as well butter his pancakes on a Sunday morning. Arrghhh.

Beyond his role as leader of the department that makes Branson one of the best STEM schools in the country, there is another quality that sets Mr. Moore apart, contributes to his popularity, and adds to his mystique: he defies the stereotype of the typical math or computer nerd.

I'm convinced he's aware of the effect he has on people. There's a certain charm and charisma that radiates from him. He's tall, with broad shoulders and lean muscles that give a commanding presence. His dark-brown skin is luxuriously smooth. A neatly trimmed moustache and close-cropped conservative haircut adds to his polished appearance. It wouldn't surprise me if Mr. Moore also has a personal stylist; his wardrobe is always on point.

Before coming to Branson, Mr. Moore earned computer science and engineering degrees from UCal Berkeley and Stanford. After that, he spent years working for JP Morgan Chase and Goldman Sachs, developing and implementing complex models and algorithms to analyze financial data, manage risk, and optimize their trading strategies.

I'm sure they were paying him insane amounts of money, so he can afford to dress well.

I push aside the nagging doubts and focus on my own task. My senior Capstone project is creating a machine learning algorithm that can detect the onset of seizures.

It's something that strikes a personal chord with me; my cousin Lynne suffered from terrible seizures as a kid, and I've always felt powerless watching her go through them. After conducting extensive research and collecting data for months, I'm finally done with the preprocessing phase.

Lynne and her parents were kind enough to provide me access to Lynne's EEG results over the years. Now I'm ready to move on to the next crucial step in my project: model development and testing.

As I pursue the goal of deploying the algorithm, I envision it being used on a device that's both functional and fashionable. Something wearable, like a headband or cap, that's comfortable, built for long-term wear, discreet in appearance, and stylish in design.

Getting FDA approval for the final product could take years, as it will require entire teams of engineers, data scientists, and industrial designers working on it, not to mention clinical trials. But I want to get the project far enough along to win the STEM award and get into MIT.

Mr. Moore has been unwavering in his support for my project. Seeing the potential for success, he even introduced me to one of his connections, the head of machine learning at a cutting edge AI company. With their expertise and resources, I can expedite the model deployment.

Charlie, with her constant presence hovering around Mr. Moore, like a puppy desperate for attention, serves as a constant reminder of her relentless campaign of sabotage against me. But I refuse to let her get the best of me.

My determination is set in stone, and I will not be distracted from my goal of blowing her out of the water. My project must not only surpass hers, but also stand out amongst all the other competitors vying for this coveted scholarship.

The stakes are high, but I've got this.

After class is over and everyone heads for the door, Charlie says loudly so I can hear, "Thanks so much for the advice, Mr. Moore. I really appreciate your helping me make my project the best it can be."

It takes everything in me not to roll my eyes and hold my tongue from the witty comeback I have all queued up and ready to go. *Ah, Charlie, you've perfected the fine art of brown-nosing. It's great for getting ahead without actually having any skills.*

I'm so caught up in my thoughts I don't see Mr. Moore approach until he's inches away from me.

"Mackenzie, is everything all right?" he asks in his deep baritone voice.

"Yes, Mr. Moore. Everything is fine."

"You shouldn't worry about your application for the Emerson-Langston STEM Award or your senior Capstone project. I don't play favorites, but you're a strong contender for both."

"Thanks. It means a lot coming from you. It's hard, but I'm persistent. I will win the award and get into MIT."

"That's the spirit," he says, smiling big and wide, as if he's been waiting on me to shore up some confidence. "Make sure nothing distracts you from your goals," he emphasizes, his words like a firm hand pushing me forward.

I feel the weight of his expectations pressing down on me.

He says, "This is important work with the potential to change the lives of people who suffer from debilitating seizures."

The air around us crackles with Mr. Moore's intensity, like a charged static electricity I can almost touch. His eyes shimmer with determination as though his reputation is riding on my success.

CHAPTER 44

My fingers fly across my phone screen. I don't care if there are spelling errors.

The dots are moving, indicating she's typing a response.

Unknown: Let's meet there. I can't be
seen, but I can text you where we should
meet.

Lucas: Seriously? I don't know if I want to do
this.

Unknown: Please, Lucas. You're my only
friend, the only person I trust. A ton of heat
is coming down on me. I can't risk being
seen. Not until the danger passes.

Mackenzie is playing on my emotions. She knows how much I care and that throwing out a word like *danger* is sure to seal my cooperation. Although to be fair, Mack is running scared. The least I can do is be there for her. It's not an ideal situation, but until I know what she's dealing with, I have to trust her.

Lucas: How can you be sure you won't be
followed this time? I don't want to get hit
again.

Unknown: You won't. I'll be wearing a
disguise so no one will recognize me.

That's a smart idea. Whoever is following Mack, and I assume it's the same person who hit me over the head, won't recognize her incognito.

Lucas: Deal. But you have to promise to tell me
everything, all of it, no holding back.

Unknown: I promise. I'll tell you all of it. You
may not like some of it though.

Lucas: Why is that?

Unknown: I have to go.

CHAPTER 45

Inside Sweet Cubes Café & Patisserie, the air is filled with an intoxicating blend of the aroma of bold, rich coffee and warm decadent pastries fresh from the oven. The smell alone is enough to make my mouth water and stomach growl in anticipation.

When Misha suggested we end our day out in the city by coming here, I jumped at the chance to eat the best croissants on the planet. Misha swears by this.

The best croissants in the world, the café's signature pastry, are artfully shaped like cubes. I might scarf down five or six, but maybe not. I don't want Misha to think I'm a glutton who can't control himself. I've been told my metabolism has a booster rocket attached to it, but still.

It's late afternoon, and I'm disappointed that our day will soon end. Today was a teacher-development day at Branson, so no school. Misha and I hopped the commuter rail into Boston and spent the day exploring the city, including stops at the Museum of Fine Arts and the New England Aquarium. She liked the sea turtles best.

We snag a table near the window and take a moment to observe our surroundings. The café is warm and cozy, so we both shed our light jackets and hang them on the backs of our chairs. Soft chatter fills the air as patrons chat over steaming cups of coffee and delectable treats, the sound of laughter mingling with the gentle hum of conversation.

Outside, the street pulses with energy, a constant flow of honking cars and bustling pedestrians. But Misha's shoulders are hunched, her usually vibrant eyes darting around anxiously.

"Is everything okay?" I ask, unable to ignore her distress.

"Nothing's wrong." She looks away, attempting to disguise her turmoil, but her voice lacks conviction.

"You can tell me," I urge, softly. "I'd hate to think anything ruined the day for you."

She hesitates briefly before giving my hand a lingering squeeze.

"Thank you."

"What for?"

"A wonderful day," she replies, her voice tinged with emotion.

"Glad you had fun. I did too."

She continues, "And also thanks for being you."

"And what's that?"

"Kind, respectful, considerate."

"I have to be kind and respectful. My parents keep tabs on my brother and me. They're determined to raise perfect gentlemen. There are consequences if we're not progressing to their satisfaction."

Misha giggles, and I can't help but return her smile. Then the smile slowly fades from her face, as though she doesn't want to alarm me with an abrupt change in expression. What's going on with her? I don't want to push, but something is weighing on her.

Misha was fine all day long. Well, that's not entirely true. During our trek to the Museum of Fine Arts, she went to the ladies' room. When she returned, there was a dark mist clinging to her, although she tried to act like nothing had changed. What happened in there? Did she encounter someone? Or did she receive bad news?

"What are you having?" I ask. "I can get our order. The line isn't too long."

As I return to our cozy booth, carrying a tray of steaming lattes and the decadent croissants, Misha quickly tucks her phone away. The way she hastily moves it out of sight reminds me of the way Mackenzie did the same before she vanished.

I take my seat and bite into my first of the delicious croissants, its flaky crumbs already settling on the plate. As it melts in my mouth, I reach over and take Misha's hand in mine once more. It's freezing, despite the cozy warmth of the café. I want her to know how much she means to me and that my heart aches for her, whatever has her down.

"You don't have to tell me what's bothering you if you're not ready. Whenever you are, I'll be here; I'm not going anywhere. Okay?"

Misha says nothing at first, and then she nods, distracted.

Reluctantly, I let go of her hand. "These croissants are as good as you claim," I say, reaching for another one. "I'm worried about getting addicted, though. Not sure I'm ready for that kind of commitment to a baked good. We might have to start a support group."

But instead of a grin or a witty comeback, Misha stands, lifts her purse from the back of the chair, and says, "Sorry, Lucas. I have to go. I'll call you later, I promise. But I have to take care of something right now."

Without waiting for a response, Misha races out of the café, weaving through customers before my stunned brain can think of stopping her.

CHAPTER 46

Suspicion forms in my heart like a cold sheet of ice as I trail behind Misha, careful to keep my distance as I navigate the bustling streets of downtown Boston.

The cool October air nips at my face. I shiver and then zip up my jacket all the way. New England weather is notoriously unpredictable; it can fluctuate by twenty degrees in the span of a single day.

The streets bustle with activity, pedestrians walking past with purpose as cars honk impatiently. I dodge around a couple arm in arm and a guy in a business suit chatting on his cell phone. It's almost dark, and I need to keep an eye on the time so I don't miss the Fitchburg Line commuter rail service to get home.

Misha is still within my line of vision. I quicken my pace, careful not to bring attention to myself. What was so urgent that she just ditched me and flew out of the café? I feel terrible for spying on her, but I shove my guilt deep down. Misha could be in trouble.

As she turns into a quieter side street, I duck behind a parked car when she looks back to make sure she's not being followed.

My heart pounds in my chest like a distant drumbeat, and my hands grow clammy. Peering cautiously around the edge of the car, I spot Misha farther down the street, engrossed in conversation with a man, his features obscured by the dim light of the streetlight.

What is she doing? Who is that guy? I stand from my crouching position and begin walking toward them. My movements are slow and deliberate, careful to stay out of sight. The narrow street makes it hard to go unseen.

Just as I'm about to get closer so I can see the man, a group of pedestrians emerges from a nearby building, temporarily blocking my view. As the last of the pedestrians disappear, I get a better look but am still not able to make out the man.

Misha stands stock-still, her body tense. The man towers over her and places his hands on her shoulders. My mind races, trying to make sense of the scene unfolding before me.

Then the man leans in closer, a gesture that feels both intimate and wrong. I squint, trying to make out his face. Just then, the streetlight illuminates his features for the briefest of moments, and my heart drops to my stomach.

Leaning over Misha and kissing her on the cheek is Mr. Moore, one of Branson's most respected teachers. *My math teacher.*

CHAPTER 47

My vision blurs with shock and confusion. The searing pain in my chest expands, taking over my entire body and making it difficult to breathe.

What the heck is going on here? My thoughts spiral, a chaotic mess of questions and accusations. Is he manipulating Misha? Is he coercing her into… are they…? I can't bring myself to finish the thought.

Feelings of betrayal and protectiveness rise up inside me in equal measure. I want to confront them, get answers. But my feet are rooted to the spot.

An endless parade of thoughts continue to swirl through my mind. Is Misha in trouble? Or is she willingly engaging in something inappropriate with a man old enough to be her father?

And why would Mr. Moore, of all people, who always seems like a man of integrity, be secretly meeting with a sixteen-year-old girl in downtown Boston? He must have followed us. Misha started acting nervous after she came from the ladies' room at the Museum of Fine Arts. Then when I returned to our table at the café, she quickly hid her phone from view.

Did Mr. Moore text her and demand to see her?

The day we spent together, laughing, teasing each other, visiting various attractions, and even the café's warmth and laughter now feel like a distant memory. The evening now seems colder, the streetlights harsher.

I need answers, but I also need to figure out how to approach this without scaring Misha away. My mind floods with scenarios, plans, and the gnawing fear that everything is spiraling out of control.

CHAPTER 48

Thanks for coming, Ivy."

"Of course. You can always count on me, Lucas."

It might be a risky move, reaching out to Ivy, but she knows everything that goes on at Branson. She might be acting stranger than usual with her chess metaphors and thinly veiled warnings, but this is exactly why I need to talk to her.

We're deep inside the library where we're least likely to be interrupted. I can't get out of my head what I saw yesterday; Mr. Moore kissing Misha on the cheek. It shocked me to the bones. If I had been within touching distance, I would have happily knifed Mr. Moore in the chest. My fury was that intense, like a raging bonfire.

Misha texted me to apologize. I've ignored her. I needed time and space to think, calm down, and get some information that might explain what I saw. There has to be a reasonable explanation.

"It's about Misha, isn't it?" Ivy says.

"How did you know?"

"You've got it bad for her, Lucas; it's no secret."

Ivy flicks her hair away from her face. She continues, "When you texted, I knew it was something huge for you to go out on a limb like that. So what did Misha do to you?"

Not sure how to explain things without making Misha look bad, even though I'm angry with her. She doesn't deserve my consideration. She ditched me at the café and ran off to meet with Mr. Moore, no explanation, no nothing, and then texted me an apology.

I deserve better, and if Ivy can shed light on the situation, so be it.

"Mr. Moore. Do you know of any reason why Misha would hang out with him?" I'm not about to share details of what I saw with Ivy.

She leans back in the chair and folds her arms. A look I can't quite identify blooms on her face, kind of a cross between a smirk and an expression of concern. Then she unfolds her arms and leans forward again.

"You don't know?" she asks, her voice soft.

"Know what?" I'm deathly afraid of what will come tumbling out of Ivy's mouth. The more I try to project a calm exterior, the more an awful dread rolls through me.

I close my eyes, trying to calm myself.

Ivy's hand rests gently on my arm. "It's okay, Lucas. You're going to be fine. Misha is…complicated."

My eyes fly open. "What does that mean?"

"Misha and Mr. Moore are close. Not a lot of people at Branson know that."

"Oh no, it's worse than I thought."

"Relax, Lucas," Ivy says. "Mr. Moore is Misha's uncle."

"What?"

Ivy shushes me, reminding me not to draw attention to our little meeting. Misha never said she had a relative working at Branson, let alone an uncle. Why wouldn't she tell me? I told her all about my family, my life, and she couldn't share with me about her uncle? What else is she keeping from me?

"How do you know that?" I ask Ivy.

"I have my ways. I can be very useful to you, Lucas. If you'd let me."

I open my mouth and then close it because I'm unsure of what to say.

Ivy says, "In a game of chess, the players will do anything to win. They'll manipulate and deceive, sacrificing their pawns to protect their queens."

"What are you getting at?"

"I'm not saying Misha is like that," Ivy hastens to add, her voice softening with sympathy. "But sometimes, people aren't who we think they are. They wear masks, hiding their true intentions behind a facade of charm and sweetness."

As Ivy's words of caution unfold, my heart sinks. Is Misha using me as a pawn in her own game, orchestrating moves behind the scenes that I'm blind to? She kept her connection to Mr. Moore a secret. What game is she playing?

"Sometimes the most dangerous opponent is the one we least suspect," Ivy says. "Be careful, Lucas. And remember to protect your king."

Ivy stands, picks up her backpack, and slings it over her shoulder. "Catch you later, babe."

Babe? Every encounter with Ivy gets increasingly bizarre, a giant puzzle I'm supposed to solve. What did she mean by *protect my king*? Obviously the chess reference is a metaphor for protecting myself from potential harm, emotional manipulation, or betrayal.

But who should I protect myself from? Mackenzie or Misha?

CHAPTER 49

'm glad you texted. I was worried you would never speak to me again. I'm so sorry, Lucas. I didn't mean to run off like that. It's just that…"

I raise a hand to interrupt her. After what I learned from Ivy, it's time to confront Misha, hear her side of the story. I'm dressed in soccer gear. Practice begins in a half hour, so I texted Misha and asked her to meet me at the field. We'll have plenty of time to straighten things out before practice starts.

"Why didn't you tell me Mr. Moore is your uncle?"

With her expression guarded, she asks, "How did you find out?"

"Ivy told me. And for the record, she didn't volunteer the information. I asked. I followed you after you ditched me at the café yesterday and saw you with Mr. Moore."

"Oh." Misha looks down, her foot making nervous circles in the grass.

I patiently wait her out. She looks up and says, "Look, Lucas, it's not that I wanted to keep it from you. I just don't want people at Branson knowing."

"Why? What's the big deal?" I ask.

"He helped me get into Branson. Introduced me to the right people, and showed me how the system works. I didn't want people thinking I was some nepo baby. I earned my place here on my own merit. My uncle just used his clout to make sure they looked at me favorably. You know how hard it is to get into Branson."

I mull over her statement. I sympathize with her logic. "So, you kept it a secret to avoid gossip and inuendo?"

She nods. "Exactly. I wanted to prove to myself, prove I deserve to be here."

"I thought we were getting close, Misha." I can barely keep the hurt and confusion out of my voice. "I thought you trusted me. Did you think I would betray you by spilling your secret?"

"Please try to understand, Lucas," she pleads. "I didn't want anyone to question my abilities because of who my uncle is. The students and faculty at Branson respect him. I couldn't compromise his well-deserved reputation, so it was best to keep our family connection hidden." Her words hang heavy in the air as she avoids my gaze.

"That doesn't explain why you didn't tell me. You just upped and left me at the café, no explanation, no consideration."

She looks down at her feet again. When she looks back at me, tears pool in her eyes. "Don't hate me. Please." She continues, "Since my parents' divorce, my father turned his back on me. My uncle stepped up. He promised my mom he would look out for me. She couldn't afford to send me to Branson on a social worker's salary. So Uncle James pays half my tuition out of his own pocket. The rest is a combination of grants and private scholarships."

Misha sniffles and then continues. "Uncle James came to find me to tell me my mom was hospitalized. She suffers from lupus and has terrible flare-ups sometimes. Lupus is unpredictable. Flare-ups have the potential to turn into life-threatening complications like kidney damage and the risk of stroke. What you saw was my uncle comforting me. He didn't want to share that kind of news over the phone."

A thousand thoughts ignite in my brain at once. I forced Misha to reveal deeply personal and painful information she clearly wasn't ready to share with me. Her trembling voice and tear-stained cheeks reveal the weight she had been carrying alone for so long. Embarrassment and guilt sweep through me. My heart breaks for her that her mother has a serious, life-threatening illness. How scared Misha must get when her mother's lupus flares up, not knowing if she could get worse.

And, it's nobody's business that Mr. Moore is her uncle. If she wants to keep it a secret, it's her right to do so. When I demanded an explanation, I wasn't expecting this.

"I'm sorry," I whisper, wiping her tears with my thumbs. "I panicked when you rushed out of the café. And when I discovered your connection to Mr. Moore, I was afraid you were playing me."

Her eyes go wide. "I would never do that to you, Lucas."

"I was unsure what to think. Since confessing my feelings for you, I've been learning to navigate this new relationship, this connection between us. I feared you might be playing games. The thought of getting my heart broken freaked me out."

Misha leans into me, her eyes shining and glossing over. Lowering her voice, she says, "You've been risk averse since birth." She recalls one of our earliest conversations. "So you're cautious. I don't blame you, Lucas. It's one of the things I like best about you. You're not reckless or rash. Even the way you think is deliberate. It's kind of unnerving and alluring at the same time."

Misha's slender index finger glides gently across my cheek, sending a shiver down my spine. The warmth of her touch is comforting. She pulls me close into a tight embrace, wrapping her arms around me as though she never wants to let go.

I hope she can't hear the rapid thumping of my heartbeat against my rib cage.

Overwhelmed by a sudden burst of emotion, I blurt out, "I love you!"

Misha's body goes rigid for a moment before she steps out of our embrace. She looks up at me, surprise in her eyes. "What did you say?"

My mind races, searching for the right words to explain myself. "Um.. I mean..."

"Hey, Rambally. Catch this."

A soccer ball comes flying through the air, hurtling toward Misha and me. I back up, and just before it lands on the ground, I kick hard, sending it scuttling across the grass toward Sergio Martinez, our team goalie.

I will owe Sergio for the rest of my life for the interruption. I can't believe I just said the L word. What was I thinking? I didn't plan to, it just spilled out of my mouth. And now, things are going to be awkward if she doesn't feel the same.

Sergio and a couple of the guys from the team circle around.

"I'll let you get on with your soccer practice," Misha says, a sweet smile plastered on her face. Then she turns and walks off the field.

I sit on the soft blades of grass and place my head between my knees. I totally blew it. What a stupid move. Dumb, horrible, ridiculous, the worst idea of worst ideas ever.

"You okay?" Sergio's voice breaks through my thoughts.

I look up and see concern in his eyes. With false confidence, I say, "Yeah, man. I'm good."

Sergio extends a hand and helps me up off the grass. "Was that your girlfriend?" he asks, looking at Misha's retreating figure.

I nod slowly, my heart sinking at the memory of my confession.

"Nice work, bro," he says. "Misha Johnson has her defenses on max. Do you know how many guys tried to make a move on her? They all got shut down."

"Really?"

"Yeah. You should be stoked she's giving you a shot." Then Sergio takes off to start drills.

My face splits into a wide grin. Now I don't feel so stupid for confessing my feelings.

CHAPTER 50

Can you repeat that?" Alexis asks, eyes wide with shock. Her gaze bounces between me and Blake and back again, as though needing confirmation that she heard me correctly.

" I…I told Misha I love her," I sputter, hardly believing it myself. It happened three hours ago. Now we're in the Bat Cave, discussing my impulsive and, in hindsight, stupid move, over delicious chocolate cake topped with toasted almonds and crushed toffee candy that Blake made just because he can on a school night.

Feeling the need to further explain myself, even though I can't, I add, "Something came over me. The words just slipped out."

"What did she say?" Blake asks.

"Sergio interrupted us, and Misha took off. If I avoid talking about it, she'll assume I didn't mean it, but if I mention it and she doesn't feel the same way about me, I'll look like a pathetic loser."

"This is huge, Lucas," Alexis says. She picks up a slice of cake from the plate on the side table next to the sectional. After a big bite, Alexis lets out a satisfied, "Soooooo good."

"Yeah, dude. Huge. You put yourself out there, and I respect that." Blake gives me a fist bump.

"But what if she's not into me like that?" I ask.

At Alexis's request, I launch into the back story that led up to the big moment where I made the confession; Misha abruptly leaving the café, me following her, and the whole Mr. Moore connection. Feeling overwhelmed by emotions when she confided in me about her mother's illness, her financial situation, that Mr. Moore pays half her tuition.

Maybe her vulnerability moved something deep inside me that came out as love.

"So you regret telling her you love her?" Alexis asks, gently.

"No. Sergio says other guys were making moves on Misha, but she turned them all down. He says I'm lucky."

Ivy's chess metaphor about protecting my king floats into my head. She said something about… what did she say? I frown, concentrating, trying to remember.

Sometimes, people aren't who we think they are. They wear masks, hiding their true intentions behind a facade of charm and sweetness.

"What's wrong? What are you thinking about?" Blake asks.

I explain what Ivy said before I realize my mistake.

"Are you serious, Lucas?" Alexis looks like she wants to grab me by the collar and shake me until I start making sense to her. "You spoke to Ivy about your feelings for Misha? Ivy!"

Alexis glares at me. She's standing now, her hands firmly planted on her hips. I can almost smell her disgust like a sweaty gym sock.

"Ivy had intel," I say, defensively. "Did you know Mr. Moore was Misha's uncle? No, you didn't."

Her hands drop from her hips, and her expression relaxes slightly, but my sister won't give up so easily.

"Don't let Ivy ruin this for you, Lucas. It's obvious she's jealous that you and Misha are a couple. I mean, how many times has she shamelessly thrown herself at you? Why are you surprised she's backstabbing Misha? She's sick with jealousy. No one ever says no to her, and she can't stand it that you're in love with Misha. Poor Ivy. Not."

Then Alexis folds her arms and plops down on the sofa.

Blake and I exchange a look. Blake shrugs as if to say, *you know how our sister gets.*

He says, "You should talk to Misha. She owes you an answer. If she's not on the same page as you, isn't it better to know?"

Doubt creeps up on me like a festering rash. But my brother is right. Misha can't leave me hanging. She has to let me know where I stand. What if she friend-zones me? Or says we should slow down and not see each other so often? Or, worse, she says I'm too intense for her and ends things?

Intensity. It's one of my character traits, either a blessing or a curse, I can't tell which. My emotions have always been larger than life. That's why I constantly work to rein in my temper, although I don't always succeed.

Even the simplest emotions are amplified, taking on a life of their own. Joy becomes euphoria, pain is agonizing, sadness becomes all-consuming, and anger can easily morph into rage. Love, to me, is like holding a burning star in my hand. Both beautiful and dangerous.

Love drove me to break Cole Parker's nose. The memory worms its way back into my consciousness. I can feel the sting of my knuckles, vivid and unbidding. It was a last attempt to reason with Cole, to tell him to stop bothering Alexis.

Cole had leaned up against his locker, as smug and unrepentant as ever. His smugness had ignited a fire inside me.

Without preamble, I'd said, "Back off Alexis, Cole. Stop being a loser who picks on unsuspecting girls. Alexis is just a kid."

"What are you going to do about it, Lucas?" he'd taunted me. "Is it my fault your sister is a hypocrite? She wants me, but she's too much of a Goody-Two-shoes to admit it. She's been sneaking out to meet up with me. So get over it."

It was the lying that did it. That was how he kept the girls he harassed silent, threatening to ruin their reputation by spreading lies.

I'd punched him hard on the nose. His head jerked back and he yelled, clutching his nose as blood spewed out. Cole unleashed a series of profanities and threats, but none of it moved me.

The little coward backed up against the locker, looking left and right, a way to escape. I admit, it made me feel powerful.

I'd leaned in and whispered, "You better come up with an excuse about what happened to your nose. Because if you tell anyone that I punched you, things will end badly for you. I know what you did to Cara Blaine. Enough to get you a jail sentence. And this time, your dad's power and influence won't save you. He has enough to worry about, keeping himself out of jail, doesn't he?"

Cole couldn't say a word, just clutched his nose and looked at me with terror in his eyes. The last ditch effort to reason with him was a formality. I knew he wouldn't back down. Guys like him never do.

Shifting my thoughts back to Misha and my impromptu declaration of love, I text her so we can straighten things out.

The twins lounge on the sofa, Alexis scrolling through her phone and Blake scarfing down another slice of cake with his ear buds on, listening to music.

> **Lucas:** We need to talk. May I call you?

The three dots are moving. She must have been waiting to hear from me.

> **Misha:** Yes.

I leave the Bat Cave and head for the privacy of my room. Staring at the wall, I try to think of the perfect opening line to set the tone for the conversation. I could have had the conversation over text, but that's a spineless wimp move.

What if the conversation turns awkward? I'll just be honest. Wait, do girls like honesty? Well, I hate liars, so I do my best to be honest and not lie to people unless it's life and death or something serious like that.

I tap her name in my favorites. She picks up on the third ring.

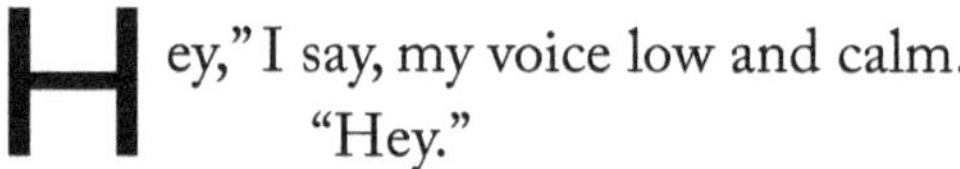# CHAPTER 51

"H ey," I say, my voice low and calm.

"Hey."

"Listen, about earlier. Sorry for dropping that bomb on you."

"Oh, don't worry about it. It's totally fine. But... what you said, it caught me off guard."

"Honestly, me too."

Awkward silence comes down the line. I rush in to fill the void. "The words just flew out of my mouth. It wasn't my intention to put you on the spot."

"No, no, you didn't. It was unexpected. Between your soccer practice and everything else, I haven't had time to process it."

This conversation will take an odd turn, regardless of my intentions. I'm curious about her feelings, but I don't want to pressure her so she feels obligated to tell me what she thinks I want to hear.

Can I handle her response, no matter what? If she doesn't reciprocate, what then? Sure, I can retreat to my room, brood, and shut everyone out, but what would that accomplish?

I leap off the bed and start pacing, my mind racing. Are the whispers about Misha and Jayden true, the ones Mackenzie warned me about? How do I stack up against Jayden, and does Misha see him as the better option? Or worse, she could be using me to make Jayden jealous. *Stop with the million questions, and just face whatever comes your way.*

Misha snaps me out of my self-pity when she says, "Lucas, you're amazing, and I really like you. A lot. But I need some time to process everything. I'm not sure if —"

I interject, "No explanation needed. Take your time. I just wanted you to know."

"Know what?" she presses.

"That I hope this won't make things awkward between us."

"It won't, if we don't let it. Expect a big hug the next time I see you, in front of everyone." She laughs.

"I'll hold you to that," I say, my shoulders relaxing. "Let's make it the dining hall. Give them a lunchtime show."

"Deal," she agrees. "Thanks for understanding, Lucas."

"Anytime," I reply."

"Talk later?"

"Yeah, talk later."

Despite our positive ending, uncertainty gnaws at me like a persistent ache. I took a risk confessing my feelings to Misha, and now doubt creeps in. Did I make a terrible mistake?

CHAPTER 52

I pocket my phone quickly as Misha absorbs our surroundings. Her distraction buys me a moment to quell my panic about this latest text and tonight's high-stakes meetup with Mackenzie. She promised to spill everything at the autumn dance, but we haven't nailed down a specific location. That's why I gambled on checking my phone when it pinged. I hoped Mack was sending our rendezvous point.

"Can you believe this place?" Misha asks, her eyes sparkling with excitement.

My gaze keeps lingering on her stunning outfit. Her champagne tulle skirt flares at the knees, shimmering under the crystal chandelier. A blush-pink sweater complements her warm-brown complexion, while gold stiletto ankle boots complete the look.

We enter the Granville Manor ballroom, marveling at the planning committee's work. The chandelier bathes the space in a warm glow, while cinnamon and vanilla scents waft from the refreshment table. A live band blends modern tunes with classic hits.

Extravagant bouquets adorn the room. The decorators went overboard. It's like they raided Home Depot's entire garden section.

Friends cluster together, laughing and posing against the enchanted forest backdrop. Others lounge on plush velvet couches, sipping cider and chatting.

Misha takes my hand as we navigate the room. Liam and Caleb give me a thumbs-up, but before we settle, Ivy approaches. Misha tenses, gripping my hand tighter. Ivy, stunning in a metallic-silver mini skirt, blue silk blouse, and hair hanging in loose waves, ignores Misha completely.

"Finally made it to an autumn dance," she says to me. "You look yummy, Lucas."

I confront Ivy about her rudeness. "Ivy, you see Misha standing next to me, right? She's not invisible." But Misha downplays it. Ivy stomps off to join her posse after a cold acknowledgment.

Couples flood the dance floor, twirling and swaying as the night unfolds. The live band alternates between upbeat tunes and romantic ballads, electrifying the atmosphere. Misha's incredible moves leave me breathless as I struggle to keep pace, but our shared laughter fills the air. I cling to this moment, pushing thoughts of my impending rendezvous with Mackenzie to the back of my mind.

I spot Alexis and Blake across the room and signal them to wait. After escorting Misha off the dance floor, I offer to get her a drink.

"Any news?" Blake asks, adjusting his suede jacket.

"Radio silence," I reply, resisting the urge to check my phone. The music might've drowned out any notifications, but Misha's waiting for her drink. I can't risk arousing suspicion.

I ladle apple cider into a plastic cup, confiding to Blake and Alexis. "I'm on edge."

"You could still bail," Alexis suggests. "Honestly, that might be wise."

"This might be my only shot at uncovering the truth and helping Mackenzie," I counter, gripping the cup tighter.

"Let's meet outside in ten minutes," I add.

Alexis agrees to cover for me with Misha when I leave to meet up with Mackenzie.

Rejoining Misha on the couch, I hand her the apple cider. She inquires about Blake and Alexis, having noticed our conversation at the refreshment table.

"They looked tense. Is everything okay?"

I lie, claiming they were concerned about Ivy's behavior. Guilt pricks at me for the deception.

After a sip of the cider, Misha places the cup on a nearby end table and rests her head on my chest. I drape my arm around her shoulder protectively and bask in the perfect moment. But not for long. The anonymous text linking Mackenzie's disappearance to my actions on Alexis's behalf nags at me. Questions swirl: Who knows these details? Mackenzie and I meticulously covered our tracks. Where is Mackenzie hiding?

My mind flashes back to when I first recruited Mackenzie to help take down Cole Parker. I'd crafted the perfect plan, determined to control every variable.

Mackenzie's response had been a combination of admiration and wariness. "Wow, Lucas, you plot payback with ice-cold precision. I almost feel sorry for Cole Parker."

The clock ticks, reminding me it's time to make a move. I fabricate a bathroom excuse to Misha and head out.

CHAPTER 53

A cool breeze rustles through the manor gardens. Blake and Alexis lurk near the hedges that border the gardens, partially hidden from partygoers.

"Check your phone," Blake urges.

"It's been silent all—" I stop abruptly when the phone pings. "Spoke too soon," I mutter, opening the message.

> **Unknown:** The wine cellar in ten minutes. Come alone.

I tilt the phone toward my siblings. Alexis's brow furrows. "You can still back out. What if someone's luring you into a trap?"

Laughter and music echo in the distance. It's decision time, before people start spilling out of the manor and into the gardens. Besides, Misha is waiting for me to return from the bathroom. I took five minutes to walk to the hedges. If my total bathroom break lasts ten minutes, that leaves five minutes to get to the cellar and hear from Mackenzie.

"Why would Mack lure me into a trap?" I ask. "A cellar guarantees no one will see us or overhear our conversation."

"You're right," Blake says.

Turning to Alexis, I say, "Make up a convincing story for Misha, one that will buy me enough time."

"I'll think of a good one. Misha won't question your absence."

Blake adds, "Good luck in the cellar."

CHAPTER 54

Apprehension tightens around my chest, a death grip that makes me want to turn tail and run. My footsteps echo softly against the cold, stone floor of the manor's corridor.

The flashlight from my phone casts dancing shadows along the walls, further heightening my paranoia. Perhaps this wasn't a good idea after all.

Holding up my phone, I open the door to the staircase that leads to the cellar. Should have brought a flashlight instead. The faint glow of the light on my phone is no match for the thick, dense darkness, as I slowly descend the stairs.

I arrive at the bottom, and with trembling hands, reach for the ornate iron door that leads into the wine cellar.

My hands freeze on the door knob. I should head back up and rejoin Misha and the twins at the autumn dance. But then I made it this far, despite my armpits beginning to sweat. I turn the knob, and the door creaks open. I step inside the room, bathed in dim light generated by a single lightbulb.

Row upon row of dusty bottles stacked neatly upon wooden racks appear. The cellar seemed to stretch on endlessly.

With cautious steps, I venture farther inside. The aroma of aged wine fills my nose as I make my way through the rows of bottles. I can't help but feel a nagging sense of unease. My phone's flashlight flickers briefly before dying completely, plunging me into semidarkness.

"Mackenzie, are you here?" I whisper. Fear licks at my nerve endings. Is this some kind of cunning trap?

"Mack, what the heck, this isn't funny. I can't help you if you're playing games."

Goose bumps form on my skin. I strain to hear anything at all that would let me know that Mackenzie is in close vicinity. The only sound is my heart hammering in my chest. I should get out of here. Pronto.

With my nerves on edge and about to snap like twigs, I head for the door. Something about this isn't right. What if the person who followed Mack when we agreed to meet up in the woods followed her here also?

This plan reeks of disaster. As I reach for the door handle to exit, Mackenzie's scream shatters the silence. "Lucas. Run!"

I spin around and race toward her voice. "Mack, where are you? I can't see you." I won't leave her here alone.

Suddenly, the light bulb flickers and dies, plunging the cellar into inky blackness.

I stand still, my muscles tense. There's someone in the cellar with me. I know this because a cold object is jammed against the back of my neck. My blood turns to ice, yet my heart beats violently as if it wants to leap out of my chest. *Don't make any sudden moves.* That's all I'm capable of thinking because both fear and adrenaline pump through my veins in equal measure.

The silent phantom in the room gives me no time to formulate an escape plan. Instead, a jolt of electricity slams into my body, horrendously painful like a thousand needles stabbing me at once. My vision blurs as I take in the sound of loud buzzing in my ears. Then my limbs convulse, and I can't control them. They give out, and I crumple to the ground.

CHAPTER 55

A pounding headache rages at the back of my skull as I struggle to sit up. With my hands tied behind my back and my muscles sore and weak, I don't have the strength to succeed.

Where am I? The surroundings seem blurred. Slowly, the wine cellar comes into focus. The lightbulb is functional again, casting eerie shadows across the cellar. Musty air fills my lungs as I fight to regain my bearings.

The memory of the electric shock hits me like a wave, bringing with it a fresh surge of pain and fear. My muscles ache, every movement sending sharp jolts through my body. I roll onto my side, feeling the cool, hard floor beneath me.

Blinking, I attempt to clear the fog from my mind and try sitting up once more.

My stomach churns with nausea. I take deep breaths, willing myself not to vomit. There's a note on the floor mere inches from me. I roll onto my stomach to get a closer look. Written in large capital letters with a red Sharpie is a threatening warning that leaves me terror-struck.

STAY OUT OF THIS, OR NEXT TIME, YOU MAY NOT WAKE UP!

I walked straight into a trap, chasing answers about Mack's disappearance.

Wait, where is Mackenzie? Her scream before the light went out still echoes in my head. Panic surges through me as I thrash against my restraints, fear blooming in my chest. Did they take Mackenzie? Is she hurt?

I gasp for air, my struggle to break free sapping what little energy I have left. My eyes dart around, searching for my phone. It's a few inches away from me and appears cracked beyond recognition. I look around the space again, hoping to find something to help me escape, but there's nothing but wine barrels and rows of wine racks.

Despair crashes over me. Only Blake and Alexis know my whereabouts. As for Mackenzie's fate…

My eyes burn as I fight back tears. Then a terrible, jolting thought occurs to me. What if they come back to finish the job?

I plop down on a leather armchair in the library of the manor house. The library provides privacy from partygoers, which I desperately need to calm down from the wine cellar trauma.

"How are you feeling?" Alexis asks, sitting across from me on a red sofa. Blake went to grab me a glass of water.

"Still sore and a little weak, but I'll be fine," I say, rubbing the abrasion on my left wrist caused by the ropes.

"What happened down there, Lucas?" Blake walks in, interrupting my response, and hands me the water in a plastic cup. I chug it down in one long gulp and then place the glass on the end table next to me. Blake leans against bookcase off to the side.

"I was ambushed. The place was empty when I got there. At first, I kept calling for Mackenzie, but there was no answer. Then she told me to run."

After I explain the incident from beginning to end, including the lights flickering and being plunged into darkness, the stun-gun attack, and waking up to find the light on and the threatening note, the room goes silent.

Blake says, "It sounds like someone was lying in wait for you. Otherwise, you would have seen them. But what's strange is Mackenzie. How come you heard her voice but never saw her?"

"I wish I knew, Blake. It was dark by the time I heard her say run. The whole incident makes no sense. There are more questions than answers."

Alexis adds, "Questions like, if the wine cellar was empty when you walked in, when did Mackenzie arrive, and where is she now?"

"Exactly," I say. "I agree with you that whoever tasered me and left the note was lying in wait, probably hiding behind a wine barrel. It's easy enough to do. But I never heard the door swing open once I was inside."

"Unless," Blake says, grabbing a seat next to Alexis on the sofa, "Mackenzie got there before you and so did the bad guy. Let's say he forced her to hide out and threatened her. Telling you to run was her only chance to warn you, but it was too late. After you were tased and passed out, they took Mackenzie and ran off."

My brother's explanation sounds logical, but something nags at me, like a piece of food stuck in your teeth. Mackenzie took off without saying a word when we agreed to meet in the woods. She only gestured for me to follow before she took off. This time though, she spoke, warning me.

Why was she quiet in the woods but not the wine cellar? She said she was followed in the woods, that's why she ran. The proof was the bump on my head when someone knocked me out. So why didn't she tell me to run then?

I'm now considering the distance, how far away I stood when Mackenzie first appeared in the woods. I'm certain it was Mackenzie. She had on her yellow trench coat, her head full of ash-brown curls streaked lavender.

Coming back to the messy present, I ask the twins how long I'd been gone before they found me.

Alexis says, "Fifteen, twenty minutes max."

Blake explains, "We didn't want to interrupt you and Mackenzie. But when we texted to see how things were going and you didn't answer, we couldn't decide whether it was because you were in trouble or you had zero bars on your phone and couldn't get a signal."

"We sensed something was off," Alexis adds. "Thank goodness for that tracker in your shoes. They could've taken you anywhere."

I nod and then hold up the cracked phone. "Was it necessary to destroy my phone? The note was scary enough. Who does that?"

The twins shrug at the rhetorical question. Alexis pulls the note from her small purse shaped like a white tea rose and scans it once more before returning it to the bag.

I ask, "Did Misha look for me while I was gone?"

"No," Blake says. "We told her you got an urgent call from your uncle Christian. She chatted with Mr. Moore and Ms. Krasnoff. And Maeve Williams."

"Maeve?"

I swallow and attempt to arrange my face into an expression that says, *I don't care if Misha talks to Jayden's sister,* who's part of Ivy's Phantastic Four clique, the same group of girls she claimed to steer clear of. But then again, it's a social event. Maybe I'm reading too much into it. My wine cellar ordeal is causing me to have paranoid thoughts about everything.

"I should return to Misha," I say, aware of the waning party. "I'm supposed to walk her back to her building, but I'm still a little woozy."

"I'll come with you to drop her off," Blake offers. "Alexis can hang out here and text Dad to pick us up soon."

"So what's next?" Alexis asks. "About Mackenzie, I mean. This is the second failed meeting."

We all stand. Blake chimes in, "We could revisit Kellen. He warned Lucas about Mackenzie's secrets. Maybe he didn't spill everything he knows."

CHAPTER 57

Dread clings to me as options dwindle. I haven't heard from Mackenzie since the wine cellar attack last night. I stayed up all night, tossing and turning, struggling to make sense of everything that's happened so far.

Wondering whether she's okay, who and what she's running from. Who keeps attacking me, and why they're so desperate to stop me from finding out the truth about what's going on with Mackenzie.

It was almost three thirty in the morning when I finally fell asleep, with a dreadful thought circling my brain: why was Misha nervous and uncomfortable when Eric Shanz gave his speech?

After the twins and I had returned to the party, Eric, a senior, picked up the microphone and addressed the crowd.

"I know we're all here tonight to enjoy the autumn dance, to take a break from our everyday worries. But as we stand here, there's a heavy weight on our hearts that we can't ignore. Mackenzie is still missing."

Misha stiffened beside me, as though the mention of Mackenzie missing upset her. I watched her carefully throughout the rest of the speech.

"Mackenzie is more than just a fellow student; she's a part of our Branson family," Eric continued. "Her disappearance has left a void in our school, a silence that echoes through the halls. It's easy to feel helpless, to think that there's nothing we can do. But I'm here to remind you that each of us has a role to play, whether it's spreading the word, keeping an eye out, handing out flyers in Concord and surrounding towns, or simply supporting each other through this difficult time.

Mackenzie wouldn't want us to give up. She's strong and resilient, and she needs us to be the same."

Misha remained stoic throughout and looked like she wanted to be anywhere but in the room during that speech. Afterward, she told me Mr. Moore would walk her back to her building which was on the way to his, and there was no reason to inconvenience me when both she and her uncle lived on campus.

I haven't had a chance to ask her about it; I'd prefer to do so face-to-face instead of texting. But I must also exercise caution. I haven't let Misha in on my not-so-secret investigation into Mack's disappearance and ditched her last night for twenty minutes while I went to the wine cellar.

If Misha finds out I've been holding out on her, she may dump me. *Will* dump me. I can't risk it, even though she gave off some weird vibes last night.

It's Friday and the end of the school day. The hallway bustles with students. I plan to ambush Kellen at his locker. And I won't stop badgering him until he gives me answers. Or threatens to get violent if I don't get out of his face. With Kellen, you never know which way things could end up.

Each step closer to confronting Kellen pulls me deeper into the vortex of uncertainty. Mackenzie's absence lingers like a dark cloud over us all, and I can't dismiss the idea that Kellen holds a piece of the puzzle, whether he realizes it or not.

Kellen is chatting with a group friends.

"Kellen," I say, trying to keep my voice steady, despite the adrenaline coursing through me.

He turns to me, his expression guarded. "Lucas, what's up?"

That's good. He's not hostile. In fact, lately, he's been almost polite during soccer practice. The friends, a couple of juniors and a senior I've seen around, nod in my direction, make their excuses to Kellen, and then take off.

"We need to talk."

"Fine. What's on your mind?"

I hesitate. How much should I tell him? Can I trust Kellen? "It's about Mackenzie."

Instantly, Kellen's demeanor shifts, his eyes narrowing with suspicion. "What about her?"

I swallow hard, steeling myself for his possible reaction. "I think you know more than you're letting on. And I'm not leaving until you spill it all."

Kellen's jaw clenches. A flicker of anger streaks across his face before he forces a tight smile.

"You still think I had something to do with her disappearance?" he asks.

I shake my head, trying to convey sincerity. "No, but I think you might have seen or heard something that can help us find her."

"I don't know what you're talking about," he mutters, his tone defensive.

With desperation pushing me forward, I say, "Stop lying, Kellen. You were dating Mackenzie. You owe it to her to tell the truth."

Kellen steps closer and then drops his voice to a dangerous whisper. "You don't know anything about it, Lucas. And you better watch yourself before you start accusing innocent people."

I hold his gaze, refusing to be intimidated. "I'll do whatever it takes to find her. Even if it means pushing you until you crack."

Kellen's fists clench as though preparing to punch me. But then, with a frustrated sigh, he shakes his head. "Fine. Hang back after today's practice."

CHAPTER 58

Standing off to the side of the field after practice, as our teammates head for the locker room, Kellen reiterates what he told me during our conversation at the library when Mackenzie first went missing. I desperately try to hold on to my temper. I hope he has new information and isn't wasting my time.

"These people, they were forcing her to hack illegally," he says. "You know she's a savant when it comes to computers. I didn't know how to help her when she started to receive threatening texts."

"What were they asking her to hack into? And what threatening texts? Who are these people?"

Reeling off the questions gives me time to think, to slow down.

Kellen nervously licks his lips. "Look, I don't know all the details. Mackenzie warned me to stay out of it. She was stressed out before she disappeared, jumpy and hiding her phone, but I managed to see a couple of texts I wasn't supposed to."

What Kellen says tracks with what I observed right before Mack went missing. She was on edge, dodgy, took mysterious phone calls. I must keep Kellen focused to get the right answers.

"What did the texts say?"

"Whoever sent them warned Mackenzie to stay in line." Kellen scrunches up his face as though trying to recall exactly what the text said.

"It was something like, 'The latest target is vulnerable. You know what to do. Stop stalling or else...'"

Were they planning to harm someone? Obviously not physically. Through blackmail? Asking her to dig up dirt on people, like we did when we set up Cole Parker?

It's getting dark. A cold breeze blows through the soccer field, bringing colder temperatures. I'll miss the late shuttle home if I don't head to the locker room to shower and change.

"Did Mackenzie react to the text?" I press.

"No. But whoever these people are, they had a tight grip on her. I'd never seen her so afraid."

"Why didn't you tell anyone? We could've helped." My hypocrisy stings, knowing I kept Mackenzie's communication a secret from everyone but the twins.

Kellen avoids my gaze. "Mackenzie insisted on handling it alone. She stonewalled me, no matter how hard I pushed."

A brief, awkward silence punctuates the conversation. Then Kellen starts sniffling, pinching his nose, trying to stop himself from crying. His voice cracks, and he says, "I miss her. I know what the kids here at school are saying. How I'm clingy and controlling, but it's not true."

"Um..." I falter, unsure of what to say or how I should react to this display of raw emotion. Kellen has been his usual tough-guy self since Mack went missing, and although I'm unsure how he deals with it privately, this raw display of vulnerability has me off balance.

"We all miss her Kellen. That's why I'm asking these questions. Trying to make sense of things. It's not easy."

Kellen looks off into the distance as though he didn't hear me. Then he says, "Mackenzie is the kindest, most patient person. If it weren't for her, I don't know how I would make it through school.

"After my mom died and my dad dumped me here and remarried, it was rough. And lonely. Mackenzie was nice to me, always checked up on me. Tried to cheer me up. That's how it started with us. But she was moody, too, and liked her space."

I stay silent, allowing him to get it all out. I've been so obsessed with my own issues and determined to find out what's going on that I never stopped to think how Mackenzie's disappearance affected Kellen. I guess the tough-guy act was just a front, like most guys. Truth be told, I sympathize.

Turning to me, Kellen says, "I didn't want to lose her. So when she wanted to break up with me, I panicked. I tried everything to convince her not to. I guess I was selfish."

"Besides your dad, do you have any other family?"

"A handful of aunts and uncles, a couple of cousins here and there. I'm not close to them. My mom held everything together when she was alive, but since she died, my dad couldn't be bothered, so I've been mostly on my own."

I place my hand on his shoulder. Kellen doesn't react. I say, "Sorry, man. I had no idea you were dealing with so much turmoil. We all got drama."

He chuckles. "Tell me about it."

"I was kidnapped as a kid and taken to Canada," I say.

Kellen's eyes pop wide in disbelief. "Seriously?"

"Yeah. When I was ten, some crazy woman pretending to be my mom's friend had her husband snatch me in the middle of the night. I'll spare you the details, but I just wanted to say I understand what it's like to feel separated from family, lonely, and scared to death of what could happen next. In a way, it gives me hope we'll find Mackenzie because I survived my kidnapping ordeal and came back to my family."

"You really think so, that Mack will come back?"

I nod with fingers crossed behind my back. Kellen can't see me waffling. I must present a one-hundred-percent-confident exterior while my insides plunge into a pool of uncertainty and dread.

A thought strikes me. Despite all I've learned about Charlie Covington, I must ask this question outright. "Kellen, do you think Mack was being bullied?"

His brows furrow, and then he shrugs. "Anything's possible. Mack mentioned an incident."

My pulse quickens. "What incident?"

"With Charlie Covington. It's like I told you the other day, she was always talking trash to Mackenzie. You know, acting like Mackenzie was beneath her. Charlie made up stories. She wanted Mack expelled from Branson."

"We already went over this, Kellen." The hashtag #thecompetitionthins comes to mind. It appeared on the BransonBuzz after Dr. Crawford announced Mackenzie was missing. The person who posted the comment referred to Charlie as a STEM-queen wannabe and implied Mackenzie wanted to get away from her.

"Charlie made threats," Kellen says.

"What kind of threats?"

"Charlie threatened to tell the dean that Mackenzie was cheating if she didn't withdraw herself from consideration for the scholarship. That's an expulsion offense."

"Whoa. Charlie took this rivalry to the extreme. But nobody would believe Mackenzie was capable of cheating," I say.

"Maybe not, but Charlie has enough clout around here to make anyone believe anything, even lies."

Kellen drops his gaze and starts picking at his fingernails.

"What? Time may be running out to find Mackenzie, Kellen. No holding back."

"There's one other thing," he says. "I totally forgot about it."

"What's that?"

"I once saw Mackenzie with this book. At the time I didn't think it was a big deal, but it had a peculiar symbol on it."

"Peculiar how?"

"A triangle with each side marked with a different mathematical symbol."

"What kind of symbols?"

"An equilateral triangle with the pi symbol, the sum symbol, and the infinity loop at each side."

"Did you ask Mackenzie about the book?"

"I did. I commented that I had never seen that book before and asked what it was. She did her usual stonewalling, told me not to worry about it."

"Do you think the book is still in her dorm room?"

"Hard to say. The police searched her room for clues. If it was there, they would have found it."

Kellen continues, "The book fell out of her backpack, and she shoved it back in, like she didn't want me to see."

Kellen frowns and scratches his temple, as though trying to recall some detail.

"What?" I ask. "Do you remember something else?"

"Nah. Never mind, it makes no sense."

"What doesn't?"

"It's a crazy idea."

"Tell me. Nothing could be crazier than Mackenzie disappearing."

"There could be a reason the police didn't find the book."

"Which is?"

"The book has been hiding in plain sight."

"What?"

When Kellen mentions something Mackenzie let slip, I stare at him incredulous. Then my brain starts to scheme. How to get my hands on that book. I push the thoughts aside for a moment because there's something else I need from Kellen. To keep an eye on someone and report back to me. Will he agree? There's only one way to find out.

I say, "Did Mackenzie's mom call you last week, when Mack first went missing?"

"Yeah. She and Mr. Fleming are scared out of their minds. None of their relatives have heard anything from Mack either. I told them I would keep in touch if I heard anything. I couldn't tell them about Charlie or the fact that Mack might be in trouble because she got in with some bad people. It would only make things worse."

"Good call." I remember how much my parents suffered when I went missing. I wouldn't wish that on the Flemings.

"You think we should tell the police about Mack acting weird and the illegal hacking?" Kellen asks. "If we find Mackenzie, she could go to jail. I thought it was best not to mention it to the investigators."

"You were protecting Mackenzie. I'm doing the same. Finding her is more urgent than whatever she's involved in. But there may be another way you can help."

"How?"

I explain the idea that had floated into my head. Kellen takes a step back, a mix of curiosity and bafflement blooming over his face. His mouth drops open for a split second, and then he quickly snaps it shut.

Kellen says, "Wow. Are you sure? That's kind of, um… out there, if you know what I mean."

"It is. But desperate times and all that."

He goes silent for a beat, and I'm afraid he'll say no. Just as I'm about to lay on the guilt, extra thick, he says, "Sure. I'll do it."

CHAPTER 59

The idea was brash and daring, with a hint of danger. Sneaking into the dorm room after hours, under the cover of darkness. It took some serious arm twisting, but she eventually agreed to sneak me into the building and into her room undetected. I kept my hoodie up for fear of being recognized by some night owl wandering through the hallway.

"Hurry up," Emily says, her voice heavy with sleep. She looks exhausted, with dark circles under her eyes, which I noticed when she appeared in the back stairway of the building to get me.

I nod, glancing around the room. A faint lavender scent fills the air. Mackenzie's bed is neatly made, her section of the room a stark contrast to Emily's. Papers, textbooks, and clothes are strewn all over.

I stride to the corner near the window and then kneel in front of the plant, carefully lifting it from its ceramic pot. Beneath the surface, instead of soil, there's a layer of small, decorative pebbles covering a block of Styrofoam, which held the plant in place.

I reach down with my free hand and scoop up a dark-brown leather book bearing the mathematical symbol Kellen explained on the cover. It's titled, *Equations of Enigma: The*

Secret Language of Numbers in Art written by Dr. Jonathan Keats.

Placing the plant back in its ceramic container, I open the book. A wad of folded sheets fall out.

"Are you done?" Emily says. "You have to go, Lucas. Make sure no one sees you on the way out."

"Okay." I pick up the wad of paper, place it in the book, and stuff the book inside my jacket.

Now to leave Emily's room undetected.

CHAPTER 60

BRANSONBUZZ

@BransonFabulous: Spotted: Midnight Rendezvous in Dorm Room!

Late-night antics at Branson? Our beloved boys' soccer captain was seen sneaking out of a certain tired and stressed-out girl's room after hours. What could they possibly be up to? #SoccerCaptainSecrets #SpillTheTea

@StraightUpBaller: Lucas+ Emily - Is that why Mackenzie disappeared? #BransonBuzz #ComeBackMack

@GossipGuru: Ooooh, sounds spicy. Could they have been studying "Biology" together? Or is our soccer hottie a playa? #Heartbreaker #LateNightStudyBuddy

@GuardianofTruth: That girl is always up past midnight... but with the soccer captain? Unexpected! #PlotTwist

@ChessGirlMagic: Heard she's into puzzles and riddles... maybe they're solving the mystery of Mackenzie's disappearance. More than just equations. #MathMystery #SneakySneaky

Reply from @StraightUpBaller: I thought he was into a certain mysterious future Oscar-winning composer with the killer dance moves. #Shady

Reply from @BransonFabulous: With Mackenzie missing, could Lucas just be comforting Emily? #StayStrongBranson #SupportiveFriend

@TheBransonWatcher: Think people. Emily and Mackenzie were roommates. Did our soccer hottie turned amateur sleuth find a clue? Maybe he's closer to the truth than we think. #BrainsandBrawn #BransonSmart

CHAPTER 61

’m so dead. My little sleuthing trip to Emily’s room last night—well, this morning—is all over the BransonBuzz. Stupid me, I pulled up the app during the shuttle ride to school.

Emily will never speak to me again. I should have known someone would see us, no matter how careful we were. Now poor Emily, who was just trying to be helpful, is the target of mean gossip and innuendo, Branson style.

I text her an apology.

As I walk through the main courtyard, the usual hum of student chatter seems to have taken on a more pointed and pervasive tone.

Eyes are on me. I can feel it. From every direction. Groups of students huddle together, their whispers stopping abruptly as I pass. The crisp morning air does nothing to dispel the fog of rumors that hang over the school.

Once inside, I approach my locker. A group of girls giggle. I catch snippets of their conversation.

"I heard they were totally making out," one girl says, her voice loud enough for me to hear.

"No way. Emily wouldn't do that," another one counters, though her voice lacks conviction.

"Why else would he be there so late?" the first girl insists, eyes gleaming with the thrill of gossip.

With fists clenched in annoyance, I arrive at my locker and turn the combination lock with more force than necessary. Just as I pop the lock open, Liam and Caleb approach.

"Dude, we need to talk," Liam says quietly, glancing around to ensure no one is eavesdropping.

"Not here," Caleb adds, his voice low and urgent. "Let's meet up at the library during lunch."

The library is safer, more private. People are whispering about me, a persistent buzz that grates on my nerves.

I want to scream at them to shut up, tell them they don't know anything. But reacting would only add fuel to the rumors and innuendo. Plus, it would come off as though I'm cracking under the pressure, which I'm not.

"So," Liam starts, looking me straight in the eye, "What's going on with you and Emily?"

"Nothing," I snap. "I mean, nothing like what people are saying. I was just... I needed to check something in Mackenzie's room. Emily helped me out."

Caleb raises an eyebrow. "And this couldn't wait until morning? You do realize how bad this looks, right?"

"I know it looks bad, Caleb, but it was important. I found something in her room, a book. It might have clues about what happened to Mackenzie."

Liam frowns. "A book? What kind of book?"

"It's an old leather-bound volume with a symbol embossed on the cover—an intricate design incorporating mathematical equations and geometric shapes. I can't provide any more details yet."

Liam says excitedly, "It sounds major, maybe a breakthrough. I feel bad for Emily though."

"I know. If I would've thought she'd get this kind of heat, I wouldn't have asked her to help me. I was so desperate to do something, anything, to find Mackenzie that I wasn't thinking about what could happen if someone saw me leaving her room."

I explain to my friends how Mackenzie hid the book under a fake plant.

"So Emily had no idea either, that the book was hidden in the plant?" Caleb asks.

"None."

"Makes you wonder what else Mackenzie could be hiding in plain sight," Liam chimes in.

My throat feels dry. I swallow, not knowing what to think of the comment.

"What do you mean, Liam?"

Liam and Caleb exchange glances and then look back at me.

"You don't know?" Caleb asks.

"Don't know what?"

"About Mackenzie secretly meeting up with Mr. Glendale, the history teacher?"

"Is this another piece of useless Branson gossip?" I ask.

I recall Glendale at the vigil, looking all somber like the sky was falling.

"Mackenzie stayed after class to talk to Mr. Glendale the day she went missing. The classroom door was closed, but apparently the argument was so heated someone heard raised voices," Caleb explains.

"Did they know what the conversation was about?"

"No."

"Then how do they know Mackenzie was in the classroom with Mr. Glendale?" I ask.

"Because they heard Glendale tell her to calm down, using her name."

"Who did you hear this from?"

"Tim Aldridge's sister has the same history class as Mackenzie. I guess she forgot something in the classroom, and when she went back to get it, the door was locked and she heard the voices. She didn't want to be caught eavesdropping, so she took off before anyone spotted her loitering outside the classroom."

A new piece to add to the puzzle. Did the police speak to Mr. Glendale? They must have spoken to all of Mackenzie's teachers.

Mackenzie wouldn't accept a bad grade, especially if she felt it was unfair. She probably gave Mr. Glendale evidence that she deserved a better grade. But then again, with everything Mackenzie had going on, it's possible she wasn't on her A-game.

Just then, the librarian walks by, giving us a stern look, reminding us to keep our voices down. We fall silent until she moves on.

Liam breaks the silence. "So, what's the plan? Suppose the book doesn't provide any real clues about where Mackenzie could be or whether she's..." He trails off.

All three of us know why. He wanted to say Mackenzie may never be found. But they don't know that she's been communicating with me via text.

"Earth to Lucas," Liam says, waving his palm in front of my face.

"Sorry. Just thinking about everything, trying to determine how the pieces fit together."

"Anything we can do to help?" Caleb asks.

Without thinking, I say, "Can you check into Cole Parker, see what you can find out? Like where he ended up after Branson?"

Both Liam and Caleb frown in confusion. Caleb says, "What does Cole Parker have to do with Mackenzie missing?"

Think. Think of an explanation. "Cole made a pass at Mackenzie, and she told him to get lost. You know how aggressive he was. It sounds ridiculous, but I thought he might have something to do with her disappearance. Cole didn't like the word *no*."

Liam looks at me like I've lost my mind. Then he nods slowly. "Revenge. It's the kind of thing Cole would go for."

"Yeah," Caleb says, agreeing.

I quickly add, "Look, I'm not saying Cole is guilty. I'm looking at all possibilities, even if they sound crazy."

"Cole was in the same year as Dylan," Caleb offers. "She might have information."

Dylan Andersson is Caleb's sister, and they're a year apart. Dylan and Cole were both juniors last year. "Would you talk to her please? Don't say anything about Mackenzie. Make up an excuse about why you're asking."

The sooner I can eliminate Cole as a suspect, the better. But where would that leave me? A thought flashes before my eyes. The BransonBuzz this morning, the very last response to the post about my late night trek to Emily's room. What was it?

He may be closer than we think.

Who made that post? Trying to find out is next to impossible since anyone can post on the app anonymously with any username they want. But maybe Liam can help me track down whoever posted the comment. He's great at research and logic, and he's connected inside Branson.

I pull up the old post and hold up my phone so Liam can read. "Do you think you could find out who made the post?"

"Why?" he asks.

"It could be nothing, but it's a funny comment. Sounds like the person knows something. Why else would they write, *He may be closer than we think?*"

"You're reading too much into it."

"Yeah, I guess you're right."

I pick up my bag and stand, signaling it's time to leave. Caleb and Liam do the same.

Caleb says, "We should do something fun, take your mind off things. Sometimes the solution to problems comes when we're not focused on the problem. At least that's what my dad always says."

Caleb's Dad may be right, but time is running out. Mackenzie provided no details about where she is and how she's coping, no matter how much I pressed. Since the proposed meetups were a bust, it's up to me to find the answers she's not in a position to provide.

Mackenzie won't come back until the danger has passed, until I figure out what's going on at Branson that caused her to flee in the first place.

It's time to eliminate Cole as a suspect. Or not.

CHAPTER 62

Mackenzie

Day of the disappearance

He did it on purpose. Low-balled me on the history test: a C. That's what he gave me. I am not, nor have I ever been, a C student from first grade until now.

Damian is behind this, trying to remind me who's in control and that I better be a good little girl. No way I'm letting Glendale get away with giving me a C. I don't care if he's afraid of Damian. This is my life they're messing with.

I wait until everyone exits the classroom and then plunk down the history test on the desk at the front of the class, my frustration barely contained.

"Mr. Glendale, I've gone over the test multiple times. My answers were accurate, my analysis of the material was spot on, and yet you gave me a C. This is going to ruin my GPA!"

This is my Global Studies course. I can tell Glendale has it in for me because I scored high on the other three essay questions. But on this one—*Analyze the Historical Evolution of Globalization from the Age of Exploration to the Digital Revolution. Discuss Key Events and Their Impacts on Global*

Interdependence—he took off a lot of points, as if he needed to justify his low grade because he couldn't find fault with the rest of the test.

He looks up from his papers, his expression calm and eyes cold. "Sit down, Mackenzie. Let's discuss this rationally."

Rationally? If he calls me hysterical, I swear I'll break his glasses and scratch his eyeballs out with a jagged piece.

I take a seat and force myself to cook up a cold expression like the one he's giving me. "You know my work. I don't do C work. And I especially wouldn't pass in C work so close to graduation, knowing what it takes to get into my top-choice college."

Glendale leans back in his chair and steeples his fingers. "Grades are not just about correct answers. These essay questions are designed to challenge your critical thinking."

My eyes narrow, and I remind myself to stay calm. "I understand that. There's nothing wrong with my critical-thinking skills. It's how I've been able to maintain a near-perfect GPA amongst a highly competitive senior class. This isn't about my performance. This is about control. You're trying to manipulate me on Damian's say-so."

A flicker of something—annoyance or guilt—crosses Glendale's face. "Honors Global Studies is meant to push you beyond memorization of facts," he says, all haughty, like I'm an idiot.

He picks up the test and scans it. Then he says, "For instance, your essay on the evolution of globalization. Your points were good, but they lacked depth in your analysis of the Industrial Revolution's impact."

"I thought I covered that well," I respond hotly. "It still doesn't explain why I was graded so harshly."

Glendale now places his hands flat on the desk. "You're ambitious, Mackenzie. MIT is a lofty goal. And while you've always been one of my top students, sometimes even the best need a reminder to push their limits. If you feel this grade is truly unfair, we can continue to discuss specific questions you struggled with and see where the misunderstanding occurred."

No misunderstanding occurred. How am I supposed to convince this man not to ruin my GPA and my future when he's clearly out to get me? It doesn't matter how reasonable I am, he'll find a way to sidestep any suggestion I make.

Without another word, I walk out of the classroom, leaving the test behind. Once outside the door, I lean against the wall, trying to keep my emotions in check, to stop the tears that are gathering from sliding down my cheeks.

Damian is determined to control me and threatening my future is the weapon of choice. I'm so very tired of playing this game. I thought I could win as long as I played by the rules and stayed one step ahead. There is only one move left now: go scorched earth.

I'm going to burn it all down to the ground.

CHAPTER 63

Blake savagely attacks an after-school snack of baked plantain chips, a grilled cheese sandwich, and grapes, as I make my way through the kitchen, past the family room, and hurry up the stairs to my bedroom. I'm anxious to examine the book Mackenzie left behind inside the fake plant.

Once I drop my bag at my feet, my text message tone pings. I plop down on the bed and pull out the phone from my pocket. *That was quick*, I think, looking at the screen.

Caleb: I spoke to my sister. Bad news.

Lucas: What did Dylan say?

Caleb: Cole Parker. He's gone.

Lucas: Gone where?

Caleb: Some super–strict boarding school for boys in England. Way in the boondocks.

Disappointment descends over me like a cold front that left Canada and settled in New England. Cole was my number-one suspect, but with this latest news, the possibility that he's the culprit fades like the waning days of autumn. If Cole is in Europe attending school, what would be the point of orchestrating Mackenzie's disappearance to get back at us both?

I change out of my uniform, and although I'm starving, I won't go downstairs to the kitchen to find a snack. Instead, I text Blake to save me some of the plantain chips. He probably ate everything Mom left, so I'll end up eating a peanut butter and jelly sandwich later. Besides, I'm too excited to eat right now.

Once I grab the book from the desk drawer, I pull out the chair and sit. Inside the book are the sheets of paper I saw last night when I swiped it from the fake potted plant plus something else. I'd gotten home past midnight and was too keyed up to look inside the book.

I couldn't risk taking it to school this morning in case Kellen wasn't the only one who saw it when Mackenzie was carrying it around. Talk about awkward questions. Why do you have a book belonging to Mackenzie? Did you do something to her?

With nervous anticipation, I spread out the contents on the desk. A photo, a group at a social event, a list of names in Mackenzie's handwriting, and articles printed from the internet. I arrange it all into three separate piles.

First, I examine the photo of the people at the social event. It looks like a cocktail party, and they're gathered around in a corner, sipping drinks.

Nothing jumps out at me at first. Then I look closer. I recognize Mr. Lennox, one of the Guidance counselors. Then Mr. Glendale, Mack's history teacher; Ms. Krasnoff from the admissions office who was conversing with Misha at the autumn dance according to Alexis; and Mr. Moore, my math teacher and head of the math and computer science department.

Why does Mackenzie have this photo? Where did she get it, and what's the significance? I place it aside for the moment and next tackle the list written in her handwriting. There are a total of seven names on the list. Most I don't recognize, but one jumps out at me.

Frank Parker, Cole's Dad.

Alexis furiously writes on sticky notes with a Sharpie and places them each on the crime board in our Bat Cave next to the list and photo. I was so flummoxed when I saw Frank Parker's name on the list that I just scooped up everything from the desk and scurried to the Bat Cave.

Blake sits on the sofa with his laptop, researching the names on the list.

"Six of the seven names on the list are Branson alumni," Blake says.

"How do you figure?" I ask. My gaze flitters back and forth between the photo and the list, trying to connect the dots.

"Google. Our school newspaper did a story about the big donor gala from a few years back."

"There has to be a connection between the list and the teachers at the cocktail party then," Alexis says.

"They're not all teachers," I remind her. "We have the assistant director of admissions, one guidance counselor, and two teachers, one of whom heads up the math and computer science department."

Bad things are going on at Branson. Mackenzie's warning echoes in my head again. We're close. I can feel it. The cocktail party photo by itself doesn't mean anything. But when combined with the alumni list, that's something interesting.

"Maybe the people in the photo wronged Mackenzie in some way?" I say. "If the rumor is true about her getting a low grade on a history test followed by a heated confrontation with Mr. Glendale, maybe she had run-ins with Mr. Moore too, the other teacher on the list."

"I don't think that's the key," Blake counters. "The way I see it, the connection is between the people in the photo and the list of Branson alumni. Otherwise, why would Mackenzie have them in her book?"

"Okay. Besides working at Branson, did any of the people in the photo actually attend as students?" I ask. "I'm trying to figure out how they would know the people on the list. Mr. Moore didn't attend our school, but what about Glendale, Lennox, and Ms. Krasnoff?"

"Not sure," Alexis says, lost in thought. "But wouldn't the people in the photo also know the alumni on the list, even if they didn't attend Branson themselves?"

"What do you mean?" I ask.

"It's obvious that's what Mackenzie is trying to tell us. Whether or not they attended Branson isn't the clue. The clue is they're connected to whatever bad stuff is going on. Besides, wouldn't teachers and administrators have access to the alumni list anyway?"

Alexis makes a strong point. The question isn't how they're connected but why. I allow my thoughts to roam freely, trying to fit the puzzle pieces together. Frank Parker is Cole's dad, and he's on a mysterious list Mackenzie left behind.

But Parker wasn't mentioned in the school newspaper article from the donor gala. He's the seventh name, and not an alum. Mr. Moore is head of math and computer science.

Branson is a leading STEM school, so I can see Mr. Moore being friendly with wealthy alumni. The proof is our brand-new, shiny STEM building that cost tens of millions of dollars to build.

What's so special about the six alumni on Mackenzie's list, and why is there an outlier, Frank Parker? I wonder.

I reach for my phone on the couch and compose a text to Liam. Research is one of Liam's gifts. Give him any subject and he has a knack for coming back with a mountain of information reaching back decades. He's the right guy for the job to find out more about the people on the list.

And despite my agreement with Alexis that the big question is why they're connected, the how could prove helpful down the road.

"Why don't you ask Misha if her uncle knows the people on the donor list?" Blake says. "He probably does. Since he heads up a major, I'm sure alumni slash donors talk to him all the time."

An interesting idea. Mr. Moore had said he wanted to help me find Mackenzie and I should let him know how he can. He seemed proud of me for trying to do something to bring Mack home, instead of solely relying on the police.

But I'm hesitant. I don't want to make Misha anxious. She might get defensive if I start asking questions about Mr. Moore. Besides, there's another angle to pursue: Cole's dad isn't a Branson alum. So what is he doing on the list? In fact, I need to dig into every single person on the list.

"I can't ask Misha," I say. "I have a better way to get answers."

The fact that Mackenzie had this information and kept it hidden is important.

Branson is the common thread. And all these people are up to their necks in whatever *bad things are happening at Branson.*

CHAPTER 65

While I grab my bike from a rack in the garage, Blake presses the panel that controls the open-and-close function. Mom and Dad will be home in approximately ninety minutes, which doesn't leave me a lot of time.

Blake and I exchange a good-luck fist bump, and I peddle out of the garage and down the street. The wind picks up, rustling the amber and crimson leaves that have fallen to the ground and on the neighbors' lawns. The chill in the air hints at the approaching evening, and I pedal faster, eager to get to Liam's house.

As I approach the corner of Maple Street, a voice calls out, "Lucas! Is that you?"

I groan inwardly and slow down, looking over to see Rachel Bennett, our neighbor, standing at the end of her driveway. She's bundled up in a thick sweater and scarf, her long dark hair flapping in the wind.

"Hi, Rachel," I say, forcing a smile and hoping to keep this brief.

"Hi, Lucas! How's everything going?" she asks, stepping closer, her eyes wide with curiosity.

Rachel doesn't go to Branson; she's a junior at Lexington high school. Her family moved into the neighborhood the summer before my freshman year. Her dad is a successful architect who works for an architectural firm in downtown Boston. They specialize in designing high-end residential and commercial buildings. Her mom runs an art gallery.

"Everything's fine, just busy with school stuff," I reply, shifting on my bike. The wind whips through the trees, carrying the scent of pine and the crispness of autumn.

"Busy with soccer too, I bet. I saw your team won last week. You were amazing!" Her words come out in a rapid stream, her eyes twinkling with admiration.

"Thanks, Rachel. Yeah, it was a tough game," I say, glancing down the street. The sky is painted with the soft hues of approaching twilight, and I can feel the minutes slipping away. "Listen, I really need to get going. I have a lot of homework."

"Oh, of course," she says, looking slightly disappointed but not deterred. "I was just wondering if you wanted to hang out sometime. Maybe grab a coffee or something?"

"That sounds nice, but I'm really swamped right now," I say, trying to sound as sincere as possible. The wind tugs at my jacket, reminding me of the urgency. "Maybe another time?"

"Sure, another time," she says, smiling brightly. "And, I'm really sorry about what's going on at your school, with Mackenzie missing and all. I saw her when she came to your house a few times. She seems nice."

I hold on tightly to the handle bars of my bike. "Yes, Mackenzie and I are close friends, and yes, she is nice. Now I really have to go. See you around, Rachel."

"See you, Lucas!" she calls out as I start pedaling again.

I turn the corner and race down the street, leaves crunching under my tires, my mind buzzing with the clues from Mackenzie's book. The urgency of getting to Liam's is like a drumbeat in my chest, propelling me forward through the crisp, autumn evening.

CHAPTER 66

Liam's room is a chaotic blend of sports posters, books, and various gadgets strewn across the desk. A large corkboard on the wall is filled with notes and photos—evidence of Liam's many interests and projects.

He's already at his desk, his computer screen alive with multiple tabs open.

"Okay, let's see what we have here," he says, glancing up as I pull the leather-bound book out of my backpack and lay it on the desk. Next, I place the printed articles on the floor, and Liam joins me.

The excitement creates a buzz in the air. My heart races as we sift through the printouts. Each article covers various prep school scandals from the past. Financial fraud, racketeering, embezzlement—every piece tells a story of corruption and deceit at elite institutions like Branson.

"This one's about a headmaster caught embezzling funds from the school's endowment. The money was funneled through several shell companies," I say, handing Liam one of the sheets. "And this one," I add, "is about a group of influential alumni and staff at a school in Connecticut who manipulated the admissions process for favors and financial gain."

Liam's eyes light up with curiosity. "Wow. That's some seriously shady stuff. But you missed one."

"What did I miss?"

"The piéce de résistance," he says, lifting a sheet with a flourish and placing it next to the others on the floor. "The prep school cocaine scandal of the 1980s."

"Never heard of it."

"Because they tried to bury it, until a curious producer dug it up and turned it into a movie."

Liam explains that a scholarship student at an elite prep school, much like Branson, was busted trying to smuggle three hundred thousand dollars' worth of cocaine into the United States from Columbia. He was a kid who didn't fit in with his privileged classmates and used the drugs as a way to fit in by supplying said classmates.

I scan all four articles splayed out on the floor. All the stories are in the past, but the people in the photo are very much present and part of the Branson community. What if Mackenzie is running from one or all of them?

It's the only explanation that makes sense, isn't it?

Unfortunately, there's no way to reach out to Mack and ask her all these questions. I haven't heard from her since the incident in the wine cellar when she told me to run. With a burner phone, I can only wait to hear from her.

Liam gets up from the floor and heads to his computer. "I've saved the most intriguing information for last," he says.

"What do you mean? What information?"

"About the seven names on the list. It didn't take me long after you texted me that you were coming over."

I follow Liam to his desk, standing over his shoulder. One by one, he goes through the open tabs on the screen.

"First up, Evelyn Harper, CEO of HarperAI, a company specializing in AI and cybersecurity. She's big into philanthropy and highly influential in the tech industry. Also a Branson alum, class of 1996."

"Okay, but that doesn't tell us anything about why she's on Mackenzie's list."

"Patience dude. She's just one of seven. I haven't gotten to the best part yet."

My palms begin to sweat as adrenaline courses through my veins. I can't decide if it's from excitement or fear of what Liam's research will reveal.

"Next up, Senator Jonathan Pierce, who has strong ties to a number of defense contractors." Liam points to a tall older man, maybe in his sixties, with a head full of graying hair and blindingly white teeth. The man is obviously tight with his dentist.

Liam goes through each tab, calling out the men and women on the list: Cameron Wolfe, a major Wall Street investment banker; Isabella Martinez, a well-known designer and owner of a global fashion brand, one of my aunt Callie's competitors; Dr. Henry Thompson, a well-known neurosurgeon and medical researcher; and Maxwell Chen, media mogul.

"What about Frank Parker?"

"I'm saving him for last."

I don't ask why. Liam just reeled off a list of powerful people who all went to Branson. Are they targets of some kind? I immediately reject the idea. These people have enough clout to protect themselves from everything and anything. A bunch of teachers and administrators at Branson would hardly be a threat to them.

"So, these powerful people. You think they're part of some secret group and the teachers in the photos work for them?"

Liam nods. "That's exactly what I'm thinking."

"Doing what, though?"

"Favors is my best guess."

"How does that tie back to the prep school scandals though, the stories Mackenzie printed out from the internet?" I ask. "As far as I know, none of them have kids or relatives who attend Branson."

"Maybe you're using the wrong tense."

"Meaning what?"

"Attended. Not attend."

My brain starts clicking, furiously putting pieces together, discarding ones that don't fit and plugging them in elsewhere. Everything I know so far. Mackenzie on the run from bad things and bad people. The text Kellen accidentally saw, *The target is vulnerable, you know what to do. Stop stalling or else…* The threatening texts I received about how Mack and I set up Cole Parker for harassing Alexis. The news articles, list, photos, all of it.

And what do I come up with? The people on the list have secrets. Kellen told me Mackenzie was involved with people who wanted her to use her hacking skills to do bad things. It totally makes sense.

Before I can think through the theory further, I share it with Liam, unloading it from my brain before I go down a rabbit hole I can't come back from.

"Blackmail," I blurt to Liam. "They're being blackmailed. Whoever Mackenzie was working for used her to dig up dirt on these powerful people. She probably refused after a while and went on the run to protect herself."

I'm breathing noisily, and my hands tremble. I don't know if what I've said is the truth, but it sounds close to it. When all the clues are put together, they fit.

"Are you okay? Do you want me to get you some water?" Liam asks.

"Nah. I'm fine."

I explain to Liam what Kellen told me about the text he accidentally read on Mackenzie's phone. I figure there could be no harm in sharing that tiny detail with him.

Liam remains calm for a minute, and then he says, "I have bad news."

"What do you mean?"

"There was a rumor going around that Mr. Parker had ties to organized crime."

"What? That's insane. Did you hear that on the BransonBuzz?" I give Liam a look that says I'm ashamed of him for listening to stupid gossip.

"No. It wasn't the Buzz. Someone overheard chatter in the teachers' lounge. You know how rumors take on a life of their own at Branson. But that was years ago. I only remembered because of the list."

We both fall silent. My mind doesn't have a destination. It's a lot to take in, and I don't know what to think. I thought I had it at least partially figured out, but with this new revelation from Liam, maybe not.

I walk over to the window and stare out, fingers absently drumming on the wooden sill. It's getting dark, and I should head home. The wind, which whipped against me on the bike ride over, now howls through the trees, causing leaves to dance in chaotic spirals on the dimly lit street below.

Leaning in closer, I scan the street. I don't know why or what I'm looking for. The glow of the streetlamp catches my attention. Then I see it. A figure in a dark hoodie, standing just beyond the reach of the streetlamp's glow. The hood is pulled low, obscuring the face, but there's no mistaking the direction of their gaze. They're looking straight up at me, their posture unnervingly still despite the wind tugging at their clothes.

My heart rate kicks up a few notches, a cold knot of fear tightening in my stomach. I blink, hoping the figure will disappear, but it remains, an ominous silhouette against the encroaching night. A shiver runs down my spine.

I take a step back, my mind racing. Who is this person? What do they want? And how long have they been standing there, unnoticed, in the dark? I turn to Liam, who is engrossed in his laptop.

"Liam," I say, my voice shaky, "I think someone's watching us."

Liam looks up, eyebrows furrowed in confusion. "What are you talking about?"

I gesture towards the window. "There's someone out there. In a hoodie. They're looking right at us."

Liam stands and moves to the window, peering out into the street. "I don't see anyone."

I have a look again, and sure enough, the figure is gone. The street is empty, the wind howling, leaves swirling.

I didn't imagine the figure in the hoodie. Someone followed me to Liam's house.

CHAPTER 67

Someone pushed Kellen Fontaine down a flight of stairs last night, breaking his right leg. That's what the text message from Liam says. I race across the quad to meet up with him at my locker. When I arrive, breathless and freaked out, the hallway is buzzing with chatter and gossip.

"What happened?" I ask, anxiously.

With a grave expression, Liam says, "One of the resident assistants was doing a final walk-through for the night to make sure everything was okay, and he found Kellen at the bottom of the stairs of the Wentworth building. It's bad. His leg was twisted at an awkward angle. At least, that's the news going around."

I drop my bag on the floor and then lean up against the locker for support.

Liam asks, "Do you think this has anything to do with Mackenzie's disappearance or the person you saw last night?"

"I don't know," I hedge. Twice I was attacked and warned to back off, although I haven't shared that information with either Liam or Caleb. How many more people are in the sights of this psycho or psychos?

As if reading my mind, Liam adds, "Be careful, Lucas." He places a hand on my shoulder. "Seems like somebody doesn't want the truth about Mackenzie to come out, and people associated with her are getting hurt."

I nod, not sure what else to say. Though tempted, I don't dare open the BransonBuzz. Poor Kellen. I should stay away from him, that's for sure. Whoever is behind this has upped the stakes. Now, the favor I asked of Kellen is up in the air while he recovers from a broken leg.

"Hey, Lucas." I turn around to see who called my name. Misha.

I've been so caught up in solving this mystery that I didn't text her after the BransonBuzz blew up with gossip about me and Emily. I hope she doesn't believe any of it. That would stink if she does and it sends her running to Jayden Williams. I hate that guy.

Liam says he'll catch me later, and I turn my attention to Misha.

"Hi. Sorry I haven't texted lately. A ton of stuff is going on, and it's all too much." I also forgot to ask Misha to meet up in the common room so I could ask about her strange reaction to Eric's speech about Mackenzie during the autumn dance.

"Yes, I know. Like sneaking out of girls' rooms in the middle of the night."

"Look, Misha, it's not what it looked like—"

She cuts me off with, "It's okay, Lucas. If you were sneaking around, it's for a good reason. I don't believe any of the nonsense rumors floating around. Emily is Mackenzie's roommate, so of course you would want to talk to her. As for why it happened in the middle of the night, I guess you didn't want anyone spotting you heading to her room or leaving. At least, that was the plan."

She gives me an understanding smile, and I'm so relieved that I hug her. Right there at my locker where anyone can see, and I don't care. She doesn't resist the hug.

She's relaxed, and it feels like Misha is melting in my arms. I can't describe how amazing it feels to hold her. The weight of Mackenzie's disappearance is a gaping wound, and Misha's hug is a huge Band-Aid that is helping me to hold it all together in the moment.

I fear that Mackenzie could be hurt or, worse, alone and terrified, uncertain, fearful of coming home, coming back to school. It's a lot to handle.

After we break apart, a few curious stares and smirks are sent our way. Who cares if the rumor mill wants to make something of the hug? I'm beyond caring.

Misha says, "You have a lot on your plate, Lucas. I can't imagine the stress you're under. I can't believe the police have zero clues about what happened to Mackenzie. I hate to say it, but I don't think they'll keep looking if there's no break in the case soon."

"Why do you say that?"

She shrugs. "Let's be honest. Missing Black girls don't exactly make national headlines. If the case goes cold, they'll move on, and we'll never know what happened. That's why what you're doing is so brave, Lucas. I respect that. Don't give up."

Now or never. I ask, "Is that why you were nervous during Eric's speech at the autumn dance?"

Frowning, Misha asks, "What are you talking about?"

"You were tense when Eric Shanz rallied us not to give up hope of finding Mackenzie. It was as if talking about her made you uncomfortable."

"Oh. Not at all. It's like I told you… there's been no break in the case, and with all the time that has passed… We're in the second week of Mackenzie's disappearance with no clues. The police may put her on the back burner and put their resources elsewhere. It upset me thinking about it."

Without giving me a chance to react, Misha plants a kiss on my cheek, and then she says I should text her later, before she saunters off.

I feel ridiculous for thinking there was something suspicious about Misha's behavior at the dance. She was just reacting to what we've all been thinking; how much time has elapsed with no word.

I break out in a big, goofy grin. It's as if the hug and kiss on the cheek were the shots of adrenaline I didn't know I needed. I had been worried Misha would berate me for going silent on her for a couple of days, but she didn't.

That's one of the things I like best about her. She doesn't need me to text her every five minutes for her to know how I feel or that she's on my mind. Misha is secure in who she is, confident. It's refreshing.

Before I swap books from my locker, a new idea floats into my head, someone who might have information on Cole Parker's dad.

CHAPTER 68

We agreed to show up for the club meeting a few minutes before anyone else arrives. That way we needn't worry about being seen and further fan the flame of rumors and innuendos.

"What's on your mind?" Ivy asks.

"Cole Parker's dad."

Ivy gives me the side eye. "Oh, so now you want to talk to me because Misha isn't around? You embarrassed me in front of her at the autumn dance."

"Come on, Ivy. You were rude. You could have just said hello and that would have been the end of it. But you acted like Misha wasn't even there. You looked right through her."

Ivy rolls her eyes, and then folds her arms defiantly.

I say, "What? You want me to apologize for calling you out when you were at fault?"

"It's a start."

"I'm leaving," I say, picking up my backpack from the floor.

"Okay, okay," Ivy says, defeated. "Sit down. Why do you want to know about Mr. Parker?"

I make up a story on the fly for Ivy's benefit. Otherwise, she'll get suspicious and won't help me.

"Just turning over every rock. I found out Cole made a pass at Mackenzie; she told him to get lost. You know Cole doesn't take rejection lightly. Yes, I'm grasping at straws, but I thought for a minute Cole might have been involved."

"Highly unlikely," Ivy says, matter of fact. "But why the question about his dad?"

"I don't know…I guess I was wondering if his dad ever paid off anyone to keep quiet about what Cole was doing."

Ivy's eyes pop wide. "Oh, snap. With all this investigating, I'm beginning to think you're auditioning for CSI: Branson Academy."

"Something doesn't feel right about this whole thing. People don't vanish into thin air. There's a clue out there. I just have to find it."

Ivy tilts her head to one side. "Well…there could be something, but I don't see what it has to do with Mackenzie going missing."

"What is it? Anything could be a thread that leads to a connection that reveals a clue."

Ivy looks toward the entrance to make sure no one is on their way in.

"Rumor is Cole's dad made a million-dollar donation to Branson to keep Cole's record clean. They didn't want any of the evidence against him as part of his record, so the Parkers made sure the official story was Cole left Branson to pursue an international opportunity that was more in line with his career aspirations."

"Seriously?"

"Dead serious."

This information tracks with what Caleb found out from his sister Dylan. Sounds like the Parkers wanted to put Branson in their rearview mirror. It would serve no purpose for Cole to dredge up his past experience by trying to get revenge on me and Mackenzie. I just assumed he somehow found out we were involved, in spite of the fact that all the information we provided was sent anonymously.

Cole Parker is truly a dead end, so I try another tactic. "Ivy, do you think Charlie Covington is capable of sending people to harm Mackenzie? You know they were in competition for that STEM award."

"Wow, Lucas. I've never seen this side of you before. I mean, everyone knows not to mess with Blake and Alexis. But this fierce loyalty to Mackenzie is very attractive."

I glare at Ivy, reminding her to tread carefully.

"What?" she says. "It's true. You're not afraid to go to bat for the people you care about. Look how you insulted me in front of Misha."

I give her the stink eye and observe her sly smile, as if she enjoys rattling me.

With a lingering gaze, Ivy leans back in her chair. She adds, her tone causal yet pointed, "In a game of chess, oftentimes the most dangerous piece isn't the one you're chasing across the board. It's the pawn you forgot about, the one that's quietly making its way to the other side, ready to become a queen and turn the whole game upside down."

She pauses, letting her words sink in, her eyes locking with mine. "Sometimes, it's the pieces you're not paying attention to that end up causing the most trouble."

Why doesn't Ivy just get to the point? All these chess references are exhausting, and they're starting to annoy me.

"What do you know that you're not telling me, and why not just say it out loud instead of turning Mackenzie's disappearance into some sinister chess game?"

Without missing a beat, Ivy looks me dead in the face. "Lucas, listen. This isn't just about Mackenzie disappearing. It's about understanding the game that's being played around us. In chess, every piece has its role, its strengths, its weaknesses.

"Just like the people at Branson Academy. Some are pawns, easily sacrificed. Others are knights, making unexpected moves. There are bishops working diagonally behind the scenes, and rooks, powerful but predictable."

Ivy stands and paces the room, arms folded, her mischievous attitude of moments ago replaced by an earnestness I've never observed in her before.

She adds, "Mackenzie? She is our queen—versatile, central to everything. Her disappearance has left the board wide open, and now everyone's scrambling to take advantage. To find her, you need to think like a chess master. Anticipate moves before they happen. Recognize patterns. See the whole board, not just the piece in front of you."

I gape at Ivy, her intensity holding me spellbound.

She continues, "I'm using chess metaphors because this isn't just a mystery, Lucas. It's a strategic game with high stakes. And right now, you're playing blindfolded. I'm trying to help you see the board. Because if you can't understand how the game is played, you'll never figure out who took our queen—or why."

CHAPTER 69

The soccer field is a cauldron of noise, the cheers and chants of the crowd, mostly Auburndale fans, echo as the final minutes of the match tick away. It's the semifinal match, the one that determines who meets Taft in the finals.

With Kellen sidelined with his broken leg, the weight of leading the team to victory rests heavier than usual on my shoulders. Even with my brother Blake playing some of the best soccer I've ever seen, and our parents and sister cheering from the sidelines, it's becoming increasingly clear our chances are slipping away. To make matters worse, it's an away game for Branson. We're on Auburndale's turf.

Auburndale has always been our toughest rival, their team a formidable force to be reckoned with. Without Kellen's skills on the field, every missed opportunity or misplaced pass adds to my growing sense of desperation.

I glance at the scoreboard, the numbers mocking me. We're down by a goal, and time is running out. The crowd's energy crackles with anticipation, their cheers morphing into a deafening roar as Auburndale launches another attack on our goal.

Rallying my teammates in a timeout, I try to instill a sense of hope in the face of impending defeat. When we return to the field, reality sets in that our efforts are in vain.

The ball sails past our goalkeeper, finding the back of the net with a sickening thud that seems to echo the finality of our loss.

The referee's whistle pierces the air, signaling the end of the match and sealing our fate. No third championship for me. I sink to my knees on the field, the weight of our defeat crushing me like a ton of bricks.

As I look around at my teammates, their faces etched with frustration and despair, I can't help but feel responsible for our failure. Without Kellen, we fell short when it mattered most, our dreams of championship glory slipping through our fingers like grains of sand.

But amidst the disappointment and heartache, a fire ignites within me, fueled by the sting of defeat and the determination to rise from the ashes. Find out who pushed Kellen and who is hunting Mackenzie. With this loss, our soccer season is now officially over, the semi-final match that was supposed to cement our spot to the finals and the championship.

I let my team down. My first year as the captain, and I'm a loser. I thought we could pull out the victory without Kellen, but if I'm being honest, my head wasn't in the game. The competitive fire that made me captain in the first place, the inferno that pushed me to bring home two prior championships, just wasn't there today.

After we form a line and congratulate Auburndale, the field slowly empties. I sit on the grass, my head between my knees, feeling the weight of defeat settle over me like a suffocating blanket. My parents and Alexis are waiting for me, but I can't face them yet. Can't face my younger brother who looks up to me. I failed him too.

"Lucas?"

I look up to see Misha standing in front of me, concern and empathy in her eyes.

"Hey," I say, forcing a weak smile.

She wraps her arms around me, pulling me into a comforting embrace. "I'm so sorry, Lucas. I know how much this meant to you, how much you wanted it."

I bury my face in her shoulder, drawing strength from her presence. "Thanks, Misha. It's hard to accept our season is over, and with everything else…"

"I know," she murmurs, running a soothing hand through my hair. "But you played your heart out."

I meet her gaze with a mixture of gratitude and frustration. "But it wasn't enough. Without Kellen, we were just… I don't know, lost."

"Kellen's injury was beyond your control, Lucas. You did the best you could with the hand you were dealt."

I sigh, the tension slowly draining away as her words sink in. "I guess you're right. I thought we had it. I feel like I let everyone down."

Misha cups my face in her hands, her touch gentle yet firm. "You didn't let anyone down, Lucas. You're a leader, a fighter. And this loss doesn't define you."

But what if Misha is wrong? What if this loss is a sign of things to come?

CHAPTER 70

Could this day get any worse? Yes, apparently it can.

I perch on my bed, unsure of my next move. Events of late bombard my mind: Kellen's fall down the stairs, the mysterious list, decades-old prep school scandals, and the constant, skin-crawling sensation of being watched.

This latest text screams outright threat. The sender has dropped all pretense, shed the kid gloves, now wielding words like weapons. They orchestrated Kellen's accident, and they're demanding I abandon my search for Mackenzie. The words pulsate with menace, daring me to defy them.

Rage coils in my gut. This faceless coward had decided to come for me. It's time I pushed back.

I've had it with this stupid game. The sender, like Mackenzie probably uses a one-way communication app. My messages to Mackenzie return undeliverable.

Mackenzie's tech skills and sinister events of late suggest one-way communication might be safer. But the threat texter? Pure coward. Big difference.

I'm starving. I should have eaten after the game, but our loss plus anger had killed my appetite. I stand, ready to head downstairs and raid the kitchen, but my phone buzzes with another incoming text. This guy won't quit.

Unknown: It's me. Mackenzie. Please watch the video. It explains everything.

I gaze at the phone, hypnotized by its message. Time stands still, stretching into an eternity. My finger hovers and then swipes, unlocking the phone.

Mackenzie's face floods the screen. Determination battles sadness in her eyes. Her cheeks look hollow, and the black T-shirt and jeans hang looser. Behind her, stark white walls reveal nothing. She could be anywhere on the planet.

"Lucas," she begins. Her voice quivers and then gains strength with each word. "If you're watching this, it means I've decided to leave Branson. My life is in danger, and I can't risk giving you any details because it will put you in danger too."

Mackenzie's eyes glisten with unshed tears. She pauses, inhaling deeply before continuing. "I know this is hard to understand. I wish I could explain everything, but I can't. Know this: I didn't come to this decision lightly. Powerful people are hunting me. They won't stop until they get what they want."

Frustration and confusion slam into me at once. I ache to reach through the screen and pull Mackenzie back to safety.

Instead, I watch helplessly as she delivers what appears to be a final farewell.

"Promise me something," she pleads, urgency sharpening her tone. "Stop investigating. Let it go. Please, your safety matters more than answers. I couldn't live with myself if you got hurt because of me."

Mackenzie's gaze drops. She swipes at her eyes and then locks on the camera again. "You've got a future, Lucas. Your talent, your brains, your creativity… don't waste them on me. Please."

Entranced, my eyes remain glued to the screen. Disbelief overwhelms me as Mackenzie's words sink in.

"I know you, Lucas," she says, her sad smile twisting my gut. "You never quit. You cling to things. But I'm begging you… let this go."

Pain laces her voice, stabbing at my heart. Questions bombard my brain, a relentless assault. Words crowd my throat, but the one-way communication silences me.

Mackenzie rakes her hair back, her voice dropping to a whisper. "This journey… I don't know where it will lead. But trust me. I'm doing what I must. I'll start over somewhere. And maybe… when it's safe… we'll meet again."

She manages a small, bittersweet smile, the kind that speaks of hope mingled with resignation.

"Until then, take care of yourself, Lucas. Don't let this darkness consume you. Remember me, but don't let my absence hold you back."

The screen flickers for a moment, a sign the recording is about to end. "Goodbye, Lucas. Be safe. And thank you… for everything."

The video cuts off. Darkness swallows the screen as silence smothers the room, my eyes locked on my now-lifeless phone. My gaze darts around, searching for answers the empty room can't provide.

Grief, fear, and anger surge through me, flooding every cell. Mackenzie faces unknown dangers alone, while I sit here, helpless.

Her plea to stop investigating echoes in my mind. But I can't walk away. Not after everything. Still, I need to outsmart my watchers. Play it cool. My anonymous texter gloated about my soccer loss, a chilling reminder of their constant surveillance.

The truth is still out there, waiting to be uncovered. Who are these people pursuing Mackenzie, and why? What do they want from her? Ivy's advice rings in my brain too. I need to see the whole board, not just the pieces in front of me. It's the only way to uncover the truth.

Danger lurks on the path ahead, and I can't see where it leads. Mackenzie begged me to stop, but I can't. I must find a way to unravel the mystery, expose the darkness that's infested our school and my tormentor.

Because one truth burns brighter than all else: that video is a lie.

CHAPTER 71

The twins and I are in the Bat Cave. They've seen the video; we've viewed it multiple times.

"So what do you guys think?" I ask.

Alexis speaks first, her voice shaky. "Do you really think it's from her? It just seems so... final. Like she's saying goodbye for good."

Blake leans forward, elbows on his knees, his expression a mix of confusion and disbelief. "But why would she send something like this? Why now?"

"I don't know," I admit. "But she sounds scared. Really scared."

Alexis shakes her head. "But why involve you at all if she didn't want you to keep looking? It makes no sense. She said it's too dangerous for her to come back and she wants you to be safe, yet she sent you a video."

"I think someone forced her to make the video and send it to me so I would stop investigating. The whole goodbye speech is a fake."

I don't mention the text I received minutes before Mackenzie's video showed up. Coincidence? Hah. I don't think so.

"So you think someone's controlling her? Using her to get to you?" Blake asks.

I bite my lip. "Could be. Anything is possible. Or maybe she's trying to protect me the only way she can think of. By pushing me away."

"But why not give you more information?" Alexis asks, frustration seeping into her voice. "Why not tell you who's after her or why?"

I shrug, a helpless gesture that speaks volumes. "Maybe she doesn't know herself or she's too scared to say."

Alexis leans back into the couch, her eyes narrowing in thought. "Do you think it could be related to that book Mackenzie left behind? The one with the math symbols on the cover?"

I nod. It could be connected to a million things. I still haven't put all the pieces together yet. "Perhaps, yes. Mackenzie wouldn't disappear without a reason. But why send me this video now, as you pointed out?"

"Maybe she found out something big," Blake suggests. "Something that made her realize how truly dangerous things are."

A thought slams into my head. Riemann. I didn't have a chance to go through the whole book, but I remember seeing the words Riemann Enigma underlined several times.

"Alexis, grab the book from my room, it's on my desk."

I pick up my phone with trembling fingers and google the name.

"What's going on?" Blake asks.

I hold up a finger to indicate I need a minute. A bunch of Riemanns come up, but they're either people, foundations, or a Garden at Iowa State University. I then realize I'm spelling it wrong. I type in the phrase again, but this time, I spell it with two ns.

Alexis arrives with the book.

"Hang on," I say.

The first article that pops up is about cracking the Riemann Hypothesis. I click on the link. As I read the article, goose bumps appear on my arm.

"What's the matter, Lucas?" Alexis asks. "You look like you've seen a ghost."

I look up from the phone, take the book from Alexis, and place it in my lap.

"Dude, you're scaring us," Blake says. "What did you find?"

I explain about the clue in the book, except Mackenzie called it an enigma, not a hypothesis.

"The Riemann Hypothesis has stumped mathematicians for over a century. No one has been able to solve it or prove it, and there's even a million-dollar reward for anyone who does."

The twins look at me like I've lost it. "It all started with this mathematician named Bernhard Riemann back in 1859 who put forth a hypothesis that the real part of every nontrivial zero of the Riemann zeta functions is half."

"Huh?" The twins say in unison.

"Exactly."

Alexis scratches her head, and Blake just frowns. I leave the book on the sofa and go to the crime board. Blake and Alexis see where my eyes are focused.

"Mr. Moore is a math teacher," Blake says.

"A very good one," I add.

"So you're saying Mr. Moore may have proven this hypothesis?" Alexis probes.

"I'm stumped," I say, my eyes traveling to the photo of Mr. Moore and the other Branson staff at a cocktail party. "What does a never-proven mathematical hypothesis have to do with the people in the photo or Frank Parker?" *Or the powerful people on the list*, I think.

All three of us go silent, lost in thought.

"I'm getting a headache," Alexis says. Math is her weakest subject, although she pulls a solid B+ in her Honors Geometry class. Alexis plops back down on the couch, leaving Blake and me to stare at the crime board.

"Unless, it's not about the hypothesis," I say.

"What do you mean?" Blake asks.

"Suppose it's not about the hypothesis but what it represents?"

"A mathematical puzzle that has never been solved," Blake says.

"Yeah," I say, excitement coursing through me. "Whatever these people are into, they're saying no one will ever figure it out."

...right under our noses. That snippet from one of Mackenzie's text messages pops into my head.

"Can we assume Mr. Moore has something to do with Mackenzie's disappearance?" Alexis asks.

"But it's not just Mr. Moore in the photo," Blake counters. "Plus, let's not forget about the list."

I almost forgot what Ivy told me about Frank Parker paying a million dollars, I mean making a million-dollar donation to ensure Cole's misdeeds stayed off his school records.

I share the tidbit with the twins. I add, "But only Mr. Moore is a math teacher. It's as if Mr. Moore, or whoever fancies himself some brilliant mastermind, thinks no one will catch him or her, and the hypothesis is a metaphor."

"Right," Alexis says, drawing out the word, her eyes bright with wonder. "It's like they're taunting us, daring us to crack the mystery of Mackenzie's disappearance."

I only have one response to that. Game on.

CHAPTER 72

Mr. Moore's classroom feels alien now. Eight of us huddle in his Linear Algebra & Matrix Theory class. Pages rustle. Whispers flutter as we settle down for the lesson.

I claim my usual spot, third row from the front. Classmates bury their noses in textbooks. I shift my gaze to Mr. Moore.

Equations flow from his marker to the whiteboard. He explains eigenvalues and eigenvectors, his voice a steady stream. But something's off. His demeanor doesn't fit. Ever since Mackenzie's photo—the one with Mr. Moore and other Branson staff—I can't shake my suspicions. There's more to him, hidden beneath the surface.

I scribble fake notes, my eyes boring into Mr. Moore. I hunt for clues, any hint of oddness. Does he scan the room more often? Does tension thread his voice? His hands tremble slightly as he writes, fidgeting more than usual.

Mr. Moore's marker squeaks to a halt. He turns to us. "Who can explain the determinant's role in solving linear equations?"

I raise my hand, more out of reflex than actual eagerness. "The determinant helps determine if a matrix is invertible and thus if a system of linear equations has a unique solution."

"Correct, Lucas," he says, his eyes locking onto mine. There's a fleeting moment where I see a flicker of something in his gaze—fear, maybe? Or is it just my imagination? He quickly looks away and continues with the lesson.

The bell rings, signaling the end of class. Everyone packs up their belongings, and I linger, pretending to finish up some notes. Mr. Moore gathers his papers, and as the last student leaves, I stand and walk toward the exit.

"Lucas, a moment?" Mr. Moore's voice stops me before I reach the door.

I turn, keeping my expression neutral. "Yes, Mr. Moore?"

He leans against his desk, arms crossed. "How's everything going? I heard you've been involved in trying to find Mackenzie." He winks at me conspiratorially and says, "Don't worry. I admire your dedication. Sneaking out of Emily Kachinski's room late at night. You're a man of action."

A nervous laugh escapes me, not sure how else to respond. "Well, the police already spoke to Emily. I just wanted to see if there was anything else she could remember. Talking to the police can be nerve-wracking. Maybe she forgot to mention something."

Mr. Moore nods, his face a mask of concern and understanding. "Did the police speak with you also? You and Mackenzie were close."

There's something in his tone, a subtle edge that makes my skin prickle. He never asked me that question before. Why now?

"Yeah, they did. But I couldn't give them anything to go on."

Mr. Moore's gaze drifts aimlessly across the classroom for a moment, his face pensive, as though pondering something of major importance. Then he says, "It's a tragedy for all of us at Branson. Mackenzie was a bright young lady with a future filled with possibilities. There's no doubt in my mind she would have taken the technology world by storm."

That's the second time he referred to Mackenzie in the past. *Mackenzie was.*

I swallow, feeling the tension tighten like a noose around my neck. Am I reading too much into an innocent comment, or did Mr. Moore inadvertently give me a clue that he knows more about Mackenzie's disappearance than he initially let on?

It's coming up on two weeks since she went missing, and although she told me in the video that she won't be coming back, that she's starting over somewhere new, something about that video still bothers me.

"Yes, Mackenzie *is* brilliant. She's a rockstar."

"Yes, that's a good word to describe her."

An awkward silence descends over the room. I take it as my cue to leave. "I have to go, Mr. Moore. Don't want to be late for my next class." It doesn't matter that my next class is a study block.

"Lucas, if there's any math involved in your investigation and you need help, you know where to find me."

I nod, forcing a smile. "Thanks, Mr. Moore."

Walking out of the classroom, my mind races. Why does Mr. Moore keep referring to Mackenzie in the past?

CHAPTER 73

I head toward the back stairwell, a shortcut to my locker, after the Alerie Club meeting. As I push open the heavy fire door, voices drift up from the landing below. I freeze, recognizing Mr. Moore's low tone and the hushed response of a woman.

Heart racing, I ease the door shut. I crouch on the top step, hidden by the turn of the staircase. The concrete stairs amplify the whispers just enough for me to catch snippets.

"...why didn't you tell me before?" the woman says, her voice strained.

"I didn't want to—" Mr. Moore cut off abruptly.

I don't dare breathe. After a tense moment, Mr. Moore continues, "We've been careful, Jocelyn. Nobody suspects."

Mrs. Ajemian. I recognize her voice. Why are she and Mr. Moore in the stairway whispering? Mrs. Ajemian teaches English Lit to mostly sophomores and juniors. I had her last year. She's also the main advisor for Branson's literary journal.

"Why didn't you tell me after all this time that she found out?" Mrs. Ajemian asks, her tone accusing.

"Shhh," Mr. Moore says. "Everything has been handled."

"You just told me one of your students found out about us. I could be ruined if this gets out. I could lose my job. Dan will divorce me and take our son."

"It won't come to that. I took care of everything. Don't you trust me to protect you? I have as much to lose as you do. Perhaps even more. Stop worrying. Everything will be fine."

Mr. Moore looks around nervously, as if expecting someone to overhear. A cold sweat breaks out across my skin as I strain to hear more.

"We need to make sure the student remains quiet," Mrs. Ajemian continues, her tone urgent. "We can't afford any more mistakes. Who's the student anyway?"

"It doesn't matter. We shouldn't worry about her. You're safe. Okay?"

Footsteps thunder up the stairs. Fearful of being discovered, I wrench the door open and bolt. My feet slap against the hard floor. My heart hammers in my chest as I zigzag through the corridor, adrenaline electrifying every muscle. Only my pounding steps and ragged breath break the silence.

I sprint across the courtyard, finally collapsing onto a bench beneath a towering tree, its branches extending out like a protective canopy.

Gradually, my breathing returns to normal. I don't think they saw me, yet tension still coils in my muscles. The danger Mr. Moore poses looms large now. He may be the reason Mackenzie is on the run, to prevent his affair with Mrs. Ajemian from being exposed. He all but confessed. His words are a chilling echo I can't shake. *We don't need to worry about her.*

CHAPTER 74

I should have canceled. But I couldn't. Not even after yesterday's stairwell revelation. Sleep eluded me all night. My brain raced, refusing to quiet. Thoughts swirled like a nightmarish merry-go-round. Mr. Moore and Mrs. Ajemian's affair spun on an endless loop.

The lively, pulsating beat of salsa music fills the dimly lit dance studio, beckoning us to join in its rhythmic sway. Misha takes my hand and guides me across the smooth wooden floor, her movements fluid and graceful like a dance of fire. Despite the heaviness of recent events weighing on my heart and the constant suspicion about her uncle's involvement, I'm glad she insisted I needed a little fun to take my mind off my troubles.

And now, as we twirl and spin to the infectious rhythm, I find solace in the simple joy of being lost in the moment with her. The scent of sweat and perfume lingers in the air, mingling with the sound of laughter and applause from other dancers. For a brief moment, all my worries fade away, and I am consumed by the pure pleasure of dancing with Misha.

She flashes me a radiant smile, her eyes sparkling with warmth and affection. "See, Lucas? Dancing is all about letting go and living in the moment."

I can't help but return her smile, the tension in my muscles loosening with each step.

"You make it look so easy," I yell above the music, marveling at her effortless grace.

"That's because I've been doing this for a while," she says, twirling me into a spin that leaves me laughing with exhilaration.

But as the music slows and we come to a stop, the weight of reality descends on me once more. Misha's smile fades, replaced by a look of concern as she reaches out to touch my arm.

"Lucas, can we talk?" she asks softly, her voice coated in trepidation.

I nod, a shaft of nervousness spiraling through my belly. "Sure. What's on your mind?"

Misha and I leave the dance studio and head to a nearby café, hoping to find some privacy. The air outside is crisp, with a light October breeze rustling the leaves that line the sidewalk. We walk in silence, our breath visible in the early evening air.

We arrive at the Princess Bakery & Café, a charming little place nestled between a bookstore and a doggy daycare. The scent of freshly brewed coffee and baked goods envelops us, instantly soothing my frayed nerves. Soft jazz music plays in the background, blending seamlessly with the low murmur of conversations.

Misha leads us to a small table by the window, away from the main crowd.

After, we order hot chocolates topped with whipped cream and cinnamon.

"Are you okay, Lucas?" she asks. "You don't have to pretend with me."

"Don't I look okay?" I ask, sipping the hot chocolate.

I can't dump my problems on Misha. Why cast a sour note on our budding relationship, such as it is? Besides, Mr. Moore is her uncle, and I'm still trying to figure out how or whether he harmed Mackenzie.

Misha is probably blissfully ignorant of Mr. Moore's affair. He confirmed nobody knew except the one student. It explains why he was nervous around me, always fishing for intel on my investigation, to learn how close I was to uncovering the truth.

Mr. Moore never mentioned Mackenzie by name, but I know he's involved somehow. I can't ignore facts: he's one of the people in the photo Mackenzie left behind. He has motive, an illicit affair with a fellow teacher that could destroy both their careers at Branson, not to mention wreck Mrs. Ajemian's marriage.

I can't confide any of this to Misha. Talk about an awkward conversation.

I carefully choose my response to her question. "It's hard, Misha. Everything is a mess. I'm not sleeping well or eating much. Mackenzie is gone, Kellen is injured…" I trail off, unable to finish.

Misha reaches across the table and rubs my shoulder. "Kellen's accident is not your fault, Lucas. You were just trying to find out what happened to Mackenzie."

Should I confide in Misha that Mackenzie sent me a video? *No.* The answer comes swiftly. With Kellen injured, and a million unanswered questions, I can't afford to drag another person into this disaster.

"I worry about you," she adds.

"Why?"

"You've been carrying this heavy burden. I know your heart is broken, although you try to hide it. We're just teenagers, Lucas. We're not trained in investigating missing persons. Things could get dangerous. Whoever hurt Kellen could come after you. I'm really scared for you," she finishes.

Everything fades away, replaced by a primal urge to comfort Misha. I want to soothe her worries about me. Tears glisten in her eyes. Instinct takes over. I grasp her hands and kiss them both. She leans in, our foreheads touching.

We remain that way for a moment. A memory flashes before me. The figure across the street from Liam's house the day I went over to go through the seven names on Mackenzie's list. Did they follow Misha and me here to this cafe?

I almost shiver but force myself still. Misha is already worried. No point in making it worse by looking around for anyone suspicious.

"I'll be okay. Mackenzie can't stay away forever, right?" I force a smile.

"Mackenzie is lucky to have you in her corner. Jealous girlfriend over here," she says, waving her hand and grinning.

Girlfriend. Misha has never used that word before. This is huge. I try to remain calm, and unaffected as I grin back at her. Happiness floods through me, warm and gooey like melted caramel. My accidental "L word" drop had left things uncertain. Misha had said she needed time to sort out her feelings. But now, I'm elated. My confession didn't crash and burn.

"There was never anything romantic between Mackenzie and me," I admit. "We're more like kindred spirits."

"Because you're both biracial."

"Among other things."

Misha's mood changes, the lightheartedness of moments ago replaced by a somber expression. She rubs her bottom lip as she looks out the window.

"What's wrong?"

She says nothing at first and then turns away from the window, her gaze focused on me.

"Lucas, I heard something about Makenzie that could be important."

Leaning closer, I ask, "What is it?"

"There are rumors floating around that Mackenzie is a highly skilled hacker. That she's even hacked into the school's mainframe before."

So Mack's technical skills are an open secret. I file the information away. It could be useful later.

"What? No way," I say, infusing my tone with what I hope is just the right amount of outrage. "Mackenzie would never do anything that unethical. Besides, the Branson network must be impenetrable. They have the money and resources to hire the best IT staff."

Mackenzie probably did hack the mainframe. And if that information is now circulating around school, it must have reached the ears of the people who forced her to hack illegally in the first place. Out of desperation, they're after her so she won't expose their secrets.

"There's more," Misha says, shifting her gaze away once more.

"It's okay," I say, encouraging her to be forthcoming. "You can tell me anything. Even if it's something negative about Mackenzie. Finding her is more important than anything else she might have done."

Misha rolls her neck, working out the kinks. "A few days before Mackenzie vanished, I stumbled upon her in the STEM building. I was visiting my uncle. As I rounded a corner, I froze. Mackenzie stood there, facing off with this older guy. A stranger. Definitely not school staff. They were going at it, voices low but intense. Mackenzie's face twisted with anger or fear—maybe both. I bolted before they spotted me."

I swallow hard. My thoughts short-circuit, as though they need to be restarted so fresh ones can start flowing again. The stranger is another piece added to the board, another player. Was this the same man who had stood across the street from Liam's house, the same person I followed during the vigil last week? What had he been doing in the STEM building?

There's a tautness in the air between us, the revelation hanging like an unwanted but necessary presence. Misha had never shared this information before, so why now? Mackenzie speaking to a strange older man who looked out of place at Branson is something the police would want to know about. It's something I wish I had known sooner.

It's fascinating how Misha spotted them in the STEM building, which suggests this older man knows both Mr. Moore and Mackenzie.

"Did you mention what you saw to anyone?" I ask Misha.

"No. Are you upset with me for not telling you sooner?"

I shake my head, forcing my racing thoughts to slow down.

"I brushed it off back then. Figured it was Mackenzie's private business. But now, with all the chaos swirling around you? I messed up. I should have spilled sooner. I'm sorry, Lucas. It was careless of me."

"Cut yourself some slack. This information is helpful. I'm grateful you shared it."

"This older man might be the key to finding Mackenzie. Or maybe not." Misha takes my hands and squeezes them as though they need warming up.

She presses on. "But Lucas, what if Mackenzie bolted on her own? Dodging the fallout from her hacking? It's tough to swallow, I know. But it doesn't make her a villain. She's just a girl who got in over her head, and she's now running scared."

Misha strokes my cheek. Then she takes in a deep, long breath and exhales, as though she needs to calm herself before continuing.

"I think," she says slowly, her words measured, "Mackenzie craved a sense of belonging at Branson. The vultures swooped in and exploited her vulnerability, dangling some vague promise of joining their exclusive circle, all to milk her talent for their own selfish gain. The allure of fitting in is powerful, especially at Branson."

CHAPTER 75

Emily and I agreed to meet up in the library. Way in the back of the library before we're seen and a new batch of rumors start up. After apologizing profusely again for sneaking out of her dorm room with the book Mackenzie left behind, we stand next to each other in the middle of a space surrounded by two massive bookshelves on either side.

She reaches into her bag. "I got something for you."

She pulls out a vinyl album and hands it to me.

"What's this for?" The album is *Melodrama* by Lorde. The cover art resembles a painting of a girl in bed. It's one of Mackenzie's favorite albums.

"Did Mackenzie leave this for me?"

"I think she did," Emily says solemnly.

"But you never said anything about it when I came to pick up the book," I say, gazing at the cover.

"Well, you know Mackenzie. She doesn't like to be obvious."

"Where did you find it then?

"The desk drawer."

"How come—"

Emily cuts me off and says, "The desk drawer has a hidden compartment. I found out by accident because it kept jamming. There's something inside the album, that's how I know Mackenzie wanted you to have it."

I crack open the album, peeking through the slit. A plain white envelope peeks back. I ease it out, fingers probing gently. There's a letter inside, alongside a small hard object. Best not to satisfy my curiosity with Emily watching.

"Thank you, Emily. I hope there's a clue in here that helps crack the case."

"I hope so too, Lucas." She pats my shoulder. "And by the way, quit apologizing. I willingly jumped into the fray of your investigation."

"Thanks again. That means a lot."

"Best of luck. Loop me in if you find anything."

As I leave the library, I wonder what secret Mackenzie is about to drop on me next.

CHAPTER 76

The envelope haunts me the rest of the school day. More secrets, tucked away in that album case, taunting my every thought. Between classes, I was tempted to read the letter, uncover the mystery object, but I resisted the urge.

Finally, I collapse onto my bed, uniform and all. Nerves set my hand trembling as I tear into the envelope. A small glittery unicorn figurine, around two to three inches tall with the mane and tail in pastel blue and pink, tumbles out. Huh?

Then I sit up and chuckle to myself, Emily's words echoing in my head. *You know Mackenzie doesn't like to be obvious.* So true. The unicorn is also a great example of Mack's playful side. I tug on the horn. It detaches to expose a USB connector. Mack left me a flash drive. For now, I place the unicorn beside me to focus my attention on the letter.

Dear Lucas,

As I write these words, my heart pounds in my chest, unsure if this letter will ever reach you or if it will remain hidden, like the feelings I've kept locked away for so long. But I can't keep pretending, can't keep burying these emotions beneath layers of fear and uncertainty. So here I am, laying bare my soul to you.

From the moment we met, something shifted inside me, like a missing piece of a puzzle falling into place. You were my anchor in a sea of uncertainty. Your laughter could brighten even the dreariest of days and chase away the shadows that haunted my thoughts.

But it wasn't just your infectious charm that drew me to you, Lucas. It was your kindness, the warmth in your eyes. You were my confidant and, in some ways, my protector.

And yet, beneath the laughter and camaraderie we shared, there was always something more. I tried to ignore it, to push it aside and bury it beneath the weight of my insecurities, but it refused to be silenced.

I love you, Lucas. More than words could ever express, more than the stars could ever count. And I can't bear the thought of not expressing the depth of my feelings.

But I understand if you don't feel the same way, if my confession fills you with discomfort or uncertainty. I wouldn't blame you for wanting to distance yourself from me, to preserve the friendship we've built. Just know that no matter what happens, I will always cherish the moments we've shared, the laughter we've exchanged, and the bond that will forever bind us together.

So if this letter finds its way into your hands, know that it was written with love, with honesty and hope. No matter what the future brings, you will always hold a special place in my heart.

With all my love,
Mackenzie

CHAPTER 77

I tumble off the bed, hitting the floor with a thud. Memories flood in, overwhelming me. Our conversations, both silly and introspective, the laughs, and the silent support she offered just by her presence. All now glaringly absent.

Regret claws at me. All the times I took her for granted, the missed opportunities to tell her what she meant to me. How special our friendship was. Words left unspoken, now lost forever.

She's out there somewhere, potential danger lurking around every corner. Yet that video... it doesn't feel like a real goodbye. Even now, wherever she is, Mackenzie is still protecting me.

Looking back, I'm guilt-ridden about all the times I went on and on about my crush on Misha. Misha this, Misha that. Do you think I should ask her out? What should I say?

I now understand why she took off in a hurry when we met in the common room to discuss the strategy for uncovering my biological father's identity.

Mackenzie had accused me of drooling over Misha. Oblivious to her feelings, my attention to Misha wounded her. Because I was too stupid to see what was right in front of me, and I came off as an insensitive jerk.

She buried her heart; suffered in silence. Her absence cuts even deeper, if that's possible. *I screwed up, Mack. I should have seen it. Should have treasured you. Foolishly, I assumed you'd always be around.*

Her eyes sparkled whenever we hung out. She bared her soul to me. Her confession about how isolated she felt at Branson and the snobbery she endured from some of the other girls. Misha had nailed it. Mackenzie wanted to fit in.

Lying on the floor won't solve anything. Time to face the unicorn flash drive, rip off the Band-Aid, and dive in. But my nerves jangle. I'm not sure how many more bombshell revelations I can withstand.

CHAPTER 78

Lucas,

Sorry I lied to you. Please forgive me. I couldn't tell you the truth about your biological father because I wanted to protect you. However, after much thought, and for the sake of our friendship, it's not my call to make. Only you can decide if you really want the truth, which is on this flash drive. It will change your life. So think carefully before you open Pandora's box.

Mackenzie

CHAPTER 79

I stumble down the stairs and somehow make it to Mom's office without losing my lunch. My throat burns, raw and aching.

I want to scream but can't pull it off. Mom is not in her office, so I slide into her leather chair. She'll be back in a minute.

I'm hyperventilating when she rushes into the office, terror in her eyes like I'm dying. No kidding; I wish I was.

"Lucas, it's okay." She puts her arm around me and speaks in a soothing tone. "You're okay. Try to breathe slowly," she says, rubbing my back in smooth, circular motions. "That's right. Inhale slowly through your nose, hold, and on the count of four, breathe out. Let's breathe together. 1….2….3….4."

After repeating the exercise several times, I begin to feel more balanced, as if the oxygen in my brain had started to reflow properly.

Mom pulls a small chair and sits across from me. "Now, please tell me what has you so upset."

I say nothing for a long while, clutching my stomach and not knowing how to begin. I'm angry, yet full of despair and grief. I'm not even sure whether to blame her or not.

"You lied, Mom. He didn't die in a car crash, did he?"

Her hand claps over her mouth, eyes widening. Then she says, "I...I can explain."

No pretense from her. No stalling or sidestepping. At least she's not insulting my intelligence.

Tears well up in Mom's eyes, and then she shuts them tight as if warding off the pain of the past. She says, "I hoped this day would never come." Her voice trembles as she speaks.

"You thought it would be better to hide the truth, to lie and say he died in a car accident? How could you keep from me that the man whose blood flows through my veins was a monster? A psychopath who sexually assaulted you?"

"Who told you this Lucas?"

"Does it matter?"

Mom's sobs fill the room, but I don't stop. I must get it all out before I choke on the horrifying truth that I exist because of what that psychopath did to my mother when she was still a teenager.

"He drugged you and threw you out of a moving car. And that's what I am, a product of pure evil."

"Don't say that!" she cries. "You're nothing like him!" Her hand reaches out to touch my face, cupping it gently. "You're my perfect boy, my sweet, incredible firstborn." Mom's sobs grow louder, and she hides her face in her hands once more, shoulders shaking with grief and emotion.

After a few moments, she composes herself and continues, "You know who your father is Lucas. Ty is your father; he has been since the day you were born."

A lump forms in my throat as I process what she's said so far. Is that why they married while still in college? Because she was pregnant with me?

I pose the question, and her body tenses. Her expression is bleak, her gorgeous face transformed into a mask of pain and misery. Her eyes plead with me to drop the subject. I've crossed a line, I'm sure, but it's too late to turn back now. I may as well see it to the end.

But perhaps I'm judging Mom too harshly. I've never seen her in such a state of anguish, an unsettling sight. She crumples inward, as if she wants to shrink. Guilt presses down on me in a vise-like grip, unpleasant and unwelcome.

Everything clicks; the family's wall of silence, my parents constantly dodging, Mom's haunted expression. That story they fed me at age ten, the first I heard about the nonexistent car accident. Mackenzie was right. I opened Pandora's box. Now a flood of regret threatens to sweep me away.

"Your dad and I would have made it down the aisle eventually, Lucas. The timeline just got moved up, that's all."

Tears ambush me, pricking my eyes. I fight them, but they won't stop. Mom had dreams of becoming a neurosurgeon. She got a full ride to Yale and was well on her way to achieving her dreams. Mom was forced to swerve off the path and chose me instead when there were other options available to her.

Zachary Rossdale robbed my mother of her dream because everything changed when she woke up at Yale New Haven Hospital seventeen years ago. Broken arm, scrapes and bruises, her memory of what happened wiped because he drugged her. The trial that followed.

The court documents Mackenzie accessed—I don't want to know how many laws she broke to get it—detailed the horrific events that led to my existence. For the rest of my life, I won't be able to unsee what's written on those pages.

Alexis had always insisted that it didn't matter who my biological father was and it would hurt Mom if I kept pushing for answers. But I couldn't let it go.

Another part of this tragedy that disgusts me even further is the fact that I look like him. The resemblance is striking. The shape of my face, the jawline, ice-blue eyes, and nose. We even have the same wavy, dark-blond hair. In a twisted way, I'm a mirror image of my murdering, psychopath of a father.

Oh yeah, Zachary Rossdale also shot his identical twin brother, Spencer, in cold blood. In front of my mother. My gene pool is so classy.

"Lucas, please try to understand. I kept the truth from you because it was the only way to protect you."

Mom attempts a reassuring smile but can't pull it off. She looks like she's aged in the few minutes we've been talking. I opened up a massive wound, and now it's just gushing with pain and despair. Seems that I have something in common with my criminally insane father: we both know how to wound my mother deeply.

I stand, and Mom does too, her arms extended, wanting a hug. I can't.

"It's okay, Mom," I say. "It's okay." Then I scurry out of her office and scramble up the stairs to my bedroom. I can't bear to look at her face.

Something in my head screams for release, but there's none to be had. I curl up in a ball on my bed, shivering uncontrollably. The desperate sounds of whimpering and moaning ricochet off my bedroom wall. It takes me a moment to orient myself, realize the sounds aren't coming from the walls, but from my shivering body.

I don't want to see or talk to anyone. In fact, I'd be fine if I never left this room for the rest of my life.

CHAPTER 80

My plan to never leave my room backfires. Both my parents sit on my bed, fidgeting, their shoulders drooping, eyes bloodshot. Looks like they didn't sleep last night either. I hope Dad didn't skip any surgeries on my account.

I'm mad at them for lying. Not just my parents, but my grandparents, Uncle Miles, Uncle Christian, Aunt Callie. They're all in on the lie. I hate liars. Been that way since I was a kid.

I'm angry about all the times I felt like an outlier in this family. And to learn I have the face of a monster is unbearable. Mackenzie had included a photo with the information she dug up. I don't want Mom and Dad in my room. I want them to leave.

Dad says, "Lucas, we did what we thought was best for you. Our number-one job as parents is to protect our kids, *all* our kids. We didn't see how any good could come from you learning the truth about who Zachary Rossdale was."

I say nothing, just stare at them as if they're strangers.

"It doesn't change anything," Mom says.

"How can you say that?" I explode. "He was a horrible human being. What if I turn out like him? I carry his genes, don't I? Every time I look in the mirror, I'll see his face."

It would've been better that I never saw the photo. Now I can't unsee it.

"You will never be like Zach, Lucas. Never. I'm your father. I raised you. Not Zach."

His words hang heavy in the air, thick and tense.

Turning to Mom, I say, "Do you see him when you look at me? Do I remind you of the horror he inflicted on you?"

Mom's bottom lip trembles, betraying her turmoil.

"After all, if it weren't for Zach's actions, I wouldn't exist. You would be living the life you dreamed of as a successful neurosurgeon instead of settling. Not that there's anything wrong with being a neuropsychologist."

When she speaks, her voice is forceful and resolute. "I have no regrets. No career, no matter how important or prestigious, can compare with the joy of being your mother. You are our firstborn. The circumstances don't take away from how special that is. Your father and I love you, and we don't regret the decision to protect you from learning something so heinous. No child should ever have to learn such things. I do have one regret, however."

Dad and I remain silent. Mom says, "I wish you'd never found out. I prayed you would never find out. I don't know how you did, and I'm not sure I want details. If we had to do it all over again, your father and I would make the same decision: shield you from ever knowing that monster's name."

She's about to break down crying, and I can't stand it. My guilt won't let me look her in the face. My guilt for bringing this ugly, dark cloud into our home, making her relive that hellish time in her life. But I can't take it back.

"Please leave, both of you. Just get out, now!"

CHAPTER 81

A half hour later, I'm still curled up in the fetal position on my bed when someone knocks on my bedroom door.

"Go away," I shout, not caring who it is.

"If you don't open this door right now, Lucas, I'm going to keep banging on it until you do."

True to her word, my sister starts banging her fists before I can respond to her threat. Reluctantly, and a little salty about being disturbed, I drag myself off the bed and open the door. She barges in.

"Alexis, I'm not in the mood, okay. Whatever it is, can it wait until later?"

"No, it can't." Her voice is low, gentle. I was expecting Hurricane Alexis. She sits at the edge of the bed. I remain standing.

"Did Mom or Dad say something?" I ask.

"Yeah. Yesterday. The sanitized version. Is that the word? When grownups need to tell us kids bad stuff? Anyway, it doesn't matter Lucas. You're still my amazing big brother. So what if our parents lied about Zach Rossdale? Wouldn't you lie to protect someone you loved if the truth could hurt them?"

I stare at my sister in astonishment. Ugly guilt works its way up from my clenched stomach and gets stuck in my throat, so I can't speak for a beat. I replay what Mackenzie and I did to Cole Parker, setting him up so he would be expelled from Branson. All to protect Alexis, and we never told her. That's exactly what my parents did. And like my parents, I have no regrets about what I did to Cole.

I can't recall how I ended up on the floor with my sister rocking me back and forth like a baby in her tiny arms. Time seems to have stopped. I can barely feel my heart beating, and the trembling I experienced yesterday after I confronted Mom returns.

"You're going to be fine, Lucas. I promise. It won't hurt like this for long. Remember what Mom taught us? We're Coopers. Coopers don't run away from their problems."

"They wrestle with it, like a math problem, until they find the solution," I finish.

CHAPTER 82

Mom called the main office to let them know I won't be in school today and neither will the twins. She said I am in no state to go to school. I guess she kept the twins home because they have a knack for calming me down when I get upset.

We sit in the Bat Cave not saying much, but I know they're dying to bring up the topic. To find out how I'm coping.

The twins want to cry. I see it in their faces. Blake keeps staring into his empty hands, his posture slumped. Alexis is breathing funny, like she's struggling to keep it in. She comes over and gives me a hug.

"Don't be mad at our parents," she says and then gently releases me.

"Why not?" I want to hear what new piece of wisdom she'll throw at me.

"Because Mom was just a kid, Lucas. Not much older than you. Can you imagine the agony she went through? If she had decided differently, you wouldn't be here. We wouldn't be the family we are."

"I'm glad Mom didn't tell you the truth," Blake says, finally speaking up. "But I understand why finding out has upset you so much. It doesn't change who you are, does it?"

Blake looks at me with expectation, as though he wants reassurances that everything will go back to the way it was before I found out.

But how can I? For years, I'd wanted to find out whose face stared back at me from the mirror because I don't look like Blake or Alexis or Mom or Dad. And to find out the face belongs to someone who hurt my mother so badly and changed her life forever, an evil man, I can't forget that. Walking around with Zach Rossdale's face is a constant reminder, no way to avoid it.

"My emotions are a tangled mess, Blake. I'm lost in a fog of confusion. I should have listened to Alexis when she told me to let it go. But you know me, I don't let go easily."

Then I confess to the twins how Mackenzie had agreed to help me search for information on Zach Rossdale before she disappeared, and how for a while, I thought her disappearance was connected to him. That Mack even tried to protect me from the horrifying truth. *I lied when I said I couldn't find any information.*

Alexis and Blake exchange an incredulous look, taken aback by the confession. Alexis says, "Whoa. We had no idea, Lucas. So where is Zach Rossdale? What happed to him?"

"He's dead. Died six years ago in prison, ten years into a life sentence for assaulting Mom and killing his twin brother. And no, I don't want to talk about it anymore. It's over and done with."

CHAPTER 83

We make the best of a terrible situation by focusing our energy and day off from school trying to solve Mackenzie's disappearance. Turning the focus on her makes me feel useful and takes my mind off my own personal drama. Mom checked in on me and said she would find me a therapist to help me deal with the trauma. My response was more of a grunt than an actual answer.

I return my attention to the crime board, scanning everything we have so far: the list of Branson alumni, the photo of the teachers at a cocktail party, the Riemann Enigma clue, Mackenzie's video about leaving.

For the first time, I share with the twins about the mysterious man across the street from Liam's house, Mr. Moore's affair with Mrs. Ajemian, what Misha told me about the mysterious older man Makenzie was talking to, and the hacking rumors. I decide to omit the letter. It can wait for another time.

"Do you think the mysterious man works for one of the people on the list? He has to be involved in Mackenzie's disappearance," Alexis says.

"Misha seems to think that Mackenzie left on her own, to get away from all the bad stuff. The video supports that theory," I say.

"How does that connect with Mr. Moore's secret affair with Mrs. Ajemian?" Blake asks. "Well, Mackenzie is on the run," I say. "He could've convinced her that there would be serious consequences if she didn't leave."

Which makes perfect sense. If rumors were starting to surface that Mack was hacking illegally, even into the Branson mainframe, that would be enough to scare her. Problem solved for Mr. Moore and Mrs. Ajemian. Still, that leaves a bunch of threads hanging loose.

I share the thought with the twins.

"The list," Alexis says. "Let's look at it again. Frank Parker was the only outlier; he didn't go to Branson, but everyone else did."

Alexis hands me the list. "If Cole Parker's dad paid a huge donation to keep Cole's record clean, what's the connection to the other people on the list?"

"Maybe they all had something to hide and paid huge donations too," Blake offers.

"Yes!" I say, grabbing a Sharpie. I stand in front of the crime board, nervous but excited energy pumping through me. "All the alumni on the list are powerful people."

"Let's go through them," Alexis says, standing up and joining me at the board.

"The tech CEO, the fashion CEO, the doctor, the media mogul, the senator, the Wall Street investment banker, and Frank Parker, who's in manufacturing," Blake says.

I go over the clues, straining to make them fit, hoping a clear picture will emerge.

"We have a list of rich, powerful people who went to Branson, minus Frank Parker; a mathematics hypothesis that has never been solved; and a photo of Branson teachers and staff at a cocktail party, including Mr. Moore, who's hooking up with another Branson teacher. What's the common denominator besides Branson?"

"I agree they're all connected," Alexis says. "But Mackenzie never mentioned any of these clues in her goodbye video. Don't you find that strange?"

I'm about to agree with Alexis when my phone chimes with an incoming text. I scoop it off the end table next to the sectional.

Kellen: We need to talk. ASAP.

Lucas: What's up?

Kellen: I did what you asked. I have urgent news. We should meet face-to-face.

Lucas: Could you come by my house after school? I'm not in today.

Then, I quickly texted back, remembering his injury.

Lucas: Oh wait, you're on crutches. I'll ask my mom to pick you up.

Kellen: TTYL.

Two hours later, Kellen joins the twins and me in the Bat Cave. Fortunately for us, he had a light schedule today. We're stuffing our faces on the tasty portobello mushroom burgers on brioche buns that Blake prepared for lunch.

"You have the floor," I tell Kellen, biting into my second burger. Kellen leans back in the sofa and pushes the side button to flip out the leg rest so he can be comfortable. The twins sit on either side of him, and I lean against the bookshelf. Kellen has our undivided attention.

"Last night, there was a fire drill in our dorm. Everyone had to evacuate quickly."

I nod, encouraging him to continue.

"It was chaos, people grabbing whatever they could. I was behind her in a wheelchair, heading to the elevator. I had help, special circumstances and all. Anyway, she had a backpack with her. Seemed odd for a fire drill, right?"

We just nod, anxious for him to get to the punchline.

Kellen continues, "Anyway, she dropped her bag when someone accidentally bumped into her hard. The bag fell, spilling some of the contents. I saw a flash of a yellow outfit with buttons. She shoved it back in quickly, but I'm sure it was a trench coat."

My eyes widen, and so do the twins'. "Are you certain?" I ask.

"Positive. And get this… when I mentioned it casually, asking if she was okay, she got all weird and defensive. Said I should mind my own business."

I trudge over to the window, my mind racing. The yellow trench coat was the final piece sliding into place, completing the intricate puzzle I've been struggling to solve. I can see it all now—the board, the players, every calculated move that led to this moment.

"It's endgame now," I murmur, more to myself than to Kellen or the twins.

"All this time, I thought I was just another pawn, being pushed around the board. But I've made it to the other side," I say out loud, my back still to them.

My hands shake with the adrenaline rushing through my body. "I've become the queen, and it's time to clear the board." I turn to face the twins and Kellen, whose faces have crumpled like sand castles at high tide, washed away by the gravity of the news.

"It's time to bring this game to an end, on my terms," I explain. "She thinks she's won, but she forgot the most important rule in chess: it's not over until the king falls."

CHAPTER 84

After Kellen leaves, we rewatch the video. On my laptop instead of my phone this time.

"Let's watch it frame by frame," I say.

There are slight but unnatural movements in Mackenzie's facial expressions I'd never observed before. Her eyes blink at odd intervals, and her mouth movements don't perfectly sync with her speech.

I play the video again, but this time, my focus is on the audio. I notice slight distortions and robotic undertones. I watch again with a hypercritical eye. The synchronization between the audio and Mackenzie's lip movements are slightly off. I replay a few sections in slow motion and notice that her lips don't always match perfectly with the sounds coming out of her mouth.

"Give me a minute," I say to the twins and take the laptop. I sit on the couch with the computer, troubling thoughts piling into my head as though they'd been waiting for me to acknowledge them all along.

Numb with worry, I say to Blake and Alexis. "It's not good. This is really bad."

"What is?" Blake asks.

"The video is a deep fake. It's not Mackenzie."

"Are you sure?" Alexis asks. "I mean, we know what a deep fake is but not the nitty gritty of how it actually works."

"I don't have any proof, but everything I've seen so far points to a setup. It's like this," I say. "Deep-fake technology uses AI to create realistic but fake images, videos, and audio. These algorithms are trained on large datasets of real videos and images of the target person—Mackenzie, in this case—by learning her facial expressions, movements, and voice patterns."

Alexis bites her lip, her eyes gleaming with anticipation. Blake sits still, his eyes never leaving my face. "Then AI generates a synthetic version that can be superimposed onto another video or audio track, creating the illusion that Mackenzie is saying or doing something she never actually did."

"So," Blake says, his eyes squinting, "if the video is a deep fake, maybe the voice you heard in the wine cellar was too."

"What do you mean?"

"Someone cloned Mackenzie's voice. She never told you to run. She was never in the wine cellar. The whole thing was staged, all part of the game."

The wine cellar. How could I forget? My brother is right. It doesn't change my final move though.

"How do we prove it's a deep fake?" Alexis asks.

"I know someone. Someone who won't make this easy for me, but I'll give them no choice. Look, we can't tell anybody about this, not a single soul. Well, except the person who's going to help me prove it."

The twins nod their understanding. Alexis rubs her arm as if warding off a chill. Blake seems to feel it too. But we're all too scared to say what we're thinking.

If the video is a deep fake, who sent it, and where is Mackenzie?

CHAPTER 85

An idea occurs to me at the end of Linear Algebra. It wasn't part of my plan, but it's time I put him to the test. What do they say on TV? Let's shake the tree and see what comes loose? I know a guy like Mr. Moore is too smooth to get rattled, but I must try.

"Mr. Moore, do you have a minute?" I approach him nervously, wiping my hands on my uniform pants.

"Of course, Lucas," he says, gesturing for me to have a seat. "What's on your mind?"

"This will only take a sec." I prefer to stand in case I have to bolt out of the classroom. Although I'm confident he and Mrs. Ajemian don't know I was listening in the stairwell, I take nothing for granted.

"Ever heard of the Riemann Hypothesis?" I watch him carefully. He's quiet, his face an inscrutable mask, but it slipped for a millisecond, as if he was trying to hide his surprise but didn't want to make it obvious.

"Why do you ask, Lucas?"

"It's a clue of sorts. You know Mackenzie has been missing for almost two weeks now. And still the police have no clues, made no progress."

"Yes, it's a sad situation. Some call the Riemann Hypothesis the Holy Grail of numbers theory," he says, and then he explains what the twins and I already gathered from our research. Mr. Moore then says, "Why would you ask about that? What does it have to do with Mackenzie?"

I shrug. "Not sure, Mr. Moore. I got an anonymous email telling me to look into it, that it might help find her. It makes no sense. And I have no idea who sent the email or why."

Please don't let him ask to see the email that doesn't exist, the one that I just made up.

"Anyway, I figured I would ask you because you're the best math teacher at Branson. Sorry to bother you."

"No bother all, Lucas. Glad you asked. We're all praying for Mackenzie to be found. My offer of help still stands."

"I appreciate it. I'm trying to keep the faith. Even now, I'm hoping someone with information will come forward."

"Yes. We all want the same thing. The whole Branson community. There are many people still on the case, putting in resources to help find her."

"Good to know. It's encouraging. Rumors are going around that Mackenzie ran away because someone threatened her."

I hadn't planned on saying that, but I had to shake the tree like they do on TV.

I wait for Mr. Moore's reaction. He looks at his watch and says nervously, "Well, I must prep for another class, Lucas. We're all rooting for Mackenzie. Keep me posted, will you?"

Then he walks out of his own classroom as though I'm carrying a deadly virus.

CHAPTER 86

The dining hall buzzes with lively chatter, the clinking of cutlery against plates, and occasional bursts of laughter. Long tables are arranged in neat rows, each one crowded with students enjoying their lunch break. I shove my nervousness deep down as I approach her.

She's seated with her usual group of friends. They're deep in conversation, but from her bored expression, she's barely listening.

"Hey, Charlie."

Charlie Covington turns around and glares at me like I'm a piece of dog poop left on her front lawn.

"What do you want, Lucas?"

"Sorry, baby," I say, my voice soft and apologetic. "I didn't mean to take so long to respond to your text message, but I'm here now. Will you forgive me?"

I hit her with my most dazzling smile. I've never seen Charlie at a loss for words, but she starts blubbering right before my eyes. Her minions just gape at me, incredulous.

I take advantage of their stunned silence to push my agenda. "Can we go somewhere private? It's important."

Charlie regains her composure and says, "Why would I go anywhere with you?"

At this point, the entire dining hall is watching, as if this is their own private soap opera unfolding live.

I lean in and whisper, "Because if you don't, I'll tell everyone we're secretly hooking up. How are you going to explain that to what's his name? Your boyfriend. Um…" I snap my fingers as if struggling to remember the name that eludes me. "Finley. Yeah, that's it. Plus the BransonBuzz will drag your name through the mud for months. Is that what you want?"

Before she has a chance to respond, I yell so everyone in the dining hall can hear. "Are you ashamed of me, Charlie? Is that why you won't introduce me to your family, why you won't tell your friends about us? You said you loved me, but I guess that was a lie. Well, Charlie, I won't be your dirty little secret anymore."

I pretend to get choked up for dramatic effect.

A plethora of emotions play across Charlie's face: loathing, fear that people may actually believe me, and anxiety. But mostly loathing.

A weak smile appears on her face. She stands and says, "He's just kidding around. You're not funny, Lucas."

Then Charlie hisses in my ear, "The library. Now!"

Ten minutes later, Charlie and I are in the back section of the library where it's quiet and no one seems to be around. She's still mad at me for that scene in the dining hall, but I don't care. I had to improvise, and what can I say, a genius idea fell into my lap.

"I don't appreciate what you just pulled in the dining hall," she practically spits at me. "I have a reputation to protect."

"Well, I wouldn't want to do anything to tarnish your reputation, especially hinting that there might be something going on between us. Don't worry, Charlie, you're safe on that score."

"What's that supposed to mean?"

It's not a good idea to be sarcastic or insult the person whose help I need, so I placate her. "Oh, I just mean that I would never have a shot at a girl like you. The incident in the dining hall might have been wishful thinking."

I'd rather stick a fork in my eyeball every hour on the hour for five days straight than date a girl like Charlie Covington: spoiled, entitled, rude, calculating, ruthless, manipulative…

She loosens up, her expression relaxed. "Okay, Lucas, stop wasting my time and tell me what all the drama is about."

"I need you to help me prove that a video I received from Mackenzie is a deep fake."

Silence. I guess I have a knack for silencing Charlie Covington. I should bottle that up. I could make a fortune.

Finally, she says, "You must be kidding."

"Do you think I embarrassed myself in the dining hall because I felt like joking?"

"Oh."

"Yeah. Are you going to help me or what?"

"A bit pushy, aren't we?"

"This goes beyond Mackenzie missing. Someone went through a lot of trouble to send me a video, supposedly from her. That's shady as heck. If I can find out more, who sent it, there's a good chance I can find out what happened to her."

Charlie's face takes on a solemn expression now, as if the seriousness of what I'm saying is finally taking root in her mind.

"Tell me what's going on, Lucas."

I lay it out for her without giving too many details, just the basics. That after Mackenzie disappeared I started receiving text messages from her and how she agreed to tell me everything, but when I showed up at the appointed place and time, she ran. Then she texted, apologizing, saying she ran because she believed she was followed.

I leave out all the other clues and events and end with the video telling me she's leaving for good.

"Wow. You're right. This does sound shady. So we're no closer to finding Mackenzie. All the text messages you received could have been fake too."

"Exactly." I make a decision on the fly to tell her about the threatening texts I've been receiving also. "Someone has been texting me too, claiming it's my fault Makenzie is gone. I think it's the same person who sent the fake video."

"I don't see how I can help you, Lucas. You're talking about a lot of different elements that need to come together You can't just log on to a computer, tap a few keys, and find out who sent you the video and texts."

"Well, how does it work? What would it take?"

She sighs, as if I'm wasting her time because I wouldn't understand the complexities of how this works. A sudden thought strikes me. Mackenzie said all of this has to do with bad things happening at Branson.

"Let's narrow the search to Branson. That should help."

"It takes a lot to do this, Lucas. I'd have to access the school's network, which is illegal; bypass the firewalls and other systems, also illegal; and then analyze the network logs to identify any unusual activities around the time you received the text messages and the video."

"Then what?" I ask, my adrenaline rising.

"IP address tracking, device mapping. Things like that."

"So will you do it?"

She gives me an evil glare like she wished I would fall under the wheel of a Mack truck going seventy-five miles an hour.

I give her my most innocent, puppy-dog look. "This is hard for me too, Charlie. I put aside my pride and asked for your help because it's important. I wouldn't bother you otherwise. And you can't tell anybody. It will mess up the police investigation and muddy the waters.

"If I'm wrong, at least I tried. No one will ever know you helped me. You have my word. If I'm right, it could have major implications for our school. You have to keep this quiet until we find answers."

Charlie rolls her eyes and lets out a disgusted, "Whatever," and leaves in a huff without giving me an answer.

"Thanks, Charlie. You're a saint," I call out to her retreating form.

CHAPTER 87

First, I'm accessing the network logs. We need to see all the traffic around the time you received the texts and video."

We're in the computer lab in the STEM building at Branson, late at night. Charlie worked her magic, bypassing security cameras and unlocking doors. I didn't ask how. Don't want to know. She insisted the lab had the right equipment for our mission. At this point, if Charlie ordered me to run a marathon in clown shoes, I'd start training tomorrow.

Charlie's fingers fly across the keyboard, cracking school security. I scan the mostly dark computer lab; the laptop's glow and Charlie's phone pierce the darkness. Suddenly, that *Jurassic Park* scene invades my thoughts—the kid with the flashlight. My brain's bizarre attempt to squash the fear percolating in my gut. I bite my tongue, fighting the urge to whisper, "Kill the lights! One wrong move and we're T-rex chow." Charlie would probably slap me upside the head if I pulled that stunt.

Instead I ask, "What are you doing now?"

"I'm accessing the network logs and monitoring all data traffic. We need to pinpoint the IP addresses used when you received those texts and when the video was sent."

She brings up a series of logs on the monitor, her eyes scanning through lines of data. "Got it. Here's the list of IP addresses active at those times. Now, I'll map these to specific devices."

She runs a program that cross-references IP addresses with MAC addresses and then narrows it down to individual devices. This is all Charlie speak. I have no clue what it all means.

"So, you know which devices were used?"

Charlie doesn't answer. She keeps typing, and more data populates the screen. "This is going to take a while."

I sit in one of the chairs, careful not to get too close to Charlie to give her breathing room. With each passing minute, my heart beats louder in my chest, like a symphony rising to a crescendo.

"This doesn't make sense," she says forty minutes later.

"What doesn't?"

"The threatening texts you received and the messages from Mackenzie, including the video, came from the same device."

"Which is?"

"Mackenzie's phone."

"But the texts were from an unknown number. I assumed they came from a burner phone in both instances. Mackenzie's texts and the threatening ones."

"Not necessarily. The person could have used a spoofing app to disguise Mackenzie's phone number so the texts would show up as unknown."

"Why go through the trouble if they wanted me to believe I was receiving texts from Mackenzie?"

"Whoever you're dealing with is seriously twisted."

"So someone has Mackenzie's phone?"

"It looks that way."

"How do we find out who has it?"

"There's one thing I can try."

Charlie explains that she can again analyze the metadata of the messages and the deep-fake video. By doing so, she can identify the IP addresses and timestamps associated with the creation and sending of the messages. This could help her pinpoint the physical location and possibly the identity of the person using Mackenzie's phone.

"I'm also checking the Wi-Fi connection history of Mackenzie's phone to see which networks it connected to recently. If the phone connected to the school's Wi-Fi, I could correlate the timing with specific locations in the school."

After another half hour, which seemed like an eternity, Charlie says, "Holy Moly, cheese and bread." She looks up from the computer screen.

"What? Don't freak me out."

"I'm so sorry, Lucas."

CHAPTER 88

Charlie tracked the location of the person who has Mackenzie's phone. After the revelation fell from her mouth, confirming my suspicions, I felt as though someone had blasted me with a high-voltage electric shock. It was worse than being tased in the wine cellar. A hundred times worse.

I couldn't think of a single response. My heart was ripped out of my chest, with extreme malice. Charlie Covington, of all people, felt sorry for me. She continued to apologize as if she was the one responsible for my world falling apart. I had less than twenty-four hours to formulate a plan.

The next day, I stake out my spot in the garden behind a tree and wait. I wanted to get here a few minutes before the appointed time, to observe the person who was capable of such treachery, deception, and betrayal.

"I'm here," they call out. "You better not be messing with me, Jacqueline. This isn't funny."

I wait a few moments more as they look around nervously for Jacqueline Krasnoff, Branson's assistant director of admissions and one of the people in the photo. Charlie had pretended to be Jacqueline messaging anonymously to lend authenticity to the urgent message.

They're on to you. Meet me at the spot. I have some information for you and then you've got to get the heck out of here before everything blows up.

Time to make my move. I step out from my hiding spot. "I'm here."

She's startled and then takes a step back. "Lucas. What are you doing here?"

"I want the truth. Once and for all. If you're capable of it, that is."

"What are you talking about? I just…"

I hold up an exhausted hand to silence her. I can't stand to hear any more lies from her traitorous lips. "Stop with the lies, please. If there's an ounce of decency left in you, please tell me where my friend is." My voice cracks with barely contained emotion. "What happened to Makenzie?"

"Mackenzie is in her favorite place," she says, softly.

"Meaning what?"

I can't look at her deceitful, conniving, manipulative face. Each time I do, the wound in my soul grows bigger. The only thing keeping me from begging her to tell me I'm mistaken—and she's really the girl I thought she was—is the desire to learn the whole truth.

Misha's chin juts out in a sharp gesture towards a tree standing tall, across from where we stand. My voice trembles with frantic urgency, fingers twitching with nervous energy as I shake her arm for emphasis.

"Where is she? Just tell me where Mackenzie is."

"I already told you, Lucas," Misha states flatly, her eyes flickering to the tree once more. "This garden was her sanctuary, and that tree over there was her favorite spot."

During my investigation, I battled against the unthinkable. I slammed shut mental doors, refusing to allow those thoughts to take root in my mind. But deep down, I always knew it was a possibility.

When Charlie came through and provided the information I needed to bring the game to an end, I could no longer stick my head in the sand.

"Did your uncle do this? Was it Mr. Moore?"

"My uncle? No. He's a nerd who doesn't have the creativity or guts to run the Riemann Society."

Misha brushes a piece of lint off her uniform sweater. Then she adds, "Mackenzie was about to ruin everything. She got cold feet, said she wanted out. I couldn't let that happen, so we started watching her, tracking her, monitoring her communication, learning her secrets and weaknesses."

"By *we* you mean Jacqueline, Mr. Glendale, Mr. Lennox?" Misha doesn't respond. Between Charlie's numerous contacts and computer skills, we learned that the people on the list had committed major crimes that could land them in prison for decades.

A big part of Mackenzie's role within the society was to dig up dirt. Then the society would turn around and blackmail the people on the list for large sums of money.

They double-dipped with Cole Parker's dad. He'd paid seven figures to keep Cole's record clean and another seven figures to the society to keep the secret from coming out. The secret leaked anyway. How else would Ivy have known?

I reach into my pocket and pull out the piece of paper. Misha needs to know that I didn't come here to mess around, that it's time to topple the Black queen. I read aloud the information on the paper.

Evelyn Harper

Secret: HarperAI has been secretly selling sensitive AI technology to a foreign government, violating international sanctions. This could ruin her career and lead to severe legal consequences.

Jonathan Pierce

Secret: Pierce has been receiving bribes from defense contractors in exchange for favorable legislation. Exposure of this could end his political career and result in criminal charges.

Cameron Wolfe

Secret: Wolfe's investment firm has been involved in a massive Ponzi scheme, deceiving investors and falsifying financial records. If uncovered, it would lead to financial ruin and imprisonment.

Isabella Martinez

Secret: Martinez has been using child labor in her overseas factories to cut costs, despite publicly advocating for ethical fashion. This would destroy her brand and lead to a public scandal.

Dr. Henry Thompson

Secret: Thompson falsified research results to gain funding and accolades, risking patient safety and committing scientific fraud. Revealing this would end his medical career and tarnish his reputation.

Maxwell Chen

Secret: Chen has been manipulating news coverage to favor certain political agendas and suppress negative stories about his allies, undermining journalistic integrity. Exposure would lead to a massive scandal and loss of his media empire's credibility.

"Was it worth it, the blackmail and extortion?" I ask.

CHAPTER 89

Misha says, "Come on, Lucas. You're no angel yourself. What you and Mackenzie did to Cole Parker, that was hardcore gangster."

Ignoring the comment, I ask, " Why did you and Mr. Moore and the other members of the Riemann Society do this?"

"My uncle is innocent. But it had to appear as if he was the one running things. Otherwise, the other members wouldn't take it seriously. They respect my uncle. Mackenzie knew who was really in charge. It's why she ran from the common room that night when she saw me."

"So this society was your idea and you used your uncle as a front man?" I say, grappling with this revelation she had so nonchalantly dropped in my lap. I thought Mr. Moore was the brains behind the operation and Misha was only a loyal soldier. Instead, it turns out she was full of cunning, a wolf in sheep's clothing.

I came here to end the game and then flee her presence. After that, I'd pray I'd never cross paths with this girl again. "Why?" I ask, loudly, my voice like chipped ice.

"I told you about my mom," she says. "Do you know how much hospital bills cost? Do you know how stressful it is to plan for the possibility your mother might go into kidney failure or have a stroke or a heart attack because of her lupus? I bet you don't. I had to find the money somehow."

"Stop!" I say, stabbing a finger in her direction. "Don't you dare use your mother's illness to justify your heinous behavior. You sent me threatening texts and pretended to be Mackenzie, manipulating me on two fronts while I blindly fell for you, thinking you were special."

She steps closer and stops inches from me. Her eyes blaze with defiance. "I did what I had to do, Lucas. Do you know how much USC's Thornton School of Music costs per year? Over sixty grand, close to seventy when you tally everything. I want to make something of myself. I refuse to fade into obscurity, end up with some low-wage job, barely scraping by.

"I don't have your cushy safety net—rich doctor parents, wealthy grandparents, billionaire uncle. It's just me and Mom against the world. So yeah, I found a lifeline, and I grabbed it."

My lips press together in a slight grimace as I consider her words. I step away from her, needing distance between us as a firestorm of conflicted emotions rage inside me.

"How about when I got a concussion in the woods, or when someone tased me in the wine cellar and tied me up? Left me alone in the dark. Will you apologize for that, or was it all part of the game?"

Misha looks down at the ground. A strained silence passes between us. I wait her out.

She lifts her head, eyes locking on to mine. "I feel bad about that. But you...you just wouldn't quit. It wasn't personal, Lucas. I didn't want you hurt, but I had to stop you from ruining my life.

"Your obsession with finding Mackenzie was a threat to me and my mom, the future I envisioned. I have only one year left at this school. One year to secure my future and my mom's. I couldn't afford to have my hard work crumble like a house of cards. I did—"

"What you had to do," I say, cutting her off and shaking my head in disgust.

"Dressing up like Mackenzie in the woods, wearing a wig similar to her hairstyle, down to the lavender streaks, I guess you had to do that too?"

Her eyes pop wide, surprised. I don't give her the chance to explain anything.

"You fooled me big time," I say, unable to keep the bitterness and grief out of my tone. "Alexis explained it to me once Kellen discovered the yellow trench coat that fell out of your bag during the fire drill. You knew Mackenzie's favorite fall coat was yellow and that I would believe it was her in the woods.

"But the hair, that was a nice twist. Your braids, that was a wig, wasn't it? It was easy to switch it out for another wig; one that was curly and streaked with lavender like Mackenzie's real hair. That's why you didn't want me getting close when we met in the woods; it's the reason you took off. I would have recognized you right away."

Misha folds her arms, defiance radiating off her. "Look, I told you why I did it. I'm not going to grovel. I explained my reasons, about my family situation."

She won't relent, still rationalizing and justifying. What did I expect? When I think about how far she was willing to go to protect her crimes—her deception, manipulation, pretending to care about me, about Mackenzie—it's mind-boggling. How could someone who seemed so normal be capable of such malice?

"You played a long game, Misha. I was your pawn for most of its duration. But you forgot, in chess, the lowliest pawn can bring down a queen."

Desperation glides onto her face. Her eyes glisten, hands twisting together. "You won't turn me in, Lucas. You love me, remember? Besides, let's not forget your own dirty laundry. How would the Parkers react if they learned you orchestrated their son's expulsion from Branson, hmm? Branson would toss you out like yesterday's garbage."

There's no end to how far she will go to cover up her crimes. Given an inch, she would rat me out in a heartbeat. I must tread carefully.

"You blackmailed people for money. You used Mackenzie to access private information about these people and then threatened to ruin their lives for profit. How can you live with yourself?" I don't know why I'm asking. It's clear Misha has no remorse and whatever I say will fall on deaf ears.

She ignores my statement and continues as though I hadn't spoken at all. "Besides, do you really want my uncle to go to jail? He's innocent after all. Your honor code, sense of justice, won't allow you to see an innocent person punished. Uncle Damian genuinely likes you. He said you're wise beyond your years and an outstanding young man. My uncle doesn't give praise easily."

I back away from her again, as if struck by a sharp object. "Damian? I thought Mr. Moore's first name was James."

"It is. But Damian is his middle name. His friends call him JD. He couldn't very well use his first name when dealing with the society, now could he?"

A wave of exhaustion cascades over me. My head aches, a dull, relentless pounding. Misha takes my silence to mean she should continue defending the indefensible.

"You talk about these people as if they're innocent. They're not, Lucas. They're terrible people who do terrible things.

"Is it fair that these millionaires and billionaires break the law and cause harm to others to fill their already overflowing bank accounts? They don't need the money, but their greed has no limit. What we got from them is less than a drop in the bucket."

CHAPTER 90

A drop in the bucket is a relative term. The society not only blackmailed the wealthy alumni on the list, but they also sold favors. Admission slots at Branson to wealthy parents whose kids couldn't cut it, embezzling funds from the endowment, accepting bribes to ensure certain kids got into elite colleges.

"So you recruited people with inside knowledge of how Branson works. People who operated in morally gray areas or could be convinced to cross over to the dark side for the right price."

"Everybody has a price, Lucas. Even you. It might not be money, but it could be something else. Don't pretend you're so perfect. You have a dark side too. If you didn't, you wouldn't have framed Cole and gotten him expelled from Branson. You wouldn't have pounded Kellen Fontaine into the ground when the two of you got into that fight during soccer practice a couple of weeks back."

I must give it to her. She was moving her pieces across the chess board with flawless precision and timing.

"I didn't force anybody to do anything they didn't want to do, Lucas. They were all willing participants who saw the big picture, what the society could mean for them and their families' financial futures.

"All the crap they put up with from these rich, privileged brats who go here—the disrespect, the threats from powerful parents if they didn't do as they're told. For not the best pay, I might add. In all fairness, don't you think they deserved something for what they put up with?"

If I keep listening to her, I'm going to be sick. I'm already barely holding back a bout of nausea that's been circling. But I need answers to my most important question.

"How did Mackenzie die? Who put her in the ground?"

"Do we have to talk about that? It's so morbid and upsetting."

"Please, please tell me," I beg. "Then I'll leave you alone. I just want to know what happened… please."

"It was an accident," she whispers.

"What?"

I wasn't expecting this. But what's even stranger is the sheen of tears forming in Misha's eyes.

Then an icy calm I can't explain floods my senses. "Tell me how it happened. Don't leave anything out. I can handle it." I gesture for her to have a seat on the stone bench, the same one Mackenzie and I had sat on countless times.

Misha sits and explains that someone told Mackenzie to run, corroborating what Emily had told me. Misha confirms that someone was Jacqueline Krasnoff, the assistant director of admissions who had met up in the garden with Mackenzie in the past. They set up Mackenzie, and Misha had sprung the trap by showing up in the garden.

"The argument was getting heated, and Mackenzie wanted to go. I kept trying to convince her not to turn us in, but she wouldn't listen. Then it started raining, and the stone pathways got slick. Mackenzie turned to go, and in her hurry, she slipped on some wet moss-covered stones."

I stare down at my empty hands and then close my eyes. I want to scream, but I can't breathe. A burning sensation expands in my chest, as if my lungs are on fire. While I struggle to collect my bearings, Misha continues.

"I reached out to grab her, but she was startled by the sudden movement and stumbled backward instead. She lost her footing on some uneven ground. As she was falling, she hit her head on the edge of the old stone fountain."

Though my mind is clouded by grief and emotion, I know she's telling the truth. It rained that day, a couple of Fridays back when Mack and I were scheduled to meet at Bonnie's. Bonnie had offered to give me a ride home because of the weather.

This garden is sorely neglected, abandoned long ago. Everything is overgrown, old and crumbling. But Mack and I loved coming here. I open my eyes, and for the first time since I got here, I notice that Mr. Gnomington is missing. A strange thing to think about given the circumstances.

Misha begins to cry. Through hiccups and ragged breathing, she explains how she panicked and called her uncle. The rest, she doesn't need to explain.

"Please, Lucas," she pleads, her voice small. "I'm sorry I didn't say anything sooner, but I figured it wouldn't bring Mackenzie back. I was trying to salvage a mess that was unsalvageable. It was a horrible accident. I just wanted to talk to Mackenzie, nothing more.

"But things got out of hand. And I got scared. I couldn't handle it, so I pretended, went along with everyone else who was wondering what happened to her. I never meant to hurt you, Lucas. I really like you, but as long as you were digging into Mackenzie's disappearance, I had to try to stop you."

I stand, and so does she. Misha senses that I want to leave.

She says, "My uncle suffers from AFib. He takes care of himself and is in really great shape, but his heart can't take the stress of a trial and possible prison sentence. You can hate me, but please, for my uncle's sake, don't say anything."

I say nothing. The weight of Misha's confession hangs heavy in the air, a suffocating blanket of truth and lies. I stand here, my mind reeling, trying to process everything she's told me. The secret garden, the argument, Mackenzie's fatal fall—it all seems surreal, like a twisted nightmare.

But the pain in Misha's eyes, the tremor in her voice, they're all too real. For a moment, I almost feel sorry for her. Almost. But then I remember Mackenzie, remember the weeks of fear and uncertainty, the lies, the manipulations. My resolve hardens. I take a deep breath, steeling myself for what comes next.

Gently, I reach out and pull Misha into an embrace, feeling her body shake with silent sobs.

"It's all over now," I soothe. "You don't have to lie anymore. Thank you for finally telling me the truth."

We separate after a moment, and I stretch my hand out to wipe the tears from her cheek with my thumb.

"Thank you, Lucas. Thanks for understanding."

"Of course. We all make mistakes, Misha. We're human."

She gives me a weak smile and then frowns. "What's that noise?"

"What noise?"

"Can't you hear it? Sounds like sirens."

I stay quiet and tilt my head to one side, listening. I say, "Yes, you're right. Those are sirens."

Confusion blooms on her face. She asks, "Why are sirens heading this way?"

"It's my final move, Misha. Checkmate."

EPILOGUE

I'm still reeling from the events of the past two months. Mackenzie's funeral was especially heartbreaking. All of Branson came out in full force. I can't help but see the irony, though. It was Charlie Covington, a girl who despised Mackenzie, who helped me crack the mystery wide open. Misha's big mistake was using the Branson network to carry out her devious scheme.

It took some convincing, but Detective Kang finally believed me when I told him about the Riemann Society and their possible involvement in Mackenzie's disappearance.

I almost blew it by confronting Misha because the pain of her betrayal was so raw. The whole Riemann Society came tumbling down. According to the police, the group had been operating for a couple of years and had raked in a few million dollars.

Branson's leadership didn't want a massive scandal like that to take down the school, so they made a deal with the cops to fully cooperate if they could partially control the narrative and portray Branson as a victim of rogue employees. They promised to have stringent rules and transparent policies in place moving forward.

The dining hall buzzes with excitement as students, faculty and visitors weave through a vibrant tapestry of global cuisines. An intoxicating blend of aromas from dishes from all over the world float in the air. It's the Alerie Club's Ethnic Eats Bonanza: Holiday Edition, which we've dedicated to Mackenzie.

Strings of twinkling lights cast a warm glow over the room, reflecting off the shiny surfaces of international flags hanging from the ceiling.

Money raised from the bonanza will be donated to one of Mackenzie's favorite charities, CURE Epilepsy, a foundation dedicated to funding research to, you guessed it, curing epilepsy.

At Mackenzie's funeral, Ivy sensed I wasn't doing well. She came over, looped her arm around mine, and didn't say a single word the whole time the ceremony went on. She didn't have to, and I didn't want to.

Ever since, we've been chatting. She understands the weight of my grief and provides a sympathetic ear. Ivy isn't so bad. She's kind of sweet, actually, but she doesn't want people to know that about her.

Ivy calls it her Branson armor. "I knew if I was going to make it through four years of Branson, I needed thick skin and to never reveal my weaknesses," she told me. "This place will eat you alive if they smell weakness."

"I think Mackenzie would be pleased with the turnout," I say.

"She sure would," Ivy agrees. We lean against the wall, taking in the commotion. After a few minutes, Eric Shanz steps up to a makeshift podium and addresses the crowd.

"As many of you know, Mackenzie was a member of the Alerie Club, and this bonanza is dedicated to her memory. But Mackenzie's true passion was tech for good, and she worked tirelessly toward that goal."

All eyes are trained on Eric, as a hush falls over the room.

He continues, "Her senior Capstone project, for example. Mackenzie wanted to create a system that could detect seizures in the form of a wearable, like a hat or headband. And because of all the hard work she put in, and the resources she was able to line up, it's my honor to announce that the winner of the Emerson-Langston STEM Award is none other than Mackenzie Fleming."

The room erupts in deafening applause, hooting and hollering. Although I should join in the celebration, all I can think is how much Mackenzie suffered for that award; not only all the work she put in, but the constant fear that Charlie Covington's efforts to undermine her would succeed.

Mackenzie more than deserves this victory. And I'm kind of mad that she's not here to see it.

"Are you okay, Lucas?" Ivy asks.

"Yeah. What's the point? She's not here to take her victory lap."

"Maybe not," Ivy says, rubbing my shoulder. "But think about the countless people with seizure conditions who could benefit from what she set in motion. The prototype could be ready in as little as two months, thanks to your aunt Callie and Kale Stafford at that AI company."

Ivy is right, but I can't help but feel resentful. The applause dies down, and a faculty member takes the podium to explain that the financial portion of the award will also be donated to CURE epilepsy. The rest of the speech fades to a dull roar.

I can barely get the words out when I say, "I need some air. See you in a bit."

Ivy calls after me, concern and panic in her voice, but I don't respond. She knows not to follow.

Sitting on the cold stone bench in the secret garden, I drop my head in my hands. It's early December, and the garden resembles a barren wasteland, the trees empty of leaves and everything cold and gray.

"You did it Mack," I say. "I'm so proud of you, but I'm mad. I'm mad you're not here to accept your award. I'm angry at myself for taking our friendship for granted. Bitter that I couldn't see how you felt.

"I keep telling myself you would be alive if you were anywhere but in this garden on that fateful Friday evening two months ago. A stupid accident. You tripped and hit your head on concrete for goodness' sake.

"I'm struggling, Mack. I'm struggling with the unfairness, the sheer randomness. But you were set up. That's the worst part. And I don't want to say goodbye, even though I attended your funeral. How can I?

"Saying goodbye would mean you're no longer part of me. And that's not true. So I won't say goodbye, Mackenzie.

"I'll simply say, see you later, queen."

ACKNOWLEDGMENTS

Writing this book was both challenging and exhilarating. Although Lucas, Blake, and Alexis appeared in the Fearless series as kids, the idea to age them and build a YA thriller series around them crystallized because of two events. A young boy came up to me at a book event and asked if I had any mysteries or thrillers for kids his age. I explained that my books were adult thrillers, and I'll never forget the look of disappointment on his face.

The second event was my own son's reaction when he saw the cover for one of the books in James Patterson's Ali Cross series. He broke out in a wide grin and said, "Mom, he looks like me." Seeing his face light up because he saw a black boy in silhouette on the cover of a mystery inspired me to take action, and voila, the Malicious Games YA trilogy was born.

A big thank you to my beta readers: Janice, Milena, Lalenthika, and Laura. Your feedback was invaluable in making the story better. I'm so grateful you took the time.

Tia Bach, thank you for challenging me during the editing process by asking tough questions, questions that made me dig even deeper to make the story stronger.

The talented team at Qamber Designs & Media, thank you for the gorgeous covers you created for the trilogy.

Word of mouth is an author's best friend, so I'm grateful to family and friends who always support my writing. Your encouragement means the world to me. A special shoutout and thanks to my brother Banjineh, who tells anyone who will listen that his big sister is a great author and they should check out her work. Apparently, it's working because I have photographic evidence. Someone reading one of my novels while on safari? That's great.

To my husband, thank you for explaining soccer formations and the role of each player on the field. And as always, for giving me the space to write these stories, and for your unwavering support. To my boys, being your mom is one of the greatest privileges of my life, and you help make me a better writer.

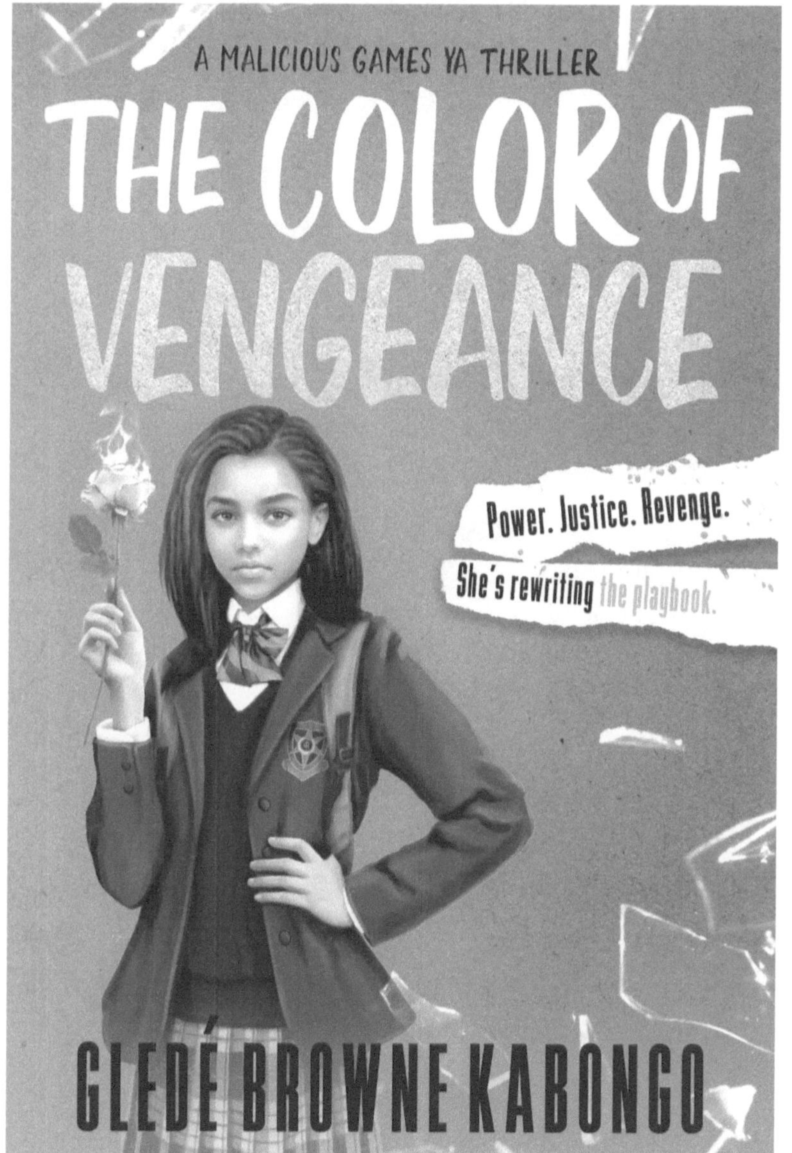
A MALICIOUS GAMES YA THRILLER
THE COLOR OF VENGEANCE
Power. Justice. Revenge.
She's rewriting the playbook.
GLEDÉ BROWNE KABONGO

CHAPTER 1

There are two types of people at Branson Academy: those who fear Kingsley Carmichael and those who haven't crossed her yet.

I'm about to become the third type.

But on this crisp March morning, blissfully unaware of the storm brewing on the horizon, I stand at my locker, still basking in the glow of applause and admiration from this morning's assembly. Being selected to represent Branson at the prestigious Future Medical Innovators Exchange program in Geneva feels like a dream. Somebody pinch me. Freaking Switzerland.

The halls buzz with energy, a cacophony of slamming lockers and excited chatter. Yet all eyes seem drawn to the larger-than-life poster plastered across the announcement board. My own face beams down at me, megawatt smile frozen in glossy perfection.

Oh, the irony. I've never been one for the spotlight, preferring the quiet satisfaction of academic success to the fickle world of high school popularity. But now, with the prestigious recognition under my belt, it seems the spotlight has found me anyway.

"I still can't believe it," my best friend Esi Boateng squeals, as she bounces on her toes beside me.

Wyatt Russo, the ever-enthusiastic student body president materializes at my other side. He says, "Do you know how many people applied from all over the country? And this is Branson's first time getting picked. You're practically famous now!"

"It's not that big a deal," I mumble, suddenly overwhelmed by all the attention.

"Not a big deal? Alexis, you just got picked for the Future Medical Innovators Exchange program. After this, you're all but guaranteed a full ride to any Ivy League school of your choice. That's beyond a big deal. It's legendary!"

A small crowd begins to gather, drawn by the commotion. A flutter of anxiety expands in my stomach. I've worked hard for this, sacrificed countless weekends and social events to prove I could make an impact, do more than get good grades. I deserve this moment. So why do I suddenly feel like an imposter?

"So, what's next for Branson's golden girl?" Olivia, captain of the debate team, asks with a grin.

I open my mouth to respond, to inform Olivia I might need her debate expertise to help prepare me for the mock UN health summit portion of the program. But the words die as my gaze drifts past the crowd, locking onto a scene unfolding across the hall.

Kingsley Carmichael stands with her back to me, her distinctive shade of auburn-red hair cascading over her uniform blazer. But it isn't Kingsley who catches my attention—it's the small figure cowering against the lockers before her.

Madelyn Bissette, a sophomore, looks like she wants nothing more than to melt into the metal behind her.

Her eyes are wide with fear, bottom lip quivering as Kingsley leans in close, whispering something that makes the younger girl flinch.

A chill runs down my spine, sharp and unexpected. The laughter and chatter around me fade as I focus on the scene unfolding across the hall. This is the Kingsley I've heard whispers about. The Kinglsey I know—the queen bee with a stinger so sharp it can reduce even the bravest souls to trembling wrecks.

"Alexis?" Esi's voice cuts through the fog. "You okay?"

Blinking, I say, "Excuse me for a minute."

Easing my way across the hall, I'm careful not to draw Kingsley's attention. Within striking distance, I tiptoe closer to hear what's being said.

"It must be exhausting, pretending to be normal all the time," Kingsley says. "Save yourself the stress. Just give up already."

Kinglsey pauses, letting the words sink in before continuing, her tone shifting to something colder, more calculating. "I see you, you know. The way you count your steps in the hallway, how you flinch when the bell rings too loud, the little twitches when someone brushes past you in the dining hall."

"I... I'm not pretending," Madelyn says, her voice quiet but with an undercurrent of frustration. "There's nothing wrong with being different. Did you know that many of history's greatest minds were likely neurodivergent? Like Einstein or Newton..."

Kingsley sighs dramatically and rolls her eyes. Then she continues her verbal attack as though Madelyn hadn't spoken at all. "Did you really think no one would notice? That you could just blend in here at Branson? This isn't some public school charity case, Madelyn. We have standards. Your special needs could be taken care of someplace else."

Near tears, Madelyn tries to reason with Kingsley, her words coming out in a rush. "Your statement is illogical. Normal is a statistical concept, not an absolute. In a diverse population, variation is the norm. Therefore, everyone is normal in their own way."

"I'm trying to help you, really," Kingsley says.

Madelyn's hands are now moving more rapidly, her agitation growing. "And exhaustion isn't exclusive to neurodivergent individuals. Studies show that masking, which is what you're implying I'm doing, is a common behavior in various social contexts, even among neurotypical individuals."

"Wow, Kingsley. I always knew you were insecure, but bullying someone for being different? That's a new low, even for you."

Madelyn's eyes go wide. Kinglsey slowly turns around to face me while a crowd gathers, their whispers floating in the hallway. Kingsley's eyes narrow, but her smile remains perfectly in place. She lets out a soft, melodic laugh that seems to ease the tension in the air around us.

"Oh, Alexis," she says, her voice dripping with false sweetness. "I've always admired your... passion. But you really should be careful about jumping to conclusions. Madelyn and I were just having a private conversation. Isn't that right, Madelyn?"

She glances at Madelyn, her gaze sharp despite her pleasant tone. Turning back to me, Kingsley continues, "You see, not everything is about academic brilliance. There are other kinds of intelligence—social intelligence, for instance. Something our dear Madelyn is still learning, bless her heart. I was merely offering some friendly advice."

I inch closer to Kinglsey, my words sharp and precise. "Let me spell it out for you, since you seem to have trouble grasping basic human decency. Madelyn's brilliance threatens you, doesn't it? Because deep down, you know that all your money, all your social status, can't buy the kind of intelligence and genuine uniqueness she has."

A collective ooohhhh erupts from the crowd of students gathered, a crowd that seems to be growing by the minute.

Kingsley lowers her voice so only those closest to us can hear. "And speaking of advice, here's some for you, Alexis. Before you go around accusing people of bullying, you might want to check your own behavior. Causing a scene, making wild accusations... some might call that bullying too. We wouldn't want your shiny reputation to get tarnished now, would we?"

My response is swift. No way I'm letting her manipulate her way out of this situation that she started. I say, "You parade around this school like you're some kind of queen, but you're just a sad, insignificant person who builds herself up by tearing others down. It's pathetic, really." I emphasize the word pathetic.

I add, "Here's a reality check for you: In ten years, Madelyn will be changing the world with her incredible mind, while you'll be desperately clinging to your fading relevance. Don't get me wrong, I totally get it. You're peaking in high school, and your cruelty is just your way of frantically trying to stay in the spotlight that will move on to someone else in oh, five minutes."

Then I saunter off without a backward glance, as the crowd begins to disperse. Standing up for Madelyn was the right thing to do, but I know that decision will cost me. Kinglsey is coming for me, there's no doubt in my mind.

All I can say is, let the games begin.

MORE FROM
GLEDE BROWNE KABONGO

Before *A Game of Malice*, there was *Fool Me Twice,* and the multi award-winning Fearless series. Dive into Lucas's origin story in these gripping thrillers.

    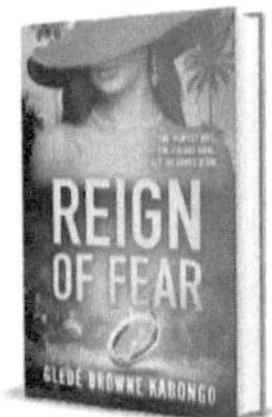

SCAN ME or visit gledekabongo.com

ABOUT THE AUTHOR

Gledé Browne Kabongo is a multiple award-winning author of eight psychological thrillers that offer a gripping exploration of themes such as deception, obsession, secrecy, and family.

Her novels, characterized by their strong emotional core, heart-pounding suspense, and jaw- dropping twists include: *A Game of Malice, Our Wicked Lies, Fool Me Twice, Conspiracy of Silence,* and the Fearless series.

Readers have described Gledé's work as "unbelievably addictive," "brilliant," "captivating," "unputdownable," "spellbinding," "deliciously duplicitous," and "haunting and complex."

Gledé has spoken at multiple industry events including the Boston Book Festival, Sisters in Crime (SinC) New England Crime Bake, and the Women in Publishing Summit. When she's not torturing her characters, she's hosting webinars and workshops on the craft of fiction writing, and working as a Content Marketing Manager for a high-tech start-up. Gledé lives outside Boston with her husband and children. You can reach her at glede@gledekabongo.com or her author website.

www.ingramcontent.com/pod-product-compliance
Lightning Source LLC
Chambersburg PA
CBHW022015310726
48972CB00006B/1663